SHATTERED WARRIOR

DARK WARRIOR ALLIANCE, BOOK 11

BRENDA TRIM
TAMI JULKA

"I feel like everything in my life has led me to you. My choices, my heartbreaks, my regrets. Everything. And when we're together, my past seems worth it. Because if I had done one thing differently, I might have never met you." ~ Author Unknown

CHAPTER 1

"Orlando!" Elsie's frantic call echoed through the house. Orlando jumped from his chair in the war room and ran into the foyer just in time to see the vampire queen flying down the main staircase.

Her long curly brown hair was sexy, whipping in every direction as she raced to him. He cursed himself every kind of fool. Apparently, he wasn't as over the Vampire Queen as he'd believed. Sure, he couldn't stop thinking about Jaidis, the cambion he'd met recently at the realm medical clinic, but he still stopped in his tracks when Elsie entered a room.

Windmilling her arms, pink fuzzy socks sailed toward him. Orlando reached out, grabbing hold of Elsie's waist to keep her from crashing into him and sending them both to the hard marble floor.

"What is it, *a ghra*?" Zander asked as he took Elsie from Orlando's grasp.

Orlando hadn't heard the vampire king follow him out of the war room, but it wasn't a surprise given the frantic sound of Elsie's voice.

Orlando's chest clenched when Elsie forgot about him

completely and gazed up at her Fated Mate with those adoring blue eyes. How many times had Orlando wished he was Elsie's mate and that she would turn that look on him? Too many to count, he thought, as he lowered his head, berating his jealousy. Elsie was not now, nor, would she ever be, his.

Shaking his head, Orlando shoved those thoughts into the back of his mind. Would that overflowing box of feelings that had Elsie's name engraved on the top ever stop tormenting him?

"Did you need me?" Orlando interjected before the couple became lost in each other. From the tremble to her voice and the way she stormed down the stairs he'd bet there was a problem.

Turning away from Zander, she gripped Orlando's shoulders and shook him. "You have to get to the pregnant lady. She's in a room and she's hurt, maybe dying. I saw you there, too, and the realm police. Youhavetogonowthebabyis-goingtodie," she blurted, her words running together at the end.

He hadn't seen Elsie this shaken up by one of her premonitions since the one she had involving her sister. He recalled how she'd seen her sister run off the road by skirm and attacked by an archdemon. It had taken the San Francisco Dark Warriors, along with, the Seattle bunch to get to Cailyn in time. After that experience, everyone took Elsie's premonitions seriously.

What Elsie had just described made Orlando's heart stop as panic threatened to buckle his knees. The only pregnant female he knew was Jaidis, his other obsession. The alluring cambion had held his mind hostage for weeks now.

"What did she look like? Did she have blonde hair? Was there a male there with her?" he asked frantically.

"There was so much blood," Elsie replied, sadness replacing some of her frenzy. "But, yes, she had blonde hair. The scene was chaotic with countless officers and a doctor. You have to go there now," she pleaded, the urgency in her voice returning.

A silver knife sliced through Orlando's heart at the picture Elsie painted. Jaidis was in trouble. It didn't surprise him given her abusive mate. How much time did he have? Unfortunately, Elsie's premonitions didn't always happen before the event. In fact, it was only last week that she'd seen a car accident after the fact and a young shifter died.

"Do you know the address, *a ghra*?" Zander asked, phone out ready to call in the cavalry.

Without thinking, Orlando blurted Jaidis' address and was in motion to the front door. As he slammed the wood panel closed he heard Zander talking to O'Haire. After jumping in his Mustang, Orlando called the realm clinic and told the receptionist Dr. Fruge needed to meet him at Jaidis' house pronto. He was relieved when the female who answered informed him the doctor wasn't already there. Maybe he had time to make it to her.

Heart racing and sweat slicking his palms, Orlando ignored speed limits and stoplights, placing his siren on the roof of his Mustang as he hurried across town to Capitol Hill. Urgency rode him like a demon. Jaidis had needed him and he wasn't there to protect her. *Fuck!*

WHEN HE ARRIVED at the scene, there were no flashing lights or caravans of vehicles parked in front of Jaidis' house. It was very different from the typical protocol of his human job at SPD. There were no patrol officers cordoning off the scene with yellow tape. In fact, from the outside, there were no visible signs that anything was going on inside the small house. It looked like any of the other houses in the dark of night.

But that ended the second Orlando stepped out of the car and the scent of blood assaulted his senses. Looks were deceiving for sure. It had to be bad if the constant Seattle rain couldn't wash away the scent. The sound of his heartbeat thrashing in his ears was deafening. Add to that the dark, winter night and his blood was like sludge in his veins. His legs threatened to give out as he trudged up the walk. Fuck, he needed to get ahold of himself. He was a seasoned warrior, after all, not some green officer.

He wondered how many realm police officers had shown up. The house wasn't very big and he imagined just a few people would make anything Elsie had seen more urgent. Closed quarters tended to skew perspective. Maybe the situation wasn't as dire as Elsie had made it sound.

Orlando already knew from a previous visit that Jaidis and her mate did not live with extended family. The faded paint on the siding was as he remembered and the porch still free of clutter. Hesitant of what he was walking into, he took several deep breaths, trying to ignore the coppery scent as he steeled his spine.

The recollection of Elsie screeching about the baby dying hastened Orlando's steps. Just as he was about to knock, the front door was pulled open and Steve O'Haire's plump face filled his vision.

"Trovatelli, thank fuck you're here. This is a damned mess," the realm police officer said by way of greeting. Orlando's heart raced in his chest, making his vision waver and his stomach churn.

The last time Orlando had seen Jaidis he had shown up

at her house hoping to save the female. He'd surmised she was being physically abused and received confirmation that night when she'd answered the door bruised and battered. Now, he cursed himself for visiting at all.

Kenny had shown up pissed off and threatened Orlando for being at his house with his pregnant mate. At the time, Orlando hadn't given the threat against him any thought, but left fearing for Jaidis' safety. And, it was that fear that had kept him away for the past weeks.

Orlando hadn't want to make matters worse for Jaidis, yet now he couldn't help but wonder if he made a mistake by staying away. A quick glance over O'Haire's shoulder had bile rising in his throat. There was a smear of blood on the wood floor of the tiny entryway. It was Kenny's blood, he repeatedly told himself, because his mind would snap if he even considered it might belong to Jaidis.

Thank the Goddess it was a habit to keep strict shields around his empathic ability because, in the next second, a toxic mix slammed into Orlando. The force of the terror made him take a step back and reach up, rubbing at the ache in his chest. Whatever happened involved more panic than he had ever experienced. More than once over his four hundred twelve years he'd wished for a different ability, but never more than right at that moment as he felt like he was going to vomit from the emotional impact.

"What happened?" Orlando snapped, hating the tremor in his voice.

O'Haire stepped aside and motioned for Orlando to enter the house. Automatically, Orlando searched for the container of protective booties for his shoes. In his position with the Seattle Police Department, there were certain protocols that clearly weren't followed by the realm police, which Orlando understood because the Tehrex Realm didn't have the same justice system as the humans.

In the realm, the leaders were the judge, jury, and executioner and they required far less formal evidence. Not that they didn't collect evidence, because they did. The realm had recently added crime scene investigators that handled cases similarly to their human counterparts with the major difference being in cataloging scents. They often called leaders to the scenes so they could gather their own impressions. These advanced senses allowed them to pick up on subtle clues that could exonerate or persecute perps.

"I came right over after Zander called me and found the male and female in the family room. I called the rest of the team right away. I've never seen such a savage attack between mates. Scenes like this usually involve demons and skirm," Steve shared as he shook his head in disbelief.

The knot in Orlando's chest expanded and further constricted his breathing. A silent prayer began in the back of his head as he entered the house. Careful of the bloodstains on the floor, his heart dropped to his feet when he looked around the room.

Blood splattered the walls of the small living room to his left and the tan couches had sprays of red across the fabric. The television was on, but the picture was marred by streaks of blood, as well. Laid in a heap next to the small fireplace, Kenny lifeless eyes stared up at the ceiling.

Right beside Kenny's body was a fifty-caliber pistol, an AMT Automag if Orlando wasn't mistaken. He prayed the son of a bitch had shot himself and Jaidis had escaped unharmed.

Orlando identified Kenny more by the familiar jumpsuit he wore than his physical appearance. One side of the male's face looked like a grenade had exploded near it.

Flesh, bone and sinew gleamed in the lighting, telling Orlando it must have been a silver bullet because nothing else would have killed the supernatural.

Skimming the room, Orlando fell to his knees when he recognized Jaidis's tiny feet behind one of the blood-soaked couches. He didn't give Kenny another thought as he crawled to her side, heedless of anything around him.

Disbelief, anger, panic and despair flooded his entire being. Part of his mind registered he was kneeling in her life's blood while the other part acknowledged nothing short of a miracle could save her.

One of her eyes was swollen shut and her lip was cut and bleeding, but that was the least of her injuries. Crimson seeped steadily from a wound to her large abdomen. The oversized t-shirt hid the injury, but he knew it was life threatening to both Jaidis and the baby. The exit wound was on her chest, precariously close to her heart.

"That sorry mother-fucker shot his mate and then turned the gun on himself," Orlando muttered. Why did he have to harm her and the baby? Why couldn't he have just killed himself and left them alone?

"Hold pressure to the chest wound," Dr. Fruge directed, startling Orlando as he entered the room and knelt on the other side of Jaidis. "I need to do a C-section right now if I want to save the baby," the doctor informed him grimly, meeting Orlando's gaze over Jaidis's inert body.

"No, you need to save them both," Orlando barked at the male. Orlando felt an instance of guilt when the doctor trembled and paled.

He knew his tone was threatening and he was frightening the male, but he couldn't help it.

As if his voice roused her, Jaidis slowly opened her eyes

and turned her head his way. "Orlando," she managed to croak. "Is that...you?"

"Yes, Jaidis. I'm here. Dr. Fruge is here and he's going to save you and the baby," Orlando murmured, trying to reassure her.

She opened her mouth and blood frothed, seeping out the sides with her labored breathing. Her shirt and pants were soaked with the liquid and he wondered how much blood a supernatural could lose and still live. The coppery scent overpowered every other scent in the room.

It was a scene he'd seen too many times to count in the human system, but never imagined between Fated Mates. Orlando had always believed the bond between mates was above abusive behavior.

Each of the Goddess Morrigan's subjects was born carrying a piece of their Fated Mate's soul. The first lesson taught in life was that it was their duty to protect their mate's soul. Once mated, their connection became so profound couples could literally hear each other's thoughts. Mates were so closely interwoven that they also knew each other's feelings. He could not imagine harming your mate in this manner, especially, when you would feel everything you did to the person you loved.

Kenny had to have felt what he'd done to Jaidis. The fear and pain he had caused. The male had to be masochistic to treat her like this and endure the consequences right alongside her. And then there was the baby to think about. How did a male harm his child when they were at their most vulnerable?

The fact that Kenny had harmed both his mate and unborn baby made Orlando want to kill him all over again. He hoped the male was burning in Hell for what he'd done. He knew from Rhys' account that there was a circle in the

Underworld where souls burned in a lake of fire for eternity. It gave him immense pleasure to picture Kenny there suffering for the rest of his days.

"Not...me," Jaidis whispered. "Save...my baby." Her eyes slipped closed and her face went lax.

"No!" Orlando shouted as he pressed on her chest wound. "You're going to live," he ordered.

"I have to operate now," Dr. Fruge cut in. "I don't know if she will make it through this. Her injuries are too severe," he added.

"You will save her!" Orlando growled at the male.

Dr. Fruge paused at the tone of Orlando's voice and swallowed hard. Orlando didn't care if the male shit his pants from his fear. He needed to save Jaidis.

"Get me some towels and move this furniture," Dr. Fruge told O'Haire in the next second. The realm officer who had been standing sentinel over their group snapped to attention.

"Search the hall closets for towels," O'Haire barked over his shoulder.

Orlando couldn't see whom he talked to, but the sofa scraping over the wood floor echoed around the room as it was pushed out of the way. It was so loud that it drowned out Jaidis's labored breathing. Orlando needed to hear her breathing to know she was still with him. He nearly snapped O'Haire's meaty neck when he moved the broken pieces of a table out of the doctor's way.

Moments later a female shifter returned with a bundle of towels in her arms. Orlando gave her a cursory glance and was instantly drawn to her. She was attractive with an average build and had a police badge clipped to her belt. He didn't sense she was a threat so he turned his attention back to Jaidis.

He smoothed the blonde hair from her face, revealing more bruises. These were a greenish-black color telling him Kenny had beaten her before this latest incident, as well. Orlando wondered how often Kenny had harmed Jaidis. The male was damn lucky he was already dead because Orlando's leopard wanted to rip him limb from limb.

The female with the towels knelt next to Dr. Fruge and hesitated before she set the towels down. Orlando knew she paused because there wasn't a clean spot on the floor.

"Just set them there. And, spread one out for me, please. I need my tools handy. Once I start the procedure I will need to move quickly to save the baby. Already his heart rate is falling," the doctor explained.

Dr. Fruge was a talented sorcerer and doctor, but he did not have the healing abilities Jace did. Orlando contemplated calling Jace, but couldn't free his hands long enough to make the call.

Tearing his gaze away from Jaidis's pale face, Orlando located O'Haire. "Call Jace and tell him to get here right away. He may be able to heal Jaidis. And tell him to bring Gerrick with him," he barked at the cop.

O'Haire's steel gray eyes bulged and then he swiveled, phone at his ear speaking to someone before Orlando blinked.

"Do you think Jace will make it? She's in pretty bad shape," the female shifter pointed out as she pushed her glasses up her nose.

Again, he was drawn to her and found it odd that in the chaos of the situation he was wondering why was she wore glasses. Shifters, like most supernaturals had perfect vision and weren't susceptible to degradation like humans.

"Jace has to make it. He has to save Jaidis," Orlando

snapped at the female, making her flinch with his harsh tone.

The female shook her head and held her hands up, palms out. That familiar frangipani scent overpowered everything else and settled the worst of Orlando's anxiety. It was rich and earthy, offering a measure of comfort and his heart slowed down a notch.

"Don't shoot the messenger. I meant nothing by it. I want the female to live and her baby, too," the female admitted, her wide amber eyes contrite. He should feel bad about his behavior towards her and the others, but he was too worried about Jaidis.

"Her name is Jaidis and she will live. You hear me, Jaidis?" Orlando asked, leaning down to whisper in Jaidis's ear. Oddly, he couldn't smell the frangipani this close to her and he questioned where it was coming from.

Jaidis stirred as Dr. Fruge cut her shirt from her body and Orlando got a glimpse of the wound to her abdomen. There was a slash diagonally across her flesh and it was flayed open, revealing her womb.

Orlando's blood went molten in his body. That piece of shit had tried to cut the baby from Jaidis's stomach, careless of the damage he caused. Orlando heard a gasp escape the female cop as he jumped up, storming towards Kenny's inert body.

Orlando's progress was cut short when O'Haire stepped into his path. "Get out of my way," Orlando gritted out. "I'm going to rip him apart."

"No. You're not. Trust me, he's dead. Stand down," Steve ordered and pushed against Orlando's effort to get to Kenny. "Gerrick and Jace will be here soon. They're going to portal here using the picture I sent them. Now, go back to Ember and Dr. Fruge," the male added as he shoved Orlando in the opposite direction of Kenny's body.

Orlando glared at the male. He contemplated fighting O'Haire, despite the fact, the male outweighed him by at least forty pounds, but the doctor's voice intruded. "Get over here, Orlando. She's asking for you and I need your help." Orlando was at Jaidis's side before the doctor finished speaking.

"I need to cut into her womb and don't have time for anesthetic. Thank the Goddess she is a month overdue instead of early because I have nothing here to deal with that scenario," the doctor explained.

Horror filled Orlando at what the doctor was about to do. Reality hit home at how dire the situation was. He'd endured his share of injuries but could not imagine the pain of having a womb cut open and your baby ripped from your stomach while you bled out.

Orlando wanted to shield Jaidis from what was going to happen and take the pain for her, but he was helpless to do anything. He fucking hated this feeling. He'd rather be skinned alive or bitten by a thousand skirm than feel so useless.

"I'm right here, Jaidis," he murmured grabbing her hand thankful when the female cop took over applying pressure to Jaidis's chest.

"Take...care...of him. Promise," Jaidis murmured, her voice barely audible.

"You will be here to help me take care of him," Orlando reassured her.

She couldn't die. The thought of her not surviving made Orlando's heart excel into overdrive and his thoughts spiral out of control.

"No...take care...of my Brantley," Jaidis said and then her eyes went vacant as a soft sigh escaped her mouth.

"We're losing her," Dr. Fruge announced. "I'm taking the baby now."

Orlando's head snapped up and locked onto the doctor's movements. As if in slow motion, he watched the male use a scalpel and swiftly cut through the flesh and muscle of the womb. In a rush, the baby was exposed. Curled into a ball, Orlando got the barest glimpse of a fuzzy blond head before the doctor's hands reached in and pulled the baby out.

Suddenly, time sped up and in a blurry haze. Orlando faintly heard Jace and Gerrick arrive just as the baby let out a loud wail and Dr. Fruge announced they'd lost Jaidis.

No! This couldn't be happening.

They were fucking wrong.

Jaidis wasn't dead.

Jace could save her. There was no other option.

As Dr. Fruge passed the tiny infant to his shaking hands, Orlando's world crumbled around him.

CHAPTER 2

"Holy fucking shit," Gerrick muttered, drawing Orlando's attention.

Compared to the realm police in the room, the warrior created an imposing picture in his black patrol gear, not to mention the scar bisecting the left side of his face. In Orlando's opinion, the scar alone made Gerrick appear menacing enough.

Emotion clogged Orlando's throat and it was nearly impossible to respond to the warrior. Anger, sadness and despair were consuming every thought. This female meant everything to him and he was losing her.

After a couple seconds, Orlando bit out, "You have to save her," he implored, pinning Jace with a bleak stare and ignoring Gerrick.

Orlando acknowledged Jace must have come straight from the hospital because he was still in his green scrubs. He'd never understood why medical staff, particularly doctors, wore clinical attire. Much like Jace with his scrubs, Dr. Fruge was never seen without his pristine white lab coat.

Did they do it to appear more capable when dealing

with the sick and injured patients? The realm police didn't wear uniforms like the human police force, but that didn't mean they were any less professional.

Orlando imagined the clothes gave a false sense of security. Anyone could throw on a pair of scrubs and everyone would assume you were a doctor who could help them. Fucking ridiculous if you asked him. Clothes didn't make you competent.

Personally, he preferred Jace in his Dark Warrior attire. That gave Orlando confidence in Jace's ability to fix the problem. He admitted he was borderline certifiable at this point, focusing on unimportant thoughts such as clothing.

His gaze shifted from Dr. Fruge to Jace and Orlando noticed the warrior was shaking his head, causing his long black braid sway. That was the straw that broke him and instantly his rage boiled over.

Jumping up, he grabbed Jace's hair, stilling his movements. Jace's eyes turned black with anger and Orlando realized what he'd done and quickly released his hold on the warrior. Jace's eyes returned to their warm amethyst hue and the small warm bundle in his arms squirmed, drawing his attention. If it weren't for Brantley keeping him in check, Orlando would swear he was trapped in the worst nightmare ever.

The baby started crying again and Orlando felt like shit. He'd startled the infant when he jumped up and he needed to calm down. Several deep breaths later and Orlando managed to steady his hands enough to cradle the infant close. The tiny being was so fragile and still covered in gunk. He had a slimy, white film all over his flesh and was wrinkled. Orlando hadn't realized babies resembled the cartoon character, Mr. Magoo when they were born. Izzy had been so cute at birth and he figured all babies were like that.

Gray eyes speckled with gold met his gaze. Brantley had his mother's beautiful eyes and Orlando amended his previous thought. This baby was perfect.

"She's gone, Orlando," Jace's voice interrupted.

Orlando lifted his head and locked eyes with the fellow warrior. "There is no heartbeat. You know I can't heal mortal wounds," Jace explained gently, his purple eyes somber and filled with regret.

Orlando already knew that, but didn't want to believe it. There had to be a way to save Jaidis.

Glancing away from Jace, Orlando noticed that Gerrick was pacing next to them, hands fisted on his hips. It was obvious the situation upset Gerrick nearly as much as it did Orlando.

"Surely the Goddess is not going to torture another warrior like this," Gerrick mused.

Orlando refused to believe what the warrior was suggesting. Jaidis wasn't Orlando's Fated Mate no matter how much he had prayed for that in the past weeks.

Gerrick was one of the happiest warriors at the compound, but he hadn't always been that way. In fact, he had been the surliest warrior at Zeum for decades. No one had understood why until Gerrick had shared how he'd lost his Fated before he'd had a chance to mate with her. And then Shae came along. She was the reincarnation of his lost love and now the warrior was content. There was a peace about him that had been missing.

"You can save her," Orlando implored which stopped Gerrick dead in his tracks.

Hope flared to life and Orlando couldn't stuff it back down as he clung to anything that meant Jaidis would come back to him.

Ordinarily, Orlando didn't allow much to ruffle his

feathers and he always saw the silver lining. That ship had sailed. The moment he'd stepped foot in the small house, everything had been clouded over by death and despair and he would give anything to turn back time. And, Gerrick was just the man for that job.

"Time trace and change all this," Orlando said gesturing wildly toward Jaidis's body while tightly securing the infant with his other arm.

He couldn't look at Jaidis because her lifeless form made the entire situation too real. The squirming baby in his arms and the blood staining the hardwood floor were reminder enough.

The pitying look in Gerrick's eyes made the ache in Orlando's chest feel as if a skirm had sunk its venomous fangs directly into his heart. He wanted to punch, or, better yet, kill something.

"I can't do that, Orlando," Gerrick informed him dourly.

"What the fuck do you mean you can't do that?" Orlando thundered which made the infant cry louder and the rest of the room's inhabitants go silent.

Everyone looked at him with apprehension as the room vibrated with the Brantley's piercing objections. Frangipani engulfed him, caressing him with buttery seduction. Again, curiosity nudged his brain as to where the scent originated. He looked sideways and noticed Ember had paused next to him. The scent had come from her, and, once again, her presence calmed the worst of his anger.

He had assumed earlier that the scent had come from Jaidis. Thinking back, he conceded what he'd smelled from Jaidis must have been a perfume because it lacked the enticing sweet coconut that Ember's held. His leopard was drawn to her like a cat was to catnip and he had to resist rubbing against her body. Regardless, the heavenly aroma soothed his frayed nerves.

"Here," Ember murmured as she held out a blanket. "Wrap him up. Infants can't regulate their body temperatures and need warmth."

Orlando looked at her sideways, noting her amber eyes held compassion. A small tattoo of a Celtic knot snagged his attention. The delicate artwork accentuated her long slender neck. Apparently, it was his day to get sidetracked by every minute detail because he couldn't stay focused for shit. Shaking off his wayward thoughts, he accepted the blanket and her assistance in wrapping Brantley in the soft material.

"Thank you," he told her before turning his frustration to Gerrick.

"Now, tell me why you refuse to help Jaidis when it's obvious she means something to me," he demanded.

Gerrick exhaled loudly and began pacing again. "First, it's too late. Too much time has passed. But, even if it hadn't been too long, I still wouldn't do it." When Orlando opened his mouth to argue, Gerrick snapped, "Shut the fuck up and listen. There are consequences for my time tracing. You know that. Remember what happened when I went back and saved Shae? We lost the amulet and Rhys had to go to Hell, literally, to retrieve it."

"Of course I remember, jackass. But, you still saved Shae knowing there would be consequences because you couldn't live without her," Orlando retorted angrily.

"Yes, because she was my Fated Mate and I had lost her once. I knew what it was like to live after losing a mate and couldn't survive that loss again. Not that I want to see anyone suffer, but, from what I see, this female belonged to the dead male over there," Gerrick pointed out and

Orlando winced at his words as the knife to his heart found purpose.

Orlando was all kinds of fucked up. From day one, he had fought for every scrap of food he'd eaten, had been called scarecrow as a stripling by his peers, and his siblings hated him for being the runt of the litter. Eventually, he grew up, filled out and became a Dark Warrior thinking he'd left all that pain behind, but his demons continued to haunt him as he kept falling for the wrong females.

"Look at this innocent baby," Orlando hedged, hoping to play on Gerrick's sympathy. "If you won't go back for me, do it for him. He deserves to have his mother raise him."

Gerrick stopped his infernal pacing and glared daggers at Orlando. "That child deserves the best, and, yes, he should have his mother raise him, but Fate had other ideas so that's not possible for him. It's too late, O. I can't help her. I would only go back so you could watch her die all over again and I refuse do that to you. I can see how devastated you are. I'm simply not able to go back far enough in time," he concluded.

Orlando hung his head and brought the child up to his nose. He inhaled deeply seeking a calm that eluded him. Jaidis's scent reached him, but it didn't affect him like Ember's tantalizing frangipani. That scent is what held his attention and soothed the worst of the hurt in his heart.

"What the hell happened?" Orlando mumbled aloud.

EMBER WATCHED the Dark Warrior as he clutched the baby to his chest. Her heart was torn to pieces for him. It had been difficult to witness his devastation. She wanted to bring Orlando into her arms and comfort him. The male was so distraught and it touched her. And, it wasn't just because she found him to be the sexiest male she'd ever seen. The moment he had walked into the house she couldn't take her eyes off him.

Like most supernaturals in the realm, Ember had grown up with stories of the Dark Warriors and how fierce and ruthless they were. The warriors were all that stood between demons and the rest of the world and battle their enemies 24-7. She wouldn't have imagined a Dark Warrior being so sensitive and compassionate, but it was clear to her Orlando had intense feelings for the female which was surprising. Ember had seen the mate mark on the dead male and noted it matched the one on the female. She had belonged to someone else.

Ember had never encountered a more gruesome scene between mates in the century she had been working with realm police. As a CSI, she was called to all crime scenes and had seen her share of shit, but nothing like this.

Based on his comments, Orlando believed the male attacked the female and then shot himself. She was still piecing the evidence together to determine what had happened, but something didn't sit right with that assertion.

"Based on what I'm seeing, this male didn't shoot himself," she responded as she donned a pair of latex gloves then bent to pick up a small piece of glass.

"Who the fuck are you to say he didn't shoot himself?" Orlando demanded.

The male's scowl and furrowed brow contradicted the delicate hold he had on the baby. Admittedly, both looks were sexy on the well-built shifter.

He was clearly pissed and his eyes darkened with his anger, but all she could think about was what his full lips would feel like against hers. Ignoring that disturbing impulse, Ember focused on the issue at hand.

"Name's Ember, in case you missed it. I'm the local CSI for realm police. It's my job to collect the evidence and determine what happened," she informed him and pushed her glasses up her nose.

"Okay, Ember," Orlando sneered.

For a split second, she was offended that he spat her name like a curse word. He acted like she was responsible for his pain and it was a punch to the gut. She didn't know this warrior from Adam and it shouldn't matter how he felt, but the first two words out of his mouth made her think he couldn't stand her and that cut deep.

"In your *expert* opinion, what happened here?" he finished and met her gaze. His emerald green eyes held her captive for s split second.

Pissed about her reaction to him, as well as, his indignation, she glared at the shifter and took pleasure when her cougar ascended. Her eyes burned then her claws extended from her fingertips, piercing the gloves she wore. Orlando's eyes flashed before his pupils became oval-shaped and she could see his leopard prowling beneath the surface.

He might be distraught over the dead female, but he wasn't unaffected by Ember. The connection she felt to Orlando was not entirely one-sided. His leopard was reaching out to her cougar, making it difficult to concentrate. It took great effort to keep control and not shift right then and there so their animals could become acquainted.

Breaking eye contact, she glanced down at the piece of glass in her hand. It looked like cell phone glass. Scanning the room, she noted the blood splatter on the floor and the sofa cushions, as well as, droplets by the windowsill. She picked her way around the room for a few seconds.

Crimson drops marred the tan fabric and the cushions were askew. The contents of a side table were all over the floor in disarray. O'Haire had moved the sofa, but she recalled its original position. Stepping back, she bent and found what she was looking for. Retrieving the cell phone, she held it and continued examining the scene.

She nearly stopped in her tracks when she heard Orlando's leopard growling as she moved closer to the dead male. The embroidered name on the pocket of the coveralls indicated Kenny was the name of the male. Turning her head, she met Orlando's black eyes. If it weren't for the infant in his arms, she had no doubt that Orlando would be dismembering Kenny even though he was already dead.

Kneeling, she remained careful to avoid the blood, but moved close enough to take in the scents surrounding the male. Gunpowder overpowered his natural scent that had faded with his death. Oddly enough, she smelled gunpowder around his face and on his hand, as well as, the hardwood floor beneath his palm.

Confident of her assessment, she straightened and addressed Orlando, noting that everyone was glued to every move she made. It seemed everyone wanted to know what had happened between the mated couple.

"From what I can see the male attacked the female, but she retaliated. She was facing him when he cut her stomach, you can see the blood sprayed across the front of his uniform," she explained as she pointed out the stains.

"She scrambled to get away form him, knocking into the table and sending its contents scattering. She was going for her cell phone, but it hit the floor along with everything else. She then grabbed the gun from beneath the couch cushions and shot the male before he knew what was happening. My guess is she dropped the gun thinking she had killed him then turned to find her cell phone and that was when the male shot her," Ember finished telling the silent room.

"She never reached her cell phone, so how did you know she was in danger?" she asked Orlando.

"The vampire queen had a premonition," he responded in a daze.

Ember had no idea the new queen had the power of premonition. All she knew was that Elsie was the first ever human-turned-vampire and had been the talk of the realm for obvious reasons.

"She saw the baby and blood and said I needed to get here. That's when we called you guys because you were closer," Orlando explained as he began pacing the room with the infant in his arms.

"That's probably what saved the baby," Dr. Fruge cut in. "If they hadn't responded when they did we would have lost them all."

The doctor's pristine white lab coat was covered in blood now, reminding her of the emergency surgery he had performed to save the baby's life. She'd never seen a baby born and had wondered what natural childbirth was like. If it was anything like she'd just witnessed she never want to have a baby.

Orlando stopped and ran his free hand through his white blond spikes, leaving red streaks through the strands. As upset as he was, he held the boy close to his chest as if his very life depended on it. He was a protective male and the shifter in her liked that trait. Pack was everything. In her opinion, the strong were responsible for protecting the weak. And, it was clear the baby sensed he was safe because he had quieted and was content for the moment in the warrior's arms.

"What do we do with the infant?" Gerrick voiced.

The warrior had a scowl on his face, and that, along with the scar, made him frightening. There was no doubt the male was a stone-cold killer. It was a good thing he used those skills to kill demons and skirm. She was grateful he was with the Dark Warriors. Otherwise, she was certain he would be a big problem for realm police.

Orlando looked at his friend and grimaced. "I have no idea. I promised Jaidis I would look after Brantley. Is there even a precedence in the realm for a situation like this?"

"What about surviving family members? Realm law dictates that the stripling be placed with them." Dr. Fruge threw in.

"I think we need to contact Dante and Hayden and ask for their help with Brantley," Jace added and Orlando bared canines at the healer.

Ember had no idea what was in store for the small infant, but she could tell by Orlando's reaction that he was prepared to fight tooth and nail to keep his promise to the female he clearly loved. An unexpected bout of jealousy startled Ember, but she quickly shoved it aside.

Orlando's loyalty and protectiveness were two of her favorite traits in a male, which only added to her attraction to the warrior.

Too bad for her it was clear his heart belonged to someone else.

CHAPTER 3

Orlando should be paying attention, but his mind refused to focus on the chatter around him. Orlando could only concentrate on Brantley. He'd finally managed to get the baby to take the bottle Elsie had made for him. He was out of his league with the infant and had never felt more helpless in his life.

He was a warrior trained to hunt and kill the enemy, not comfort and cajole a baby. He refused Elsie and the other females when they offered to feed the stripling. It was his job. Jaidis had made him promise to take care of her son and he was going to fulfill that no matter what. Not to mention, Brantley trusted him. He had been through quite an ordeal since his birth and needed to know he could count on someone.

The soft breaths against Orlando's neck made his chest tighten. What the fuck had happened? He had prayed a million times over the past day to wake up from the nightmare he'd found himself in, but that wasn't going to happen and he had no frame of reference of where to go from here.

This was unchartered territory for Orlando and he was scared shitless of the outcome.

This was not how he saw his life going. Despite the centuries old "mating curse" that had dominated the Tehrex Realm until Zander found Elsie, Orlando had always believed he would find his Fated Mate and live happily ever after. Now, he doubted his judgment, as well as, everything having to do with mating.

Kenny was missing half of his face in the realm morgue, thanks to Jaidis, and she was on the steel table next to him. Both dead and their infant orphaned. The entire cluster fuck should not have happened. The Goddess should never have allowed the mating to go so wrong. It still stunned Orlando that Kenny could harm Jaidis at all, let alone, to such terrible lengths. Not only did she deserve to be loved and cherished, it would be like harming yourself when inflicting pain on a mate.

Everything Orlando had seen in the mated couples in the compound went against the abusive relationship Kenny and Jaidis had. What had happened between them that it devolved to this point?

Against his better judgment, he had allowed himself to fall for Jaidis, much like he had with Elsie, and now she was gone. The worst part was at one point he'd had this justification rolling through his head that Jaidis wasn't Kenny's mate, but his, and one day he was going to go to her house and convince her to run off with him.

What a fucking idiot he'd been.

Instead, he was mourning her death and holding her baby, waiting to hear what was going to happen next. Orlando's cat came alert as he sensed the presence of his Omega before Hayden entered the war room.

"Now, that's a sight you don't see everyday," Hayden

chuckled as he saw Orlando cradling the baby. "A warrior in full combat gear feeding an infant."

Normally Orlando would have a humorous comeback, but he didn't have the energy. "Then you must not come around often," he informed his Omega flatly.

"I'm going to let that slide given what you've been through tonight. Don't forget who you're talking to," Hayden growled as he took his seat, his chocolate brown eyes glaring daggers at Orlando.

Orlando swallowed hard. He had been so caught up in the grief and despair that he had forgotten he was addressing his Omega. Not only was Hayden huge, standing at six and a half feet tall with shoulders as wide as a house, he also had the ability to cause Orlando and his leopard significant pain for their disrespect.

If Hayden wanted to, he could reach out with his power and seize control of Orlando's animal. It was unpleasant, not to mention humiliating. The Omega typically only did so with striplings just past their transition when they struggled to control themselves.

"Sorry, Sire. It's been a shitty day. Thank you for coming," Orlando murmured.

Slightly mollified, Hayden pushed his long brown hair over his shoulders and rested his arms on the table. Orlando had never realized exactly how big Hayden was, but when he reached out to touch Brantley, he couldn't help but notice that the baby would fit in the palm of his hand. Orlando's protective instincts immediately went on alert and had him clutching Brantley a bit tighter.

Hayden quirked his eyebrow at Orlando before addressing the rest of the room. Yeah, it was odd behavior, but Orlando was helpless to control it. Brantley's own parents hadn't protected him while in the womb and Orlando felt it was up to him to ensure his safety.

As much as he cared about Jaidis, he was upset at her for not accepting his offer of a safe home while she was pregnant. He didn't blame her for being abused and could understand not seeing a way out, but when he gave her the solution and she denied it, she was knowingly placing her and her unborn child in danger.

Dante walked in and took a seat on the other side of Orlando, startling him. He hadn't heard the male enter the room. When had Elsie gotten up? She'd been sitting next to him a moment ago. There was a time that Orlando could have told anyone every move Elsie made when they were in the same room together, but not now.

At least that was one positive that had come out of the catastrophe. He was no longer completely obsessed with Zander's Fated Mate.

"Is this the little guy?" Dante asked as he stroked the baby's cheek.

Where Hayden's power was stifling, and almost felt like being buried alive, Dante's was more seductive, like a warm breeze caressing your skin. That was fitting given Dante was the Cambion Lord and a sex demon.

When more than a few of the Dark Alliance council were in the same room, their power made the space feel incredibly small. Zander's power was pervasive and tended to sink into your being despite any shields you had in place. Orlando pulled at the collar of his black t-shirt as he adjusted to the competing sensations. Thank fuck Evzen, the Guild Master of the sorcerers, wasn't also in the room or Orlando would be sweating.

"Aye, 'tis Jaidis's *bairn*. Were you able to learn anything before coming over?" Zander asked.

The vampire king sat at the head of the large wooden conference table with Elsie at his side, holding his hand on top of the table. Orlando smiled slightly at the sight.

As an empath, Orlando sensed the love and affection the couple shared. No matter how exasperated the couple was or how many cross words were exchanged, it was never anything but respect and devotion. This was how it should be between mates. He never thought he'd lose faith in the Goddess, but that was exactly what happened after Jaidis and Kenny.

For longer than he could remember, Orlando had yearned for his Fated Mate and it had only intensified since Zander found Elsie, but now he questioned things. Mating was no longer the perfect union he had imagined and he wasn't certain he wanted anything to do with it.

"Well, I learned that Kenny has family in Mississippi. Jaidis's family was killed in a skirm attack two decades ago. She had been on her own until she met Kenny last year," Dante explained.

"What did his family say? Are they coming for Brantley?" Orlando blurted as his heart raced in his chest. He didn't want to give the baby up, but he knew he didn't have a legal right to keep him.

"They aren't coming. His brother said he *wanted nothing to do with that asshole's baby*. Apparently, they disowned him after he strangled their mother," Dante said with a shake of his head.

That quick Orlando's rage was back. It wasn't surprising to hear Kenny had murdered his mother and it made him question the Goddess's wisdom even more. Why the fuck would she put Jaidis in his care? Why not give her to a male like Orlando who would treat her like a queen?

"Oh my gosh," Elsie interjected. Her hand fluttered over

her heart and Orlando was bombarded by her sympathy. He had always experienced Elsie's emotions stronger than most others and now was no different.

"The baby isn't his father. Why would they reject him because of that? That's so unfair. Whatever happened to make Kenny abusive has nothing to do with this child. What is going to happen to him now?" the queen asked.

"I'm keeping him," Orlando blurted as he held the sleeping infant close. He may not be the child's blood, but they belonged together.

Dante shook his head while the rest of the room watched in silence. "Besides being a cop, you're a Dark Warrior. If that's not bad enough, you aren't a cambion, Orlando. You won't know how to care for him," Dante declared.

Orlando bristled at the assumption that he wouldn't make a fit parent. He liked Dante, considered him a friend even, but at that moment Orlando wanted to deck him.

"Fuck that," Orlando spat, clenching his free fist in his lap to keep from lashing out.

"Isn't that something for your social services to decide?" Elsie asked, confusion clear on her beautiful heart-shaped face.

"We doona have social services, *a ghra*," Zander informed her. "The leaders make these decisions for their people."

"What? You guys aren't qualified to decide that. If you don't have social services, do you have domestic violence shelters?" Elsie asked incredulously.

Orlando normally enjoyed when she challenged Zander and what she called the realm's backward ways, but this was different. He didn't want strangers to decide if he was fit in raising the child and he certainly didn't want to wait or be temporarily separated from him. Brantley's future needed to be decided and he wanted the people that knew him best to make that decision.

"Nay, we doona have any shelters," Zander replied as he tried to wrap his arm around Elsie's shoulders. Orlando didn't miss when she shoved his arm off and scooted away. "The Tehrex Realm is different, *a ghra*. We doona need shelters. Our families take care of our own. As you know, we live in large family groups often with three or four generations in the same house and this is rarely an issue."

"Obviously, you do need shelters. Did you learn nothing from this situation? I can't believe you are still sitting here spouting this BS to me. Your families aren't better than humans because you live together. There are still abusers in the realm, children are still orphaned, and, in no way, do you three men know what is best for children or abused women. You guys know fighting and killing," Elsie exclaimed angrily.

Orlando chuckled at the way Zander paled and Hayden looked a touch panicked. Orlando knew the Omega would never put the vampire queen in her place, but he could tell that her words had struck a cord with him. Dante smirked and didn't appear bothered in the least by Elsie's outburst.

"That's what's up," Nate added, laughing as he set the tray of snacks in the middle of the table.

"This doesna concern you, dragon" Zander warned the majordomo.

Nate ignored the vampire king's gruff tone. "No offense Liege, but I beg to differ. If this child remains at Zeum, he will very much be my business. And, I happen to agree with the Queen. Even on Khoth we have a system of trained individuals who are responsible for children in such situations, as well as, adults in need," Nate shared.

The dragon shifter was walking a fine line. Orlando wasn't sure his deference was enough to ameliorate Zander's ire as the veins at the king's temple looked ready to blow.

"Don't get mad at Nate," Elsie murmured as she placed her palm over Zander's chest.

The king met his mate's clear blue eyes and instantly calmed. Orlando had always envied the connection they shared, but he was convinced that he was cursed and would ever experience the same so he mentally stabbed that dream with his switchblade. He was done hoping for things not meant for him. It only led to heartbreak and loss.

"We need to change this and now. How you survived without an official system to help those in need baffles me. Elsie's Hope has just expanded. During the day, we will still help the humans, but at night we will begin assisting supernaturals in need," she declared. Elsie's determination impressed him, as well as, her confidence.

It struck him how far she had come since becoming the vampire queen. He recalled how timid and unsure she had been. She believed she wasn't *queen material* and had little faith in her abilities, but he'd seen the potential like many others and wasn't surprised by how easily she'd adapted to the role. There was a time when he'd have said it was because the Goddess created her for the role, but after losing Jaidis like he had, his beliefs had been rocked to the core.

"*A ghra,*" Zander began, but she held her hand up stopping his next words.

"I'm not done. Each faction will put money into organizing shelters in each of the major cities. I understand that the supernatural population in rural areas isn't big enough to warrant such services, but they can go to the nearest city. The question remains what we do with children like Brantley. Do we begin training social workers who can make those decisions?" Elsie finished.

"I will set up an alliance meeting in the next few days so we can work oot all the details," Zander conceded, earning him a triumphant smile from Elsie. "Tonight, we need to decide Brantley's fate. That canna wait."

"Jaidis's dying words were for me to take care of her son and that is what I plan to do," Orlando reiterated for what felt like the hundredth time as resolve steeled his spine.

The affable warrior he had always been was gone at that moment. He couldn't help but admit he was acting more like Gerrick than himself. "I may not be a cambion, Dante, but I live with one and I have no doubt I can ask Rhys for advice or help when I need it," Orlando declared, pinning Dante with a glare.

Dante sighed and shook his head. Orlando knew his friend well enough to know he was wavering. "I won't argue with a mother's wishes. Are you okay with this infant coming into your home?" Dante asked Zander.

Suddenly, he panicked. He hadn't asked Zander his opinion in the matter. Fortunately, they were a family at Zeum and he hoped his leader and friend would support him.

"Aye, the *bairn* is welcome here. Although, Isobel may see him as one of her dolls," the king laughed and met Orlando's gaze. The sincerity he saw in the king's eyes was comforting and Orlando smiled his appreciation.

"And, the infant will be welcomed into the pack," Hayden announced, shocking Orlando. "If you ever need a babysitter, the females in the nursery would love to help take care of him." That was more that Orlando expected from the Omega.

He recalled his days in the nursery. At the Grove, there

was a nursery where infants and children went while their parents worked or performed pack duties. He had always preferred to spend his days at the nursery because the dynamics he lived with at home weren't present. Helga refused to allow his siblings to pick on him, unlike his mother.

He envisioned Brantley amongst the various shifter children and thought he would get a kick out being around them. Shifters didn't have control over their animal and shifted with the slightest emotion and he imagined they'd make the perfect playmates.

Orlando would take Brantley to the nursery if for no other reason than to give the females at Zeum a break. He couldn't do this without their support and refused to take advantage of them. His schedule didn't allow for him to travel daily to the east side where the pack was located, but he would get there on the days he could.

"That's great, but what happens when you can't get to Jesaray house? Who will take care of him then?" Dante asked as he leaned back, arms crossed over his chest.

Orlando didn't get the feeling he was being difficult and creating obstacles, but was genuinely concerned for Brantley's well being and that was the only reason he didn't lash out at the cambion lord.

Orlando met Elsie's gaze and her smile told him the answer he was seeking.

"I will take care of him and when I'm not here there are five other females who are available, not to mention Nate, the other warriors, and the gnomes. Pepper and Dipple have been amazing with Izzy. Besides, everyone at Zeum pitches in to take care of the kids. That's what family does," Elsie answered Dante, but kept her gaze on Orlando. Emotion clogged his throat at the unwavering support she showed him.

"Thank you," Orlando mouthed and she nodded in return.

Zander raked a hand through his shoulder length black hair, the familiar movement telling Orlando exactly how stressed the vampire king was.

"Are you sure you want to take this on? I know the *bairn* needs to be taken care of, but this is a lot for a single male. Trust me, I know how hard caring for him will be. Feedings every couple hours, countless diaper changes," Zander said with a shake of his head. "It never ends."

It was a struggle to think past anything else. Orlando knew Zander wasn't asking because he didn't support him, but because he wanted to make sure he was thinking it through. Truth was he'd been doing nothing but thinking about this situation for the past twenty-four hours.

"Brantley belongs with me. I know that in my heart. There is a reason I was so drawn to Jaidis when she wasn't my Fated Mate and I think it is because I was destined to care for this little guy," Orlando said, sharing his epiphany.

Before he could continue, his cell phone vibrated in his pocket. In a roomful of supernaturals with extraordinary hearing, that was like being in a crowded theater and having your phone ring during a tender love scene. Shifting his hold on Brantley, the infant woke and wailed his displeasure at being disturbed.

Without a word, Elsie was at his side and taking the baby from him. He stood and fished out his phone, checked the caller ID, and answered as he stepped into the hall.

"Trovatelli here," he murmured by way of greeting.

"O, we've got a case that I need your expertise on. And, before I forget, have you heard from Reyes? How's his mom doing?" Captain Rowley asked in his raspy, phlegm-laden voice.

Orlando heard the distinctive sound of the male inhaling and knew he was puffing on a cigar. There wasn't a time he didn't have one of the foul-smelling addictions in his mouth. Even in the station house, the captain chewed on a cigar and lit up the moment he was stepped outside.

"Santiago is hanging in there. Not the happiest right now. His mom is in a bad way and he will be out the next month for sure," Orlando responded, trying to be as cryptic as he could and still stick to the cover story of Santi needing FMLA time off to take care of his ailing mother. Thank the Goddess Jace worked in a human hospital and filed the necessary paperwork to get Santi the time off.

Truth was, he was serving his sentence in the dungeons of Zeum for going rogue and still had time left. From what Nate had seen, it had been hell on his best friend.

Santi had been mated to Tori right before he was stuck in the dungeons. The couple had agreed to the sentence so Santi could earn his place back at Zeum, but it wasn't easy. Of everyone in the house, Orlando sensed exactly how much it tortured both Santi and Tori to have him so close but unavailable. No one could see Santi. Nate brought him three meals a day and fresh clothing and linens when needed but that was the extent of his visitors.

Orlando had begged Zander to allow Tori to spend time with Santi, as much for his own sanity as for theirs, but the king refused. Zander was a stickler for the rules. Thankfully, Santi's wolf could run the halls of the dungeon so it didn't go insane. It would have been better if he was allowed outside, but that wasn't part of his deal. As a result, Santi could be feral when he was released.

"Tell me about the case," Orlando prompted the captain, wanting to think about something he could impact.

"There has been an attack in the middle of a club and some of the victims...they aren't right. And, from what the responding officers are hearing from survivors, sounds like something from a horror movie. I'm not sure if this is another hoax like the TwiKills or something else altogether. That's where you come in."

The hair on Orlando's arms stood on end and his leopard went on alert. A couple years ago, supernatural's existence was almost revealed when newly turned skirm had gone on a rampage, killing indiscriminately. When archdemons created skirm they took control of the victim's mind and the new archdemon at that time hadn't been aware of how easily skirm lost control, but Kadir caught on quickly and the open killings stopped.

The media dubbed the attacks TwiKills because they believed it was people *pretending* to be vampires. Orlando wondered if Lucifer had sent another archdemon to fill Kadir's empty shoes.

Quickly jotting down the address, he returned to the room, aware that they had all heard the conversation.

"Fuck," Zander snarled. "I had hoped it would take Lucifer longer to send another demon. Get your arse down there ASAP and see what damage has been done. And, call if you need help with the scene."

"This is exactly what has me concerned," Dante cut in before Orlando could talk to Elsie about the baby. "You've had Brantley less than forty-eight hours and you have to leave him."

Elsie turned to glare at the cambion lord. "No one can be with any baby 24-7. We have a house full of caretakers that will be here for Brantley. You wouldn't suggest taking Isobel from Zander because he was called to a meeting or a battle. This is no different," she spat and her face turned red with her anger.

Orlando shot her a grateful smile. It was nice to know he didn't have to worry that they would be there for him when it was needed.

"I have to admit that you're right, Elsie," Dante murmured before turning to Orlando. "Don't make me regret drawing up the adoption papers. And, if you need any help with him, call me. That's an order, not a request."

"You have my word," Orlando promised.

His priorities had shifted in the past days. Typically, he went into situations with his first thought to protect the realm and innocents at all cost. He never gave much thought to his own safety. Now, he had eighteen inches of responsibility depending on him and a bigger reason to return home. He'd always assumed his reason to return home would have been a female, but he was done with that. He would focus on Brantley and nothing else. He didn't need a female in his life.

On that thought, Orlando leaned down and kissed Brantley's head then headed out the front door. He hadn't made it two feet out of the house before the memory of sweet frangipani called him a big fat fucking liar.

CHAPTER 4

E xcitement and anticipation bubbled beneath Ember's skin as she parked her SUV near the curb. She loved her job almost as much as she loved her pack. In fact, she was obsessed with anything related to CSI, even the popular TV show. Everything from her Escalade to most objects in her kit were things she'd seen from the series. She had immediately connected with the show and its extensive knowledge of criminal psychology. She had a knack for cataloguing and processing a scene and took pride in her ability to discover clues others typically missed. It kept her mind sharp and focused.

Originally, it was Ember's idea for the realm police to employ crime scene investigators and she had fought tooth and nail for it. There had been no precedence for it in the Tehrex Realm. Standard procedure had always been realm officers handled every aspect of investigations and then reported their opinions to the leaders of the factions involved whom then punished offenders. There was no trial or delay unless the leader asked for more information.

Admittedly, there were fewer crimes in the realm than

there was the human world, but in her opinion they still needed to be investigated thoroughly. The realm had fallen down on the job and she believed more diligence was needed with crimes committed by supernaturals. Punishments were swift and severe. In fact, many carried a death sentence because of the danger to realm exposure.

She was proud to say that her track record was ninety-eight percent accurate. A recent case that she had been wrong about still gave her nightmares. A few months ago, she had been called to a scene involving a vampire and a dead human female. After her investigation, she concluded Caine DuBray had lost control and drained his human girl-friend, which resulted in his comatose state from overfeeding. Her mistake had nearly cost him his life.

Thankfully, Caine met his Fated Mate in the three days the vampire king gave him to find proof of his innocence. If Caine had been mated to anyone other than Suvi Rowan, one of the infamous Rowan triplets, he would not have uncovered the evil witchcraft behind the setup to frame him. He would've been put to death and it would have been Ember's fault. It was a lesson to all involved and further proved why her job was so important.

Setting aside those morose thoughts, she looked out the driver's window and noticed the activity around the club. It was a human establishment and it was crawling with human police. Instinct told her to leave and return home. She didn't hate humans, but she wasn't comfortable around so many. It made her skin itch.

For the hundredth time, she wondered what made the Dark Warriors call her to the scene. It wasn't as if they had ever called her before, and, aside from the incident the other day when the female delivered her baby right before dying, she had never met any of the warriors. All she knew was that the Dark Warriors had asked for her assistance and a fellow realm officer was meeting her there.

Scanning the chaotic scene, she looked for O'Haire, but didn't see him. Did she go in without him? She had no idea who was at the scene and she didn't like the idea of waltzing around a human crime scene. Invariably, her mind went back to wondering if Orlando had asked for her.

Had he been thinking of her as much as she'd been obsessing over him? It was highly unlikely given how upset he'd been over the dead female. She, on the other hand, had been fixating on the feline shifter with his full mouth and sexy smirk.

Never in her life would she have imagined one of the Dark Warriors being so gentle with an infant. However, the loyalty and determination he exhibited was no surprise. That was common among shifters.

Most supernaturals remained close to their family, often living with them in the same house, but shifters had an additional family with pack mates. Pack had your back no matter the circumstance and it didn't matter whether they lived in the Grove, as they called pack land, or not. There were always a few bad apples, but most would never hesitate to jump in and help a fellow shifter.

She remembered the time she had been buying fish at Pike's Market and encountered a mom and her young son. They were canine shifters and the boy couldn't control his urge to shift. The mom was panicking and a group of humans was trying to see around her as she shielded her son.

Without a second thought, Ember jumped in and helped shield the boy while ushering her and the stroller out of the limelight. After getting them to a private area, she'd helped calm the boy down and sent them home, offering to finish the female's shopping. She hated to think what might have happened if the humans had seen the boy shift. Exposure carried an automatic death sentence in the Tehrex Realm.

Of all the supernaturals, shifters felt they were at the highest risk if the humans discovered their existence. Historically, humans used animals to test everything from lotion, makeup, soap, and medications for humans. There was no doubt that shifters would be highly valued and sough after if they were discovered. They were a lab's wet dream as perfect subjects to dissect and study and were her reason for avoiding the very type of scenario she found herself in.

Despite her vehemence that she was going to stop obsessing over Orlando, her mind traveled back to thoughts of him. It had been obvious he was a feline. When they'd locked gazes after the baby had been born her instinct screamed he was a leopard and everything she'd mulled over since then confirmed that suspicion. Now she wanted to know what his coat looked like. Was his fur the darkest midnight or white as snow like his unruly hair?

She had never been so affected by a male. The fact that she wanted Orlando more than she wanted to breathe irked her, but also reminded her that she'd been celibate too long.

She had gone through one too many heat cycles with no partner to sate her sexual needs. Her best friend, Faith, repeatedly told her that she needed to get laid and had been trying to lure her to Confetti Too for weeks, but Ember wasn't interested. Not that she was against the idea. A night of wild sex sounded pretty damn good, but she'd been too busy between work and patrols around pack land to entertain the thought.

As much as she loved her job as a CSI, she had bigger

dreams. Some may laugh and scoff, but she wanted to become Hayden's first female Lieutenant. She knew he trusted her to take on patrols around their land and keep the pack safe, but she wanted more. It was just a matter of time before she convinced him she would make a capable C.L.A.W. (Core of Lieutenants Against the Wrathful), as his group of Lieutenants was known.

A tap at her window startled her and she jumped. She'd been daydreaming for Goddess only knew how long and let her guard down. Cursing herself, she glanced over and was relieved to see O'Haire standing at her window.

"You gonna sit there all day?" he quipped as he huddled into his leather jacket.

Shaking her head, she opened the door and instantly shivered. The arctic front was bitter this time of year. "Steeeeve, you scared the shit out of me!"

"Damn, where were you girl? I've been standing her for five minutes. You're losing your edge," he teased as he shut the vehicle door after she'd climbed out.

O'Haire turned and began a quick pace, trusting she would follow as he started across the parking lot. "I'm not losing my edge, just wondering why we were called to a human crime scene," she said as she caught up to him and they made their way across the pavement.

Darkness hid most of their progress because someone had broken most of the streetlights. Leaves and sticks broke under her boots, sounding like gunshots. She expected the humans to turn to them, but no one paid any attention and she had to remind herself they didn't have the sensitive hearing of a supernatural.

"We were asked to be here. You didn't exactly dress for the weather," Steve replied as he glanced at her attire.

"Don't they care that we are here?" she asked O'Haire, ignoring his question.

The wind cut right through her dress slacks as if they were tissue paper. Normally, she wore jeans with a nice shirt under her lab coat. She was grateful that she had forgone the lab coat this time. Human authorities were the boogey man in her opinion and her goal was to fly so far under the radar she was skimming blades of grass. Nothing special or different here, she thought as they approached the throng of cops.

"They haven't heard us yet, but they will care very shortly. Orlando is something of a celebrity among them so I imagine they will follow his orders," O'Haire explained.

Her heart rate increased at the mere mention of Orlando. In the next blink, she was sweating from nervousness. She smoothed down her blouse and pushed her glasses up her nose, wishing she had a mirror so she could check her makeup to make certain that she didn't look like a clown.

Normally, she wore a little eye shadow and mascara along with lip-gloss, but today she'd gone to town in case she encountered Orlando. Unfortunately, it didn't feel natural and the foundation was heavy on her face. The smell of the cosmetics permeated her nose. Steve hadn't mentioned anything so she must not look that bad, she reasoned. They had the type of relationship that was direct and honest and she appreciated that. No bullshit necessary.

"What makes him so important?" she asked, sticking to a safer question than the ones she wanted to ask.

Chances were Steve didn't know if Orlando was open to public sex or what his favorite position might be. The mere thought of the powerful male taking her had her core clenching with need.

Everything about Orlando was intimidating from his black clothing to his intense emerald green eyes. She wondered if he ever smiled. He'd been grim and a bit broody when she'd met him and couldn't imagine him grinning, let alone laughing.

"Is this the special investigator Trovatelli called in?" a female voice interrupted before O'Haire could respond.

Taking a step closer to the human, Steve smiled and turned on his considerable charm. It had never affected Ember because she didn't like her males so big and beefy. He was a good-looking bear shifter and she'd toyed with the idea of them hooking up in the beginning, but decided against it. His neck was as big as one of her thighs for crying out loud and she had heard rumors that his dangle was just as thick.

"You know you were hoping I'd come back, Stacy," he teased, making the female smile and shake her head. "Of course, I was happy to personally escort the investigator to Orlando." Ember thought he was laying it on pretty thick until she smelled his arousal. He wanted this human female.

"I'll never tell," Stacy said then winked at Steve. "He's through there. Come see me before you leave."

Ember rolled her eyes and bumped her shoulder into O'Haire's side as they entered the club. Every light was on, making the room oddly bright. Nightclubs were typically dim as owners wanted to create a more intimate ambiance.

Tables were overturned, shattered glasses were strewn about, and there were several prone bodies on the floor. Some were writhing in obvious pain with humans tending to them. It was the ones lying still with sightless eyes focused on nothing that made her shiver. It was always eerie to see death, but to have so many in one location was highly disturbing.

Her stomach churned, but whether it was from the stale smoke and alcohol that tainted the air, or the foul stench of the victims, she wasn't certain.

"How can you flirt and be thinking of sex when we're surrounded by all this?" she remarked. The big cop blushed and lifted his shoulders in response. Males.

"Orlando," O'Haire called out without answering her.

When the Dark Warrior stood up and turned to face them, Ember's mind went blank and her mouth watered. He was the sexiest male she'd ever seen. And, as her body went all kinds of molten, she realized she had no right to make fun of Steve. That fast her thoughts had traveled down the same road as his where Orlando was concerned. And their grotesque surroundings didn't factor in one bit. Her body refused to listen to reason.

She wanted to rush to his side and offer her sex-deprived body to him without reservation. She had no shame in that moment. There was no doubt about the degree to which she wanted Orlando. Her body flooded with heat and her core ached with need.

She would've sworn her eggs dropped regardless of the block still on them. It was as if she was in heat, but that was impossible. It wasn't her time of year yet and she had never released a single egg in her two hundred thirty two years. That didn't happen for female shifters until she had sex with her Fated Mate.

"Thank the Goddess you guys are here," Orlando responded before he walked to a male bending over a body a few feet away. Ember enjoyed the way his tight black pants stretched over his firm ass. Her cougar wanted to bite that fine ass.

Moments later, he turned around and walked towards her and Steve. She would have been disappointed but the front view was just as luscious as the rear. His tight black shirt displayed his muscles to perfection. What attracted her most was that he wasn't some huge bodybuilder type. He was the perfect size. His leather jacket currently covered his arms, but she recalled his bulging biceps. She craved to know what his other bulges might feel like inside of her.

"What happened here?" O'Haire asked interrupting her fantasy.

She nearly snarled at her co-worker, but caught herself in time. She must not have hidden her annoyance very well because Orlando gave her a confused look.

"Club-goers reported a monster attacking them, but I can't seem to find any evidence of demon or skirm involvement here. I interviewed a couple shifters, a vampire and three sorceresses who had been dancing and they reported it was a demon. If this were a demon it would be out of character. Kadir had pushed the limit, but never did anything that risked exposure like this," Orlando shared as he took a switchblade out and began flipping it.

It was such a casual and natural movement that she assumed he must have done it a million times. If she attempted that with the blade she'd end up with it stuck through her hand. She had to squint against the bright flash caused by the light bouncing off the weapon and it made her wonder if the thing was silver. It would certainly fit him if it were.

Orlando seemed cocky enough to toss around a weapon capable of killing him. The thought should've been a turn-off but it wasn't. No supernatural in their right mind would play with silver like that so why it made her find him even sexier she had no idea. She must be over worked *and* under-sexed to be attracted to such danger. She wasn't one of those females that wanted a bad boy.

"Please tell me that's not silver," she told the warrior with a shake of her head. She needed slam the brakes on her attraction or every supernatural in the club was going to know exactly what she was thinking.

Orlando smiled and cocked his head while he continued to toss the blade. How the hell was he able to do that without even looking?

"It wouldn't be any fun, otherwise. Don't worry, Wildcat. I never miss," Orlando replied with a chuckle.

His half-smile struck her like a bolt of lightning. This male was meant to smile and joke, not be the angry, serious warrior she'd seen the last time. The clouds parted and the sun came out when he smiled. It warmed her to her toes and set other parts on fire.

She finally understood what her friends meant when they said a sexy smile made their panties drop. She had never been that female to become weak in the knees by such an insignificant gesture from a male but damn if she wasn't hot and bothered from his flash of pearly whites.

His nickname finally registered through her desire. She was a wildcat, but she wasn't sure she liked him calling her that. It was something you'd say to your best friend's little sister, not a female you wanted to ravish. She was aching to be spend a night sweaty and naked with this male and it seemed he had no interest in her at all.

"If that's your idea of fun, you need to get out more," she snarked to cover the hurt she felt over his disinterest. All she'd been able to think about since she'd met him was tearing off his clothes and satiating her burning desire for him, but apparently, he didn't feel the same.

Good news was that realization sobered her and her arousal shriveled up like a grape in the sun.

"Tough to get out when all you do is work," Orlando quipped to the beautiful female. "Speaking of work. I called you out here to see if you could work your magic again and tell me what happened."

He wanted to tell them they could handle the investigation so he could go home to be with Brantley, but had to admit he was glad he hadn't passed the case off. It would be easy to leave Ember and O'Haire to run a more thorough examination. Funny enough, the desire to be done and home wasn't as strong now that this female was near. He needed a nice distraction from the shit in his life.

With confident steps, Ember crossed the room and her nostrils flared. No doubt she was following a scent trail. It was difficult to discern what was what with so many competing odors overwhelming the room. One thing he couldn't deny was that her boldness was alluring and her lithe movement was reminiscent of her cougar. Both called to his leopard.

She was an attractive female. He hadn't realized how tall she was when he'd met her before. He swallowed hard as he watched her mile-long legs move around the room. Her delicate frangipani scent soothed and aroused him, making him want to take her. Suddenly, she bent over and to reach one gloved hand to a pile of goop and a growl left his throat.

He wanted to bend her over while taking her from behind, claiming her. Whoa there buddy, he chastised. He reminded himself she was a female and he wanted no part of that. It would only lead him to disaster. No, it was best not to get involved. With his luck, she was involved or mated. There was no mate mark obvious, but there was too much that was hidden from view.

His body ignored his command and continued to peruse her body. She had legs made to wrap around a male's hips and pull him close. Ember wouldn't submit easily. It was obvious she was an alpha female and didn't hesitate to take control. The scar running under her left eye told him she was a scrapper. He wondered if that had anything to do with why she wore glasses.

Normally supernaturals didn't need them, but perhaps she was self-conscious about the imperfection. He found scars highly attractive because they hinted at a fire within. It showed she was a fighter.

Watching her, he realized there was something about her presence that brought him back to life. Ever since falling for Elsie, his head had been tangled and confused. And then Jaidis came along and everything crumbled, he thought bitterly. But somehow, Ember walked into the room and the fog cleared.

"We gonna follow her?" O'Haire asked, breaking into Orlando's thoughts.

Ember was walking down the back hall of the club. "A patrol officer cleared that area already," Orlando called out.

Ember turned her beautiful face his way and pushed her glasses up her nose. Her amber eyes glowed briefly. "Yes, but they weren't me," she muttered with a smirk as she held up several evidence bags. "They clearly need more training. I mean, some pretty obvious evidence was missed—."

Wood flew into the air behind Ember, cutting her off. The lights flickered before several bulbs burst in a loud pop and pandemonium erupted as they were encased in blackness. His SPD colleagues began running around franticly trying to find a light source. Orlando was in motion before he fully registered what was happening.

"What the fuck is that?" O'Haire blurted.

Orlando didn't stop to respond, but made it to Ember's side just as a demon charged from the room. If Orlando hadn't felt the malice exuding from the creature, he may have mistaken it for an angel. Well, until closer inspection.

Black as night eyes were a dead giveaway of its lifelessness and malevolence. This demon was a female, scantily dressed with enormous blue wings that seemed to take up the entire hallway. Strips of charcoal-colored cloth rapped around her limbs and across her torso, barely covering her breasts and sex. At first, he didn't realize she wore clothing because her skin was only a couple shades lighter than the fabric. Her long black hair flew about her head in the wind her sudden appearance created.

The sight made his skin crawl and his stomach revolt. What the hell were they dealing with now?

He realized now wasn't the time to get caught up in analyzing the new demon. It was about to attack Ember and Orlando needed to get his ass in gear. Keeping most of his attention focused on protecting Ember, he glanced around to gage if the demon was alone.

Moving closer, Orlando noted the wings were nothing like Illianna's diamond-tipped gold wings or Tori's smaller bat-like wings. Instead, these were a deformed version of both. Blue feathers covered blue leathery flesh and the ends were pointed with claws. This demon could slice and dice its victim while the razor-like fingernails disemboweled them. Not a pleasant thought.

"I am Crocell," the demon answered haughtily before she moved to grab Ember.

Her movements were almost as quick as Kyran's when he sifted, but Orlando didn't let that deter him. His switchblade left his hand before his racing heart took another beat. Sailing through the air, it embedded to the hilt in Crocell's forehead.

Screeching, the demon raked her claws across Ember's shoulder. Ember cried out and Orlando lunged, grabbing her arm before the demon could portal her away. It was a risk, but he had no choice. The way he saw it, better to be alive and without an arm than dead. Santiago's mate, Tori, had suffered a similar injury but was learning to live with her handicap. Ember would cope, too. At least she'd be alive.

With one arm wrapped around Ember, Orlando withdrew a *sgian dubh* from his boot and tossed it at the same time O'Haire took aim and fired. Crocell shrieked then disappeared a second later.

Orlando remained on alert, grabbing another blade with his free hand. "Call Zeum, get Jace and one of the princes here now," he ordered O'Haire.

They had some memories to erase after this shitstorm and only vampires were capable of that. Jace needed to heal Ember because he could feel her warm blood seeping through his fingers.

Meeting Ember's amber gaze, he felt her fear, pain and determination reflected. This female was as tough as nails and wouldn't go down without a fight.

Lifting his hand from her shoulder, he cursed as he got a good look at the four deep furrows that left her arm hanging by threads. The cuts went all the way to the bone and a couple went through it.

"It's just a scratch, put a Band-Aid on it," Ember muttered in a tight voice.

Startled he looked up and realized she was joking with him. He appreciated her humor. It was how he dealt with life. He'd rather be laughing than yelling or crying any day, but he could tell this was her trying to deal with the pain.

"I've got a box in my car. Hope you like SpongeBob," Orlando teased back. "I'm not familiar with that demon, but I think its safe to say this is gonna leave some nasty scars. Hold tight, Jace is coming to stitch you up. This is gonna hurt for a while. I wish to fuck he could heal demon wounds. I'm sorry I couldn't stop her," Orlando admitted, feeling like he had failed yet another female.

The scene surrounding them was gruesome. It was impossible to determine how many victims the demon had in there. He didn't envy the coroner who would try to figure out which parts went with which body. Blood and gore spattered every surface. Thank the Goddess Bhric and Kyran would be here to erase the human's memories of the demon. Otherwise, this would be written off as a horrendous massacre.

His heart skipped a beat when he realized that Ember had almost been part of that carnage.

He should have protected her. It was his job and he wanted to kick his own ass for being so lax with the scene. He'd been too focused on keeping any hint of supernaturals from the human's attention and she'd almost paid the ultimate price. Glancing down he expected to see hatred behind her amber eyes, but was shocked to feel gratitude and admiration.

"I guess that means our dinner date is going to have to wait a few days," she quipped, drawing his attention away from the bloody mess of her injury.

Did she just ask him out? He hadn't realized she was interested in him. Hell, he hadn't anyone, aside from Jaidis and Brantley, much thought in the past couple days.

Unable to stop his reaction, his eyes went wide and his

mouth dropped open. Shaking his head, he murmured, "Dinner? I can't."

Ember narrowed her eyes at him. "Can't or won't?"

"Does it matter?"

Trying to sit up, Ember winced from the pain her movement caused. "Steve," she called out and the male quickly rushed over. "I need you to put pressure on my arm so I don't bleed out," she said as she glared at Orlando.

He opened his mouth to tell Steve he had it, but she shook her head violently and her complexion turned gray. Not wanting to cause her more pain, Orlando relinquished her care to O'Haire, but the act was harder than he expected.

His leopard howled to return to her side and he found it impossible to move more than a foot from her side. He didn't even care that some of the humans who'd seen the attack could be getting away. His chest twisted at the sight of her blood and even more at her obvious disdain for him.

He hated the look in her eyes and wanted to explain, but no words came. This was best for her. The Goddess had shown him he wasn't meant to have happiness and the last thing he wanted was to pull her down with him.

CHAPTER 5

Ember clenched her hand and rotated her injured shoulder as she got dressed. It moved much better than it had when she'd gone to bed that morning. With the ability to heal quickly, she wasn't used to being out of commission for so long. Typically, she'd be back to fighting condition the next day. It sucked knowing that demon injuries took twice as long to heal because of the venom poisoning their systems. The pain had been excruciating and unlike anything she'd ever experienced. Thankfully, Jace had given her the antidote. She hated to think how long it would have taken without the shot. Two days was enough for her.

She wasn't a very good patient and Jace had tried his best to soothe her. Unfortunately, she couldn't totally blame her piss-poor attitude on the pain. After Orlando's rejection, she been surly and short-tempered and the injury only added to it, causing her to act like a flat-out bitch. She'd cursed and snapped at Jace, but it hadn't ruffled his feathers.

One positive had come out of the awful experience. She was no longer interested in Orlando. Okay, that was a total lie, but she was determined she could convince her mind and body that he was worse looking than the demon. Surely, she could do that. She considered herself intelligent in many areas including chemistry, blood analysis, finger printing, as well as, fighting and even rock collecting. Yet, she couldn't seem to teach her mind and body not to react to the mere mention of Orlando's name. Her new approach was to ignore the subject altogether.

Leaving her cottage, she headed to Jesaray house and wondered what her Omega wanted. Her heavy boots crunched on the frozen ground cover. It was cold this time of year, but the Grove was located on the eastside of the lake in the forested area around Snoqualmie and it seemed bitterly cold amidst all the trees. The scent of the various shifters permeated the air, connecting her to her pack through the feedback loop of shared energy.

The temperature couldn't abate the anticipation that bubbled beneath her newly healed skin. Was Hayden finally going to make her a C.L.A.W.? Throwing a couple practice punches, she tested the bone. Her skin was healed, but the slight ache could mean the bone wasn't done fusing back together.

No matter, she could do the job or die trying. If Hayden offered the position to her there was no way she was going to turn it down. She had worked too hard for far too long. She understood the need to protect the females, but it was just as important to protect the males. The females wouldn't be the future of the race without the males. And sadly, there were some in the pack that still believed females were weaker than males.

That notion irritated Ember. Generally, females were weaker than males, but there were also males not equipped to patrol and protect the pack, just as there were females who sucked at nurturing the striplings. It was based on the individual, but so many of the elders in the pack were stuck in their old way of thinking. They weren't in the stone ages anymore.

For all that supernaturals held themselves apart from humans she found it curious how both groups had a history of treating their females as inferiors. When the vampire king had sent out an open call for Dark Warriors decades ago she had contemplated joining since it was the only group where females were accepted into male roles, but she refused to leave her pack to live at Zeum. There was strength in being close to the pack and she doubted her cougar could survive without that energy. Besides, she felt protecting her pack members took precedence.

As she walked along, she enjoyed the quiet near her cottage. Her place was on the outskirts of Jesaray house where all the activity radiated from. In the center was also the common dining hall, nursery, and the school, but she preferred to live where it was calm and peaceful.

Nodding to John, a wolf shifter who looked to be on his way to the dining hall with his family, it reminded her that she hadn't eaten dinner yet. Ember quickened her steps anxious to hear what Hayden wanted, but acknowledged she didn't want to miss out on the home-cooked meal.

Ember reached Jesaray and took the steps leading to the huge wrap around porch and large front door. Wiping her boots on the mat, she knocked on the door, wondering if Zeke and his new mate were home, as well. Grimacing at the thought of running into him, she prayed he wasn't.

Her hope dashed a second later when Zeke opened the door. For the first time in months, the sight of his smiling blue eyes didn't cause her chest to ache.

"Hey, Em. Good to see you," Zeke murmured as he

pulled her into a friendly embrace. Pack was touchy-feely and this was their way of greeting one another. Of all supernaturals, they shared physical affection without thought. It soothed their beasts and grounded them, but this was the last male she wanted to hug. Well, next to last anyway.

Returning the hug, Ember glanced over his shoulder to see who was in the house. "Who's here?" she asked, not able to return the friendly sentiment.

Zeke broke his hold and held the door open for her to enter. Immediately, the scent of food reached her and her stomach rumbled, reminding her again that she was hungry. The air was filled with rich spices, but she detected seafood and pork.

"I hope you brought your appetite," Zeke chuckled when he heard her stomach. "My Tia has been cooking up a storm and her gumbo is legendary."

Hearing the pride in Zeke's tone and seeing the way he gazed goofily at the exotic bombshell in the kitchen made Ember want to use his legs as a scratching post.

Jesaray house was comfortable and intimate and typically Ember loved the atmosphere, but it seemed too intimate today. The soft, brown leather sofas and rustic wood accents were so familiar and magnified the fact that the female waltzing around the kitchen was an interloper.

"I'm sure we will wrap up this meeting and I'll just head to Flo's," Ember replied, referring to the main dining hall.

Hayden's grandmother, Flo, had been cooking for the pack way before Ember had been born and everyone called her Grandma Flo, although there wasn't a single gray hair on the elderly female.

"There's no need for that," Zeke objected.

She knew he was aware how uncomfortable she was around him and his mate and wanted to ease the situation for them all. That's one thing she loved about Zeke and what made him a good beta. He was always playing the peacemaker.

Ignoring the comment, Ember was tempted to take a seat on the large sofa away from the crowd in the kitchen, but that would be petty. She'd have to look at Tia anyway, thanks to the open floor plan. She might as well join the other C.L.A.W.s surrounding the island. She couldn't regret the relationship she'd had with Zeke, but it hurt more than she'd expected when she had lost him to his Fated Mate a few months back.

When Tia had first come to the Grove, Ember wanted to hunt her down and use her for a chew toy. The worst part was she didn't even know why. Sure, she had loved Zeke, but they both knew that they could lose each other to their mates at any point in time. She wasn't angry that he pursued Tia. Ember understood that there was an irresistible pull to your Fated Mate that few could deny. Maybe it was the fact that the female could control animals. That made her hackles rise and was enough to convince her to keep a safe distance.

"Is Hayden around?" she asked as she took a stool next to Grant.

Grant trained her for patrols and was a great soldier. Plus, she liked that he was a huge bear shifter and would block her smaller frame in a battle.

"I'm right here," came the husky reply. Cigar in mouth, Hayden descended the wide stairs and crossed the hardwood floor to join them. "Thanks for coming on such short notice."

"No problem, Sire," they murmured as a group.

Zeke reached into the cabinets and grabbed bowls, holding them while Tia ladled the thick soup into them.

Focusing on Hayden, Ember waited for him to explain why they were there. Her heart dropped as she realized it wasn't likely he was going to promote her. That was a private affair and there were too many C.L.A.W.s standing around the kitchen.

Hayden's internal animals rose to the surface in rapid succession, inciting the animal in each of them. Ember's gut tightened and she automatically went on alert in response, as did every other shifter present.

"We have a big fucking problem," Hayden announced then nodded his thanks to Zeke when he was handed a bowl of food.

Hayden set the soup down and began pacing. "There have been attacks on the pack. In my fucking back yard," the Omega snarled. "More than a dozen have been left fighting for their life and five are dead. Two of them were striplings and one was a female."

A gasp filled the room and Ember inched closer to Grant in response. The male wrapped his arm around her shoulders, needing the comfort as much as she did. Their children were their most prized possessions because there were so few. Having spent seven centuries without a mate blessing, every group within the Tehrex Realm saw a drastic decline in birth rate and the shifters were no exception.

"Who attacked us?" Ember growled without thought and quickly looked around the room.

She'd never attended a meeting with the C.L.A.W.s and had no idea what was proper etiquette, but no one seemed shocked by her outburst.

"From everything Zeke and I have gathered, we've been attacked by demons," Hayden explained. "The scent of brimstone was unmistakable. Not to mention, some of the wounds are consistent with skirm attacks. I know the vampire princess killed Kadir so I have no idea who is now targeting us, or why, but I don't like it and I will not tolerate it!" Hayden growled, his power rippling through the large room.

"Were there any blue feathers in the area by chance?" Ember asked, thinking of the feather she'd managed to yank from the demon's wing when she was attacked.

It was in a bag under her mattress. Why she had kept it she had no idea. Instinct had driven her actions and she wasn't ready to part with it yet.

Zeke placed a bowl of soup in front of her and gave her one of his sympathetic smiles which made her want punch him in the face. She wasn't a scorned female who couldn't imagine life without him. They had a thing and it ended, simple as that. She didn't need or want pity from him.

"Not that I know of, why?" Hayden asked then stopped pacing.

"The night I was attacked the demon was a female with giant blue wings. She seemed fond of fanfare and making a statement. She didn't give a second thought to exposing our existence to the humans. This is a move I could see her making," Ember explained as she tried to focus on her omega and not the dozen pair of eyes staring her way.

The tension in the air nearly suffocated her. No one liked the idea of being the target of a powerful archdemon. Most shifters were happy to have the focus of the archdemons and their minions remain on the vampire royal family who had a group of the most skilled warriors in the realm surrounding them.

Before Hayden could respond to her admission, Ember's body went on full alert. The distinctive masculine scent of Orlando reached her nose and made her turn in her seat to watch the warrior saunter into the house.

What was it about a male dressed from head to toe in black? His tight t-shirt under a leather jacket combined with tight leather pants oozed sexiness and confidence like nothing else. He moved with feline grace and his beautiful emerald eyes penetrated to her very soul. *Yeah, you're over him all right.*

ORLANDO'S GAZE locked on Ember and refused to let go. He hadn't seen her for a couple days. Her presence punched him in the gut and practically had him panting. The more he was around her the more she affected him. Her beautiful face scrunched as if she'd tasted something she didn't like and she pointedly looked away from him, suddenly focused on eating whatever sat in front of her.

Part of him wanted to explain why he couldn't go on a date with her, but then he thought better of it. This was not the time or place. If he thought she was pissed now, there was no doubt she would chew him a new asshole if he mentioned anything with Hayden and the pack Lieutenants as an audience.

That didn't stop him from admiring her pert backside as she shifted on the stool where she was sitting. Her amber eyes had glowed enticingly before she shut him out and he wanted to see it again. There was a time he would have been dying to taste her lips and explore every inch of her delectable body. And, what a body it was. She was tall with an athletic build with breasts begging for male attention.

It wasn't a different time, he reminded himself, before he got lost in her allure. Jaidis had been killed and he was now the parent of an infant. He didn't have time for a female or the trouble that came with relationships.

Turning to Hayden, he clasped the Omega's forearm and greeted the group. It had been a long time since he had been back in Jesaray house. With his busy schedule, he didn't come often. He had lived in a cabin close to the school for a long time, but Zeum had been home for the past two centuries.

He stopped coming to the pack hunts long ago, as well, but seeing fellow shifters made him miss it. His leopard became restless every full moon, forcing him to find an alternative to the hunts. Running through the forest around Zeum wasn't the same, even with Santiago. The pack had an energy that was irreplaceable, not to mention, fun with the females after the hunt.

He couldn't remember Ember being a part of the pack when he'd lived there. Either she was far younger than his four hundred twelve years or she'd moved from another area. It would be exciting to run next to Ember's cougar. Maybe he would find the time to make it back for the next one.

"What can you tell me about this new demon, Orlando? I have a hunch the recent attacks on our land are connected to that piece of shit. From what Ember said she got a taste of her blood," Hayden surmised as he picked up a crystal snifter of what looked like brandy.

Tia approached him with a smile. "Good ta see you, Orlando. I tink you will enjoy dis gumbo. Eat, eat," the voodoo mambo ordered as she shoved a bowl of the soup into his hand.

"Good to see you, too," he told Zeke's mate.

Santiago had told him the female had taken on the role of caretaker for Hayden and Zeke. Orlando smiled, wondering what Hayden's grandmother thought of him not going to the main dinning hall as often. If given the choice,

Orlando would eat this food over Flo's any day. Tia cooked foods rich with spice where Flo served what he called comfort food. Ever since Elsie joined their ranks at Zeum, he'd come to crave rich flavorful food.

"We don't know too much about the archdemon Lucifer sent this time. She is bold and brazen for sure. And, doesn't give a shit about exposing us. We've talked with Rhys and Dante and they don't know anything about her. Rhys's mate Illianna couldn't recall seeing a winged demon during her century in hell and her brothers are going to do some research. Hopefully those warrior angels will have some information soon. What happened here?" Orlando asked.

There was no doubt in Orlando's mind that Lucifer hadn't wasted time in sending a new archdemon. The bastard was slick, no doubt. This bitch could wreak enough havoc if she exposed them and their attention would be split between the humans and skirm, putting them at a huge disadvantage.

Hayden was solemn as he told Orlando about the attacks. There was entirely too many females and striplings being harmed. This was far beyond anything they'd ever faced. Skirm couldn't feed from supernaturals so they didn't generally target their population.

"From this point on, we are on high alert," Hayden informed them. "We are now doing patrols in pairs and there will be a thirty-minute overlap at shift changes. Every able-bodied male will be taking shifts. So will you, Ember." Orlando's gaze jerked to the female who snapped to attention and sat straight on her stool.

It was clear she was proud to be asked to assist. He, however, didn't like it one bit and wanted to object. The thought of another female, especially this one, being hurt or killed had him resisting the urge to punch Hayden.

"We will not leave a window of vulnerability. I will let the pack know that kids are to be kept close to the center and can never be left alone. Same goes for females. Monthly hunts are postponed until this threat is eliminated," Hayden finished.

"Zander has issued the same orders for the Dark Warriors and our patrols. Looks like none of us will be getting much sleep until this demon is caught," Orlando mused. Ember's gaze finally jerked his way and she glared daggers at him.

What the hell was that about, he wondered. Was she still pissed that he turned her down for dinner? They had bigger matters to deal with and he couldn't become sidetracked.

Unfortunately, her hatred stung, telling him he would need to make this right with her or he'd never have a moment's peace.

CHAPTER 6

"How did you manage to survive on this planet for so long, Sire?" Lorne asked Angus as they brushed passed another group on a street in Inverness, the heart of Scotland. They had been traveling across the world trying to locate Keira, but kept coming up empty.

Shortly after Angus had felt the power of his home realm surrounding Mack's house many months ago, he'd been hit by a sensation he'd resigned himself to never feel again. Keira's magic was unique and was a blow to his gut. It had been that way from the moment he met her over a thousand years before.

He hadn't hesitated to ask her to be his queen, but before they could complete their mating she had disappeared. Without thought, he'd followed the faint trace of her magical signature from Khoth to Earth and had been stranded on the planet for a thousand years. He had all but given up on finding her after endless searches that led to dead ends.

That was, until a few weeks ago, when he felt her again.

It had been muted, but still knocked the breath from his body. He had wanted to leave immediately to find her, but duty made him remain until Zander and the others were safer. Now, he worried that delay had cost him the one chance at finding his love.

He couldn't regret helping those who had become his family, but he wanted to curse Fate for toying with him. Angus knew he had to return to Khoth, but he refused to leave Earth until he found his queen. He had to find Keira. He would never be complete without her.

"Having to hide what you are. Not to mention, having your powers diminished." Lorne continued, oblivious to Angus' anguish.

"At first it wasna that difficult. The population wasna so dense and there were plenty of locations I could shift withoot being seen. It was lonely until I found Zander and joined his household. Since then I've had a family. It wasna the same as my people on Khoth, but a family I came to love. Och, the hardest for me was feeling as if a blanket surrounded my dragon," Angus shared with Lorne, one of his best Máahes.

At first his drive to find Keira kept him going, but after two centuries of searching, without a single clue to her whereabouts, grief had debilitated him. Not only could he not find Keira, but also he didn't have Legette or any of his Máahes. He had nothing. Leading his people had been his purpose for longer than he could remember. He tried to return to Khoth, but discovered that when the portal had snapped shut, something blocked it from reopening.

He'd tried everything to reopen it and get back to his people. Portals didn't naturally disintegrate which told him someone or something had done this on purpose. There was magic at play, so he went to various magic practitioners, but nothing could force the portal open.

Over the next several hundred years, he became a violent destructive creature that he hoped and prayed he never saw again. Eventually, depression and loneliness had him searching for a place to belong. He needed a new purpose and beings he could devote himself to. As king that was all he knew how to do, serve and protect others and was eternally grateful for the day he found Zander and Zeum.

"I still can't get used to your accent and the way you speak, Sire. You sound and act so different from the king I served for so long," Lorne admitted as he gave Angus a sideways look.

Stopping outside the car they'd rented, Angus looked over the hood and met Lorne's deep green eyes. Chuckling, Angus said, "Aye, I lived here in Scotland for so long because that was where I originally sensed her and I eventually adopted the brogue. Now 'tis part of me."

"It suits you," Lorne said as he climbed into the car. "Where are we going now?"

Angus started the car and pulled into traffic. He knew Lorne may not approve and wanted to go home, but Angus was not giving up yet. He knew the kingdom and Legette needed him, but he had been gone for over a thousand years and he trusted they could last a bit longer. Like one of Pavlov's dogs, he'd catch a trace of Keira's presence in this realm. It didn't matter that it would disappear as soon as it appeared. The point was that it manifested and renewed his hope to find her.

He was certain his queen was still alive and on earth, but someone or something was blocking him from locating her. It was the only thing that explained what he was feeling. It wasn't mere wishful thinking on his part. He had mourned her loss long ago. Even now, he held the thin thread of hope at bay despite his convictions. He recalled the pain of her loss all too well to allow for more.

"To the stone circle again. There must be a clue we missed. And, if not, then we go home. I've been gone long enough and I know it's time," Angus growled as his frustration rose.

He'd been to the stone circle and searched the surrounding area countless times, but he couldn't shake the feeling. His Cuelebre instincts were screaming that this location mattered.

"So we're not going home then?" Lorne asked, forlornly.

Angus glanced over and patted his Máahes on the shoulder. "Nay, but I can send you home before we begin the last search if you'd like. I doona want to keep you when you are needed on Khoth."

Lorne turned wide eyes at him and shook his head. "Never, Sire. I don't go home until you do. If I return without you, Legette will have my head. I am by your side no matter what. I swore to serve you and that is what I will do until the day I die," Lorne vowed.

Emotion clogged Angus's throat. All this time, he had worried his people hated him for abandoning them, but that wasn't the case. It was Lorne and Nate who had explained to him why the portal wouldn't open. His one-time friend, Cyril, was behind it all.

Seemed the Unseelie King placed a spell prohibiting all travel from Khoth. The key Cyril placed on the portal was an impossible combination to unlock. Thankfully, the male had underestimated the Gods and Fate because they found a way around what he had done.

The Goddess Morrigan had sent Kyran, a vampire prince, and Mack, a human female, through a one-time portal to Khoth. Once there, the couple had to join forces, battle Unseelie Creatures, discover Keira's tablet and perform a mating to open the portal again, but they overcame each obstacle and ultimately discovered the hex.

All spells require a counter measure and Cyril thought a nightwalker mating a human would never surface because neither existed on Khoth. After all, how could a vampire mate a human and use their blood to break the spell when there were none in the realm? The Unseelie King had made the fatal error of underestimating Fate and the power of the Gods and Goddesses.

Thinking of Cyril and his wicked ways only added to Angus's determination find Keira. Given the events that had occurred, he was certain Cyril was behind Keira's disappearance and was likely the culprit blocking her from Angus. No doubt the powerful king felt when Mack broke the spell and took immediate action in hiding Keira. He'd be damned if he allowed the male to take anymore from him or the dragons of Khoth.

"Your loyalty humbles me," Angus murmured with a nod. "I promise when we get back I will bring the mighty Cuelebre back and restore Khoth to its former splendor."

"I know you will, Sire. But first, let's find your queen," Lorne stated.

"Our last hope is this potion Marie gave us," Angus said, holding up a glass container with glowing blue liquid inside. "It should remove any lingering spells and reveal what was being hidden."

Their trek to the Louisiana bayou had been harrowing, but not as bad as it could have been thanks to Jace and Zander. The vampire king and the Dark Warriors had been forced to visit the voodoo queen a year ago to save Cailyn, Elsie's sister and Jace's Fated Mate. They shared their experience along with tips and tricks, which helped Angus and Lorne avoid the worst of the traps.

"I mean no disrespect, Sire, but why are you so convinced there is anything there? We've gone over that area so much I could tell you the placement of every stone," Lorne asked curiously.

As they drove along, the magic of Khoth called to Angus the closer they got to Calanais and the stone circle. It woke his dragon, invigorating the beast. He had been half asleep for so long he forgot what it felt like.

"Instinct, Lorne. This is where her presence has been strongest. I just hope we will find something that can help us."

"Or, at least something the witches could use to cast a spell," Lorne added thoughtfully.

"Aye," Angus agreed as he found a spot to park on the hillside.

Stepping out of the vehicle, he was awed again by the large stones that dated back to the Bronze Age. Placed in upright position, the dozen or so pillars of rock were a mysterious wonderment surrounded by majestic beauty.

"Stand back here while I dispatch the potion in case something goes wrong," Angus ordered as Lorne came up beside him.

"Not going to happen, Sire," Lorne quipped then suddenly grabbed the small glass bottle before Angus could react.

On swift feet, Lorne ran towards the stone circle where their portal was located and tossed the vial into the middle. Immediately upon hitting the rocky ground, the small container shattered and sent shock waves exploding through the area. The force of the spell threw them both into the air and Angus lost site of his knight as he sailed over the car and landed awkwardly on his arm.

Barely managing to stifle the shout of pain from his broken arm, Angus stood to shaky legs and was pleased to see Lorne standing with his hands on his hips none the worse for wear.

Cradling his arm, Angus made his way to Lorne's side. "You're injured, Sire. You need to shift," Lorne observed.

Angus glanced down and saw the odd angle to his forearm and knew Lorne was right. As much as Angus didn't want to take the time, he had to or his injury would slow them down.

"Och, you're right. Give me a minute," Angus said as he stripped off his clothing and shifted into his dragon.

The instant his reptilian beast took over, Angus felt his arm mend and the call of his home realm reach through the portal, feeding his animal energy.

He had been away far too long and a sudden longing to return had Angus flying toward the portal. He opened his snout and let out a loud roar as a flame of fire shot forty feet in front of him. It had been over a thousand years since he had felt this whole and complete. He knew once he was back on Khoth it would be more intense and he couldn't wait to return.

A small amount of clarity returned and he could hear Lorne cursing behind him. Angus glanced back to see the Máahes gathering his clothes and following towards the portal.

"*Keep up, pup*," Angus taunted in Lorne's mind. "*I smell her.*"

"*I hope to all Gods she is in the cave where you are headed. I am tired of the chase*," Lorne griped in return.

The male wasn't annoyed by having to chase after

Angus. It was the continual disappointment of coming up empty-handed.

Angus flew through the portal and landed outside a cave then changed back to his human form with Lorne following suit.

As Lorne handed him his clothes, Angus carefully scanned the area and stated, "I don't scent any danger here, but I sense a presence I haven't felt for thousands of years."

"Unseelie," Lorne growled, claws extending from his fingertips.

Angus understood his hatred. The Unseelie had turned on them and were destroying their planet. Angus had been relieved to learn that Legette and his Máahes had been able to hold off the Buggane, although they were losing more and more of the lush forests as the Unseelie robbed Khoth of its natural resources.

Angus recalled a time long ago when he and Cyril had been friends. They'd roamed Khoth together hunting treasure and bedding females. Their easy camaraderie had ended when Angus discovered Cyril was responsible for creating the Buggane, as well as, the death of Angus's parents. Cyril believed he could control Angus through their friendship after he became king.

Refocusing on Keira before he got lost in his rage, Angus slowly crept into the small cave. The ceiling was low at the entrance, but about fifty feet in, he noticed it had been manually raised and altered, opening into a larger space where runes were carved into the walls. He detected the strong scent of Unseelie along with Keira's tangy salt and sand, reminding him of the ocean.

"She was held somewhere close," Angus muttered excitedly at having found the epicenter for the spell.

Lorne lifted his hand to a rune, but paused and looked

around. "Yeah, but where. I don't see another opening and there is no evidence there was anyone here."

"Och, keep looking around. There's another room or path somewhere," Angus ordered as he searched the outer walls.

"Here," Lorne called out seconds later. Peeking his blond head around a large stalactite he waved his arms frantically. "There's an opening over here. Come on."

Angus was at his side and rushing through the opening before Lorne could stop him. "Fuck," Angus snarled as he stepped inside a smaller chamber and was greeted by a giant serpent, Suddenly, the creature turned into a vision of Keira lying dead on the floor.

"Watch oot!" Angus yelled to Lorne. "It's an *uabhas*." The Unseelie creature snarled and snapped to attention and turned back into the large serpent then reared up to tower over them. "It turns into what you fear most."

The room was too small for either of them to shift into their dragon. An empty stone table off to one side took up most of the space and another table was topped with some of the same implements they'd seen in the outer chamber.

"Why does it have to turn into a viper? I hate those wankers," Lorne muttered. Having drawn the snake's attention, Lorne danced out of the way as Angus searched for a weapon.

The small titanium *sgian dubh* they both carried would do little against the serpent's razor fins and dagger-sized fangs. Without warning, Angus suddenly found himself sailing through the air as blades sliced into his side. Grunting in pain, he braced himself to hit the stone wall as he tried to track the beast's movements.

He rolled to the floor and noticed that Lorne had partially shifted and was using his talons to slice away the numerous fins from the snake's head. It had been one of those fins along its tail that had cut Angus's side open.

The *uabhas* was one of Cyril's nastier creations. Angus recalled how the Unseelie King created it from jealousy against Angus. It was shortly after his first encounter with the *uabhas* that his greatest fear had come true and his parents had been brutally slain in their beds.

Another swipe of the powerful tail had Angus jumping to his feet. His side was bleeding badly, but he couldn't let that stop him. He climbed onto the creature's back while Lorne distracted it. Glancing down, Angus noted how shimmery blue fins riddled the floor.

Ducking under the largest fins on its back, Angus withdrew his titanium blade and buried it in the creature's skull. The leathery hide didn't afford the beast enough protection and the weapon slid in easily and met its target. Rearing up, Angus was dislodged from the viper and fell to the stone bed with a hard thud.

He lay there panting for breath and holding his side while Lorne rushed to his side. The knight was scratched and cut, but whole and walking. They both looked on as the viper disappeared and a man-sized white worm took shape.

"Its not dead yet," Angus shouted to Lorne. "Kill it before it burrows underground."

"Of course its not. That would've been too easy," the male grumbled as he rushed to the worm and used his claws to slice through its middle.

It was a thing of beauty as the male chopped and diced the slimy creature to bits. Pieces fell and flopped on the ground for several seconds before going still.

"Did you see that shit? I'm the fucking snake-master!" Lorne boasted with a grin as he did a victory dance, fist-pumping the air.

"Och, I hate those things. You definitely have skills, my friend. I'm quite certain it's dead now," Angus relayed as he stood to shaky legs.

"You need to shift and heal," Lorne observed as he stopped and pointed to Angus's injured side.

"I know, but first we need to see if there is anything of Keira's here," he ordered as he hobbled into the small chamber. Angus made his way to the overturned table and searched the contents scattered on the dirt floor. "She was here. And for a very long time by the strength of her scent, but she isna here now."

"I found something, Sire. I think we finally have something to take to the Rowan sisters," Lorne said, holding up a small piece of fabric that had been stuck under the corner of the bed.

Angus's heart raced as he recognized the pattern as the last dress he'd seen Keira wearing. After a thousand years of suppressing his hope he set it free to spread its wings and fly.

His queen would soon be in his arms again.

EMBER STOOD rigid while her Omega paced in circles around her. She'd asked for a private meeting after the C.L.A.W. and Orlando had left the lodge. "You don't have to allow them to remain at Zeum, Sire. You can force them to come home," Ember insisted for the tenth time. "Pack comes first."

Hayden stopped and glared at her. "You would have me force Zander to relieve all shifters worldwide from their obligation as Dark Warriors to come and help find who is stalking and killing our people? What about the innocent humans? What about the vow they pledged not only to Zander, but the Goddess? They cannot simply walk away from that," he explained.

Ember tried to hide her annoyance. Hayden was a stubborn male at times and was not seeing how the pack needed protection just as much as the humans, if not more. Ember felt the Goddess would agree with her.

"Sire, the pack is in grave danger. Our children and females are being killed. We need to find the demon responsible for this before we lose more," she insisted.

Hayden crossed to the bar and grabbed his crystal glass and poured another healthy dose of brandy. She loved the earthy scent of the liquor even if she hated to drink it.

"I have thought about the same thing but you must consider the bigger picture, Ember. This is one reason you would not make a good C.L.A.W." The comment stung and made Ember wince at the reminder he continually denied her.

"Yes, the pack is in danger, but perhaps the demon is attacking us on purpose. Shifters have played a major role in the fight against the archdemons, especially in locating lairs, and if we pull the shifter Dark Warriors we leave the vampire royal family at a disadvantage. This is what the enemy wants. Us chasing our tails and depleting Zander's protection. Their goal is to get to Princess Isobel," Hayden said but Ember could see the wheels turning. He was questioning his decisions.

"I understand that and I don't want her hurt, but we are trading many lives for one. That hardly seems right," she added, hoping to sway him.

Hayden took a gulp of his drink before shaking his head. "No one possesses the power this young vampire does. She can teleport, kill demons with a touch, and talk directly to the Goddess. And, that's what she can do at less than a year old. Who knows what she will be able to do when she matures. We are on the same side as the Dark Warriors, Ember. We fight the same enemy. They are looking for this female and she needs protection, too," he finished and Ember saw his resolve and knew she couldn't change his mind.

"If you won't call Orlando and Santiago back then I wish you would reconsider making me a C.L.A.W. I can help with more than simple patrols. I'm ready, Sire," Ember informed him, holding her head high.

"No you're not, Ember. I had been denying you because you are female, but now I see your impatience and that could endanger far more than fellow shifters. This conversation is over. I entertained your objections, but my decision is firm," Hayden barked, his tone layered with the power of his animals.

Ember nodded her head. "Yes, Sire. Thank you," she mumbled before she walked out the door.

Her Omega's words reverberating through her head. She understood the danger the demons posed to every being on the planet, but pack was everything. She had to protect them first or everyone weakened, including her Omega.

And she would die before she allowed that to happen.

CHAPTER 7

Orlando gagged as he pulled the tabs on Brantley's diaper. "How can something so sweet smell so foul? Are you sure you won't change him while I play with my Princess?" he asked the vampire queen as he looked over to Elsie who was playing a game with Isobel in the corner of the nursery.

"Not on your life," Elsie replied and laughed. "You're his father now which means you get the good, the bad, and the stinky."

"I'm sure you didn't make Zander change Izzy's diapers," Orlando grumbled as he pulled one side open.

The smell intensified and he saw the disaster had exploded up his back. When Orlando reached up and pinched his nose to dull the stench, Brantley tried to crawl away.

"No, don't let him get away," Elsie cried out as she jumped to her feet. The instant the queen was in motion, five gnomes appeared by Izzy's side, watching the events unfold.

Orlando reacted on instinct and caught Brantley's leg

before he managed to wiggle away and was rewarded with a dirty palm. "Ugh, that is disgusting. I'd rather fight skirm and be covered in black blood than this mess." The baby rolled over and giggled and Orlando couldn't help but laugh, as well.

He was glad Brantley didn't seem impacted by the death of his parents and circumstance of his birth. Not to mention he was growing like a weed. Supernaturals' growth rates were expedited and he recalled Elsie's shock over how rapidly Izzy had grown. She had only been a few months old, yet was walking and talking. Brantley was just a couple weeks old and crawling everywhere.

Every milestone Brantley made lifted a weight off Orlando's chest while making him sad at the same time. The baby would never know his mother. How beautiful and strong she was. How she loved him enough to put his life ahead of her own. Orlando vowed Brantley would know as much information as possible about his mother even though he'd only known her for a short time.

"Stop being a baby, O. Grab his legs and take off the old diaper and clean up the mess," Elsie ordered, bringing him out of his thoughts.

"There's so much of it. Can you guys do this?" Orlando asked the gnomes hopefully.

Izzy laughed and tossed a ball to Pepper, or maybe it was Dipple. He could never keep their names straight. They all looked so similar with their black trousers and green and blue striped shirts. Izzy loved their pointy shoes and had asked her mom for her own pair, adding that she wanted hers to sparkle.

"We will be back after we clean this mess, Princess," the gnome cooed at Izzy.

"Pepper play. Dipple is Mr. Poopy man," Izzy insisted to the gnome sitting next to her.

"You heard the Princess, Mr. Poopy man," Pepper said to Dipple.

Dipple didn't appear happy about the comment, but didn't argue or show Izzy his displeasure. Instead, he walked over and took charge of the diaper disaster.

Izzy was the perfect combination of Elsie and Zander. She had her father's black hair, but Elsie's Loch-blue eyes. She was headstrong, yet caring and loving and very intuitive. She could kill demons with a touch and could teleport. Izzy represented the amulet and was their link to the Goddess. She could call weapons of light at will.

She had the makings of a born leader and he couldn't wait to see her grow into her power, but he wished she didn't carry such a heavy burden on her tiny shoulders.

Dipple turned to Orlando. "Get that contraption off him and hand him here" the gnome ordered in a raspy voice that contradicted his small stature.

Orlando looked down at the two-foot tall gnome and wondered what Brantley would think of them when he grew older. They looked like dolls with bulging blue eyes and fire-red hair, at least until they smiled. Their razor-sharp teeth were anything but friendly.

Orlando kept hold of Brantley's ankles like he'd seen Elsie do with Izzy and lifted his legs as he removed the dirty diaper. He couldn't manage the one-handed swipe like Elsie who seemed to get Izzy practically clean before she ever took a wipe to her bottom.

"You're a lifesaver," Orlando told Dipple as he handed a messy Brantley over. Before the gnome walked away with the baby, Orlando couldn't stop from running his hand through his soft hair before kissing his forehead.

It was bittersweet to be given the privilege of raising Jaidis's son. The baby had his mother's eyes and soft temperament, making him miss Jaidis that much more. She would have been so proud of this easy-going stripling. Brantley preferred sleeping in the bed with Orlando to the crib in the nursery where the gnomes stayed and Orlando was okay with that for now.

He enjoyed every moment with the baby and was happy to share his bed even if it made him long more for Jaidis to be at his side. He had imagined them all living at Zeum while he helped her raise her child, but never had he thought he'd be doing it alone.

A sudden flash of bright light grabbed Orlando's attention. It wasn't the same light he emitted when shifting to his leopard, but it wasn't entirely unfamiliar.

Turning around, Orlando half-expected to see Rhys's Fated Mate, Illianna. Orlando enjoyed the angel's presence. She was a bearer of joy and happiness and he couldn't help but feel at peace when she was in the room. Occasionally she was called upon for assignments in her home realm and Orlando thought the white light was her returning from Heaven and was surprised to see Isobel's guardian angel, Ramiel, instead.

Immediately tension filled the room, while Izzy burst into her round of clapping and jumping up and down.

"Rami, Rami. You came to play ball, Yay!" Izzy exclaimed as she grabbed up the green ball and tossed it at the surly angel.

Unlike Illianna, Rami represented the Angel's of Retribution and his presence was intimidating and suffocating. His large black wings filled the room, taking up all the space. The male didn't bother retracting them and he didn't smile when Izzy called out to him. He caught the ball and knelt to address the Princess as she ran for him, her fluffy purple dress flying about her legs. Her sparkly shoes caught the light with each step and Orlando was certain the outfit was courtesy her Aunt Breslin.

Orlando knew Breslin influenced her niece more than Elsie cared for. He had witnessed more than one argument between Elsie and Breslin as they battled over a pair of sparkly shoes or a designer dress Breslin had bought for the little princess, but ultimately Izzy chose girly garments over practicality.

Elsie, bringing his attention back to the matter at hand, suddenly bombarded Orlando's empathic senses. He watched Elsie wring her hands in front of her pink sweater as she eyed the angel who had once been her husband. Orlando recalled the hell Elsie had gone through after Dalton had been killed, and now it wasn't much better after he had returned to her life as her daughter's guardian angel, Ramiel. Things had been tense, to say the least.

When Rami first came to Zeum, everyone in the house could see he still carried a torch for Elsie. Of course, Orlando could relate to that. But now, he saw a male filled with nothing but hatred and bitterness. Dressed in his black leathers and black boots, the male was unapproachable and it was clear he had no desire to be around Elsie. But Izzy adored him and he would always come for her. It was his duty and obligation and he would never fail her.

"Izzy," The angel greeted as he hugged her close then stood, enclosing her in his strong arms. "Haven't I told you that you are only to call me when you are in danger?"

Izzy wasn't afraid of the angel's gruff tone as she smiled back. "Pepper and I play ball. Rami, play with us," the princess insisted.

A harsh smile graced Rami's face as he tickled under

Izzy's arm. "And I told you that I don't have time to play. My job is to protect you," he replied sternly.

Izzy put her chubby little hand on his chest and held his gaze. "You need to hab fun, Rami. You too sad."

Before Rami could respond, Elsie greeted him, "Rami. It's been awhile. How are you?"

The cold, narrowed eyes Rami threw Elsie's way made Orlando's hackles rise and he stepped up beside the Queen. A knowing smirk graced Rami's lips, telling Orlando the angel knew how he'd felt about Elsie. Orlando didn't care. Elsie was his to protect when Zander wasn't around and he would do that without hesitation.

"Word is there's a new archdemon on earth," Rami said by way of answering.

None of them bothered hiding the conversation from Izzy who listened to the conversation raptly. Orlando wished he could shield the princess from the harsh realities of life, but it was pointless. She was given an incredible position the day she was born and she would have to accept it.

"What do you know about her?" Elsie asked as she looked to Orlando then back to the angel. Orlando hoped the male had come with helpful news about the latest terror to the realm.

Rami tossed the ball back to Pepper and shifted Izzy to his other arm. "Not much. The warrior angels are being tight-lipped, but Abraxos and Ayil said it was because they didn't know much other than she is a very dangerous fallen angel," Rami shared.

"Makes sense given her blue wings," Orlando replied, thinking about the demon that had injured Ember in the club. "She was brazen in her attack and seems intent on exposing supernaturals."

"But why?" Rami asked as he began to pace with Izzy.

"Exposing you would create another barrier to getting hands on Isobel. They have to know I would take her to Heaven with me to keep her from human authorities and then they would never get to her."

"I can't even think about that. My daughter is going nowhere," Elsie declared.

Before anyone could respond, Orlando's cell rang. Digging it from his pocket his heart kicked into gear when he saw Zander's number. Why was he calling him and not his mate?

Elsie watched Orlando closely. He half expected her to start screaming with another premonition, but she stood silently.

"Yes, Liege," he answered as he turned his back to Elsie.

"I doona have much time. Get Santiago from the dungeons and the two of you get to Gasworks Park. There's a shitstorm going on and I need you two ASAP," Zander barked into the phone before the line went dead.

Orlando turned around to see Elsie's pale face. She had grabbed Isobel and was holding her tightly. Orlando was bombarded by Izzy's worry through his empathic ability which was most disconcerting. Supernaturals grew at a rapid pace, but their emotions and awareness didn't and Isobel was extremely alert to the dire situation.

Shaking off the disturbing thought, Orlando turned to Rami. "Can you teleport Santi and I to Gasworks?"

Rami nodded once and headed out the door. Orlando hurried after him, calling back to Elsie, "Take care of Brantley."

"I will. And you bring my mate home to me," Elsie ordered before they turned a corner in the hall.

Diverting Rami to grab weapons first, Orlando wondered if Hayden had received a call also. Could Ember be heading, as well? He remembered their last encounter and the attack she suffered. A chill rushed through his body and he quickened his pace. If ember was in trouble he had to get to her.

He couldn't fail another female.

CHAPTER 8

Stumbling, Orlando's previous meal was lodged in his throat and his head was spinning. Nothing was in focus, but he heard chaos surrounding him.

"Fuck me, running. Teleporting sucks," Santi griped.

After several blinks, blurry shapes were highlighted by a subtle glow. "I really enjoyed Elsie's stroganoff going down. Coming back up, not so much," Orlando added.

Beside him, he felt Rami stiffen at the mention of Elsie and his emotions nearly laid Orlando on his back. He'd rarely come across so much rage, sadness and pain in one being. The angel had some serious unresolved issues. A check yourself moment slammed home, forcing Orlando to realize if he didn't watch it he could end up just as angry and bitter. The thought was sobering.

"Speak for yourself, bro. I'd do that twenty times in a row cause my ass is out of that dungeon, even if it's temporary. You don't know how good it feels to be outside breathing fresh air," Santiago countered.

Orlando knew his best friend and partner was relieved to be out of his cell. He didn't know how he was staying sane

88 BRENDA TRIM & TAMI JULKA

but if Santi was feral it didn't show. Orlando thought for sure his wolf was climbing the walls in the dungeons of Zeum.

"Are you two pansies done complaining?" Rami interjected with a snarl. "I believe your comrades may need some help."

The levity of the moment fled with the reminder as their vision slowly cleared. Without pausing to contemplate the dozens of skirm surrounding Zander and his brothers, Orlando removed one of his titanium *sgian dubhs* and raced into the fray.

Thrusting his blade into the back of the first skirm he encountered, the demon-created minion instantly turned to ash. It was unfair of the archdemons to turn young human males into mindless slaves. Even if they had agreed to the transformation, there was no way they understood the full scope of what would be done to them.

Suddenly, Orlando was knocked so hard his body flew forward. He quickly shifted, landing on four paws. As soon as he had his bearings, he searched for what had knocked him hard enough to sail through the air. There was so much terror and chaos he could hardly make sense of the situation.

Glancing to his paws, a mangled corpse had been trampled, but there was no mistaking the injury to its throat. Skirm had attacked this human. Scanning the field, Orlando saw countless more human victims. He had never seen more humans at the sight of a supernatural battle in his four hundred twelve years. Dozens of cups and candles littered the area.

These people were holding a candlelight vigil, Orlando thought with horror as his leopard howled in outrage.

Pain radiated through Orlando's ribs as his animal was

tossed in the air. This was getting old, Orlando thought. Twisting his head, he saw the skirm that had kicked him. The idiot thought he could take on a snow leopard? Time to show this asshat who was boss.

Landing easily on his feet, Orlando ran forward and locked his jaws around the male's throat and ripped it out. Black blood spurted, burning Orlando's mouth and esophagus. He felt the liquid coating his white fur. Thankfully, his hide was thick enough that it protected him from being burned by the toxic substance.

The skirm fell to the ground and Orlando moved on, leaving it for a warrior to ash with their titanium weapon. He was confident the skirm couldn't heal from a wound that severe and he had bigger fish to fry.

Bhric was twenty feet away surrounded by three skirm. Claws finding purchase, Orlando tore into one of the skirm attacking the Vampire Prince. Bhric and Orlando fell into familiar teamwork.

"Feel the freeze, motherfucker," Bhric shouted as ice shot out of his hands and pierced one of the skirm.

Bhric used his weapon to turn another to ash while Orlando incapacitated the third. Thank the Goddess for titanium weapons, Orlando mused. They made cleanup easy. Until the lesser demons began crossing into this realm from the Underworld, there had rarely been evidence left behind after one of their battles.

Orlando didn't want to think about what was going to happen this time. There were too many human bodies for he and Santiago to cover this up. He feared the media would be all over this.

Bhric patted Orlando between the ears and pointed to his brother Kyran who was sifting around the largest group of skirm. "Och, let's go help my *brathair*," Bhric murmured as he pulled a flask from his back pocket and took a hefty swig. Tossing it to the ground, he yelled, "Time to finish this shit," before taking off in Kyran's direction.

Concern about Bhric's drinking vied for attention with Orlando's need to focus on the battle at hand. The warrior drank all the time at home, but he'd never seen Bhric drinking during a battle. The problem was clearly worsening, Orlando thought as he followed the vampire prince.

Black mist shrouded the park for several seconds, blinding everyone and causing further chaos. Using his other senses, Orlando targeted as many skirm as he could before the mist began to clear.

Moments later, the blue-winged demon stood facing Zander with a black sword in hand. "How nice of you to join my party," the demon cooed.

Orlando had hoped to never see this bitch again. The cloths wrapped around her torso and limbs seemed more torn than before, but her blue wings looked just as vile.

"Crocell, I presume," Zander growled after ashing a skirm.

The king's black leathers were torn and his faced cut and bleeding, but he appeared as regal and confident as if he were sitting on a throne greeting his loyal subjects. How the male did it Orlando didn't understand because the archdemon had his four legs shaking uncontrollably.

The demon's eyes widened before she cocked her head and a slow smile spread across her face. Orlando continued attacking skirm while trying to keep his eyes on the pair as they stood in the middle of the mêlée speaking. It was noisy but his keen ears picked up the conversation.

"I wanted to introduce myself so you know who is coming after your daughter. I don't play the same game as my male counterparts, as you can see. You can't beat me. I don't know how you managed to kill Kadir, but mark my word, Vampire King, I will not fail. Your daughter will be mine and she will free Lucifer from his frozen prison," Crocell purred seductively to Zander.

That had Orlando pausing, which was a mistake. He knew better than to become distracted. Next thing he knew a skirm stabbed him in the shoulder. Claws ripped into skin and blood flowed as Orlando sank his sharp fangs into the neck of the skirm. Orlando thrashed his head back and forth until he felt the enemy go lax in his mouth.

An ear-piercing screech rent the air and Orlando caught sight of ice leaving Bhric's palms before encompassing her wings. Kyran sifted, appearing behind the demon and lifted his hand to thrust one of his blades into the demon's back. She turned at the last minute and his blade sank into a frozen wing, missing its target.

Wrenching herself free, she spread her wings and shook off the ice, black droplets falling with it. "Your ploys will not work with me. I will have the Princess. Humans will continue to die until she is mine. It's on your head how many innocent lives are lost," she snarled as her eyes turned black.

"I have stopped every demon Lucifer has sent and I will stop you, too," Zander replied calmly as if the demon hadn't just threatened every human on the planet.

Crocell threw her head back and laughed. "I am going to enjoy this battle, Vampire King. This is just the beginning," she vowed before disappearing.

Car doors slammed shut and Breslin, Rhys, Gerrick and Jace rushed onto the field with Cade and Caell following on their heels. The Dark Warriors wasted no time in eliminated the remaining skirm.

Orlando felt the brush of Breslin's flames followed

closely by Bhric's ice. The twins were more in sync than the others and to watch them together was a thing of beauty. It was hard to tell where one stopped and the other began as their fire and ice swirled around them.

Orlando searched the field for survivors, but found none. When the dust settled and no more demons or skirm came out of the woodwork, Orlando took the time to shift back and made his way to Zander's side.

"This is a huge fucking mess," Orlando stated, surveying the carnage.

"Bluidy hell. That bitch is going to pay for this," Zander promised as he clenched his fists at his sides.

"This is a massacre we won't be able to cover," Santiago added, voicing what Orlando had been thinking.

"The media will definitely get wind of this. We need to come up with a plan and fast," Orlando suggested.

"Och, you're right. I need to bring the council in on this. This affects us all. The possibility for exposure is high. Crocell is going to continue attacking," Zander said.

"I could set fire to this field and cover evidence of super-natural involvement," Breslin offered.

Orlando winced at the princess's suggestion. He hated desecrating the victims anymore. He knew how human families needed and deserved closure. Unfortunately, something had to be done or every being in the Tehrex Realm was at risk.

"I doona like it, but there is no other option. Even now the human authorities are racing this way," Zander pointed out.

Orlando directed his keen hearing outward and realized the king was right, sirens were blaring in the distance. They needed to leave pronto or be caught in the middle of a giant massacre.

'Take care of this, Bre, and fast. We need to get oot of here," Zander finished as he headed to the car.

"You guys go ahead. I'll teleport Breslin home when she's done," Rami offered.

Zander glanced at the angel and they shared a long silent look. The two males had come to an awkward truce based on the love and concern for Isobel, but they would never completely trust one another. Finally, Zander nodded and their group headed to the vehicles.

Sweltering heat radiated behind Orlando and he glanced over his shoulder. His heart was in his throat. This was not a simple cover up. The humans were going to have a field day with this and he had a sinking feeling that nothing was ever going to be the same after tonight.

THE ENORMITY of the infamous Zeum compound awed Ember as she and Hayden followed a shifter down a long hallway. She couldn't identify Nate's animal, but she loved the way he teased Hayden and flirted with her. Surprisingly, the hotel-sized home was warm and inviting rather than cold and impersonal. She would have expected with the sheer size that she would feel out of place and uncomfortable. She admitted that Nate's friendly demeanor added to its charm.

Voices drifted out of a room ahead and curiosity had Ember trying to catch any details she could. She felt honored Hayden had asked her to attend with him, especially since this was something his Lieutenants usually did.

Still simmering with irritation at Orlando, she hoped he wasn't there. She didn't want to face him yet. Okay, that was a flat out lie, she acknowledged. She wanted more than anything to see him again, but she *was* pissed off at the male. His order of priorities needed to be rearranged and she was more than happy to do it for him.

Unfortunately, she vacillated between wanting to strangle the annoying male and needing to strip his clothes and ravage his sexy body. As if her thoughts had conjured the shifter, she heard his voice above the cacophony. It was the most seductive sound she'd ever heard. Not too deep, but full of life.

The room fell silent the moment she and Hayden entered and several seated around the table looked to Hayden with raised eyebrows. She didn't pay them any attention as her gaze went right to Orlando.

He smiled at her and her damn panties nearly melted off her body. Damn if his grin didn't need to be registered as a deadly weapon. Frustrated with her reaction to him, she reminded herself she was annoyed with him for not only ignoring the pack's needs, but also rejecting her advances.

Twisting her face into a scowl, she shook her head at him and turned back to the group seated around a huge wooden table. She contemplated asking Nate into helping her heft the nice table out the front door because Grandma Flo would love to have something like this in the dining hall.

She didn't know all the faces in the room, but she certainly knew which two were the king and queen. Elsie narrowed her eyes suspiciously at Ember. What the hell was her problem? Ember had never even met the female before.

"Who's your beautiful companion?" a male with seductive blue eyes asked Hayden, drawing her attention away from the stick-up-her-butt queen.

"This is Ember. Ember this is Dante, the Cambion Lord," Hayden murmured.

"I must say you have the most exquisite eyes, my love,"

the cambion said as he reached over and grabbed Ember's hand, placing a warm kiss to each knuckle.

Dante's lips were soft and she could feel his sexual power at play on her. She knew the lure of a sex demon and placed up her mental barrier. Sex demons had the ability to bed anyone that let down their defenses and the Cambion Lord was oozing with seduction.

"You are a silver-tongued devil," she replied, smiling. She could've sworn she saw Orlando bristle at her reaction to the attractive male.

Hayden proceeded to introduce her to the rest of the table's occupants and Dante released her hand and took his seat. Her palms began sweating when she realized he had brought her to a Dark Alliance Council meeting. It would have been nice to know so she could change into something nicer, she mused. Her holey jeans and Led Zeppelin t-shirt didn't seem appropriate. Although, the snotty vampire queen was dressed nearly identically so she guessed it was acceptable.

"Love your sweatshirt. It's classic," Mack drawled.

Ember smiled at the spiky-haired female whose whiskey eyes were full of fire. She couldn't help but notice the female's huge breasts and almost laughed out loud at her tight-fitting t-shirt that read 'Don't worry its only kinky the first time'.

"Yours, too. I've heard that more than once," Ember laughed as she gestured to Mack's shirt.

A growl echoed throughout the room and she glanced in Orlando's direction. Surely that hadn't been him. She hoped her responding smirk told him he shouldn't have turned down her offer for dinner.

Mack chuckled and gave her mate, Kyran, a knowing

look. "My bloodsucker says it so often I'm considering it for my next tattoo," she said and winked toward Kyran.

Ember's gaze darted to the ink running up both of Mack's arms. She had the small one on her neck and was itching for another, but couldn't imagine being bold enough to pull off something that ostentatious. Somehow, it worked on this female, though.

"And, I havena been wrong, have I, Firecracker?" Kyran murmured before he placed a kiss on Mack's neck.

The female didn't shiver or melt from his comment, but rolled her eyes instead. What she couldn't hide was her arousal. It perfumed the air and every supernatural in the room had to be aware of it. These two had it bad for one another and Ember couldn't stop the spark of jealousy that ignited. Who wouldn't want that kind of passion, she amended. It was enticing.

"Och, let's start this meeting before things go too far off track," Zander ordered. "Thank you for coming. Last night, my Dark Warriors and I faced a horde of skirm and one bluidy fucking archdemon who didn't think twice about the massacre she left behind. We need a plan of how to deal with this new demon and how we are going to handle the inevitable evidence she is going to leave behind. Seems the bitch is bound and determined to expose our existence," the vampire king finished then took a swig of his drink; Scotch, if Ember wasn't mistaken.

"She left at least a hundred dead humans in Gas Works Park and we had to have Breslin burn the scene. There was no way Santi and I could contain that amount of evidence," Orlando admitted.

"She's a conniving cunt, for sure. She launched an attack on us around the same time. She was testing our boundaries for weaknesses. Ember detected her first and called in reinforcements," Hayden shared with the group, which had every eye turning her way.

Clearing her throat, Ember voiced, "I wasn't about to allow her to take another member of my pack. I managed to cut her but then she disappeared."

Ember recalled the minor wound and the small amount of her black blood had that had splattered to the ground. To Ember's shock it had burned all the ferns and ground cover in a two-foot radius.

"What are we going to do about this one? How do we cover up a hundred human deaths without raising suspicion?" Dante asked. All hint of the sex demon's previous flirting was gone, replaced by a sharp edge of seriousness and concern.

"This time they will chalk it up to an explosion at the old factory. Breslin made sure of that, but who knows where she will target next," Orlando interjected as he took his switchblade out and started flipping it. Still sexy, Ember thought.

"And, we canna use fire every time. That will look suspicious," Zander added.

"So we don't," Hayden said and sat forward. He folded his large hands on the table and projected a calm Ember didn't quite understand. "Let them find out. I'm tired of trying to stay one step ahead of the humans, as well as, the demons. Besides, we need them as allies at this point. They can help us beat the demons," the omega stated.

Ember's jaw fell along with everyone else's in the room. The gasps, growls and glares spoke volumes about the reaction to the bomb Hayden dropped. Zander turned a deep shade of red and was leaning over the table in Hayden's direction.

"Are you fucking insane?" Zander snarled. "Not only has

the Goddess forbid it, the humans canna handle that knowledge."

"They would turn on us," Dante said with a slam of his fist to the table. "I for one don't want to become the government's next experiment. Think of your people, Hayden. They would be chained and put in cages."

Ember wrapped her arms around her middle at Dante's words. She would never survive in a cage. Her cougar would go insane and so would she.

"We don't know that," Hayden insisted. "Your opinion underestimates humans." She inched closer to her Omega, needing the strength of his animals, as well as, wanting to support him.

"No offense, Hayden, but you're wrong," Cailyn interjected. From what Ember recalled of the introductions she was Elsie's sister and Jace's mate. "My sister's initial reaction is a perfect example. She is Zander's Fated Mate, yet she was terrified at first."

"She's right," Mack added. "It's why I formed SOVA. We attacked and killed vampires." Ember cocked her head at that bit of irony. Mack had hunted and killed vampires, yet was now mated to one. Interesting story she wanted to hear more about at some point.

"Sure, they turned out to be skirm, but we didn't know that. We thought they were vampires and needed to be killed. No one stopped to think there could be *good* vampires. We wanted them all exterminated," the feisty female added and Ember could see that Mack was an asset to the Dark Warriors.

"I willna incur the Goddess's wrath by exposing the realm when she has ordered otherwise," Zander declared and resounding nods around the room followed.

"I concede for now, but you have to realize that we may

not have a choice. This demon may do it for us and we need to be prepared for that outcome," Hayden countered and folded massive arms over his chest.

Her Omega was wise and had made a perfect point. This demon was taking risks and none of them could stop her. Wanting to gage Orlando's reaction, her gaze sought him out. He was nodding in agreement with Zander and looked at Hayden in disbelief. Her rage bubbled to the surface again over this male's alliance with the vampire king. She might be undeniably attracted to the male, but if this ever came to blows, she swore to skin his leopard alive.

CHAPTER 9

Orlando watched Ember's tempting backside as she bent over sifting through ash and burnt debris. It was impossible to stop the erection that sprang to life or the desire to mount her and stake a claim. He knew it was from wanting a female of his own. It was the desire for a female of his own that had led him down two paths he never should have traveled. Jaidis and Elsie belonged to other males and it was wrong for him to feel anything for either female. Jaidis's death had hardened his heart.

If he could stop his attraction to the brown-haired beauty with her penetrating golden eyes he would. He had no fucking desire to care for any female at this point. Besides, he had his hands full with Brantley.

"Are you just gonna stand there all day staring at my ass or are you going to come help me?" Ember asked, the amber of her eyes catching fire.

He liked her spunk. He especially liked how she didn't back down. He'd sensed her reticence upon entering the war room and watched her scan the room. Her gulp wasn't obvious to most, but he'd been watching her like a hawk. She was exquisite, from the slender line of her throat to the way her chin lifted with her pride and determination.

"I think I'll keep watching. The view is making me hungry, Wildcat." he said, truthfully with a small smile at the corner of his mouth.

She gathered her torso up and stood tall while planting her fists on her hips. She was piqued, but he knew her true feelings. Not only was her arousal perfuming the air with its sweet frangipani, his ability told him she wanted him as fiercely as he wanted her. He also knew she wasn't happy over the fact that she was attracted to him.

He'd never struggled for female companionship and had certainly had his share of lovers, but the fact that this female shared his desires soothed some of his ache. Having gone so long with unreciprocated feelings, this stole his reserve and he nearly pounced on the female. As much as Ember may want him, but she would rip his nuts off if he tried to push her to her hands and knees in this charred scene.

"That's funny. Seems to me like you're just being lazy. If I remember correctly, you turned down my dinner invitation. So be a good little kitty and help me," she ordered as she dismissed him and turned back to her task.

"Ouch," he winced as he threw his hand over his heart in mock hurt. "Your claws are lethal. Why did Hayden send you to do this investigation? I'd have thought he'd send Zeke and his mate, Tia, with her voodoo powers."

Ember stiffened at the mention of Zeke and Orlando had to hold back his reaction to her feelings over another male.

He hadn't been prepared when she'd joked with Mack about males talking her into kinky sex. His claws had shot from the tips of his fingers and his growl had rumbled from his throat before he knew what hit him. He still didn't understand why he'd been so pissed by the thought of any male tying Ember up and having his way with her, but he was unable to deny his displeasure.

It seemed his long-denied libido was going to take over his mind given that he was unable to stop imagining her on all fours in front of him.

"Zeke and his precious mate can't do what I can," Ember snapped.

Orlando lifted one eyebrow at that. Interesting. She was jealous over Zeke being with Tia. He wondered if she'd been seeing him when he discovered his mate. Instant camaraderie formed with the stubborn cougar.

"Sucks when you want something you can't have," Orlando observed as he went to work looking through the debris.

Digging through a scene, let alone one so gruesome, and looking for clues was not part of his normal job. At SPD they had a CSI unit to perform these duties and with the Dark Warriors most of their enemies became ash.

His chest tightened and regret was a bitter pill on his tongue as he saw a tiny blackened bone. The child was young, so very innocent, and deserved better in life.

"I have no idea what you're talking about. I don't want Zeke. I just don't like an outsider being considered one of us," Ember replied without pausing.

"You've been cocooned within the pack too long. When you find your Fated Mate they become one of us no matter who, or what, they are. Don't forget that Tia carries the soul of a wolf, even if she can't shift into the beast," he pointed out.

Ember stood and pushed her glasses up her nose in that sexy way of hers. "Why do you always take their side? If I didn't smell your leopard I would swear you weren't even a shifter," she countered.

"Damn, Wildcat. That's harsh. I am more shifter than you will ever know. But I am also one of the Goddess's children and I will fulfill her calling for me. The world is bigger than the acres around Jesaray house," Orlando informed her.

Orlando pulled a rubber glove from his front packet and used it to pick up the tiny bone. Thrusting it in her direction he allowed his irritation to surface. This female was insufferable at times.

"This little boy needed me to be here and protect him. Dark Warriors are the only thing standing between the demons and humans. Supernaturals, too, for that matter. That job falls to all of us, not just the vampires. Or are you saying it's their problem and we don't need to bother ourselves with it?" he challenged.

Ember shook her head, her brown hair flying wildly about her head. "What happened to these humans is unfortunate and I hate that they died, but shifters are being killed, too. Are you going to be there for them?" she spat and fire sparked behind her amber eyes.

"I am always there for Hayden, but he has C.L.A.W.s to keep pack safe. That's the reason hundreds of them haven't been killed like they were here. Humans have nothing. I go where the Goddess sends me. I fight this war in her name, not Zander's, not Hayden's. No one's but hers," he amended, frustrated that she was making him explain his calling.

He might question Fated Mates and the Goddess's reasoning behind those choices, but he was steadfast in his commitment to protecting human and realm members from the vile archdemons.

That shut the feisty female up for a millisecond as she

cocked her head to the side and considered his words. Her breath fogged in front of her as she breathed and her nose was turning pink, reminding him how cold it was outside. The sight of her heated his blood and had him sweating beneath his clothes.

"I get what you're saying, Warrior. But, there always comes a time when something happens and people must choose a side. I can't help but wonder if you'll pick the right side," she muttered with a shrug before she turned back to her work.

Orlando had to look away as her comment struck home. What would he do if he ever had to choose between Hayden and Zander? Would it be that simple?

After several silent seconds of his pushing charred bits and pieces around, he finally said, "Right or wrong, I'll always choose the side of the Goddess, no matter who that happens to align with."

Before Ember had a chance to respond, she stood up with something clutched in her gloved hand. Waving the appendage around she exclaimed, "There are two. I knew something was off."

She was so animated and truly pleased with her find that Orlando found himself hurrying to her side. "What is it? Two what? Demons?" he asked, giving voice to his suspicion.

"Yes!" she practically shouted. "There are two of those bitches. I knew the time frame didn't add up. And, here is my proof," she declared as she waved something in her fist as a broad grin broke out over her face.

Her excitement was infectious, and, before he knew what he was doing, he wrapped his arms around her waist and pulled her close. Her plush breasts felt perfect smashed against his chest and her startled gasp was music to his ears.

Her softness was the perfect compliment to his hard defini-
tion. And, she smelled incredible. As he gazed into glowing
amber eyes, he instantly fell under her spell.

The thought of falling for another female had his gut in
knots, but it wasn't enough to dampen his desire for her.
The stiff erection poking into her stomach was proof
enough of that. The way her eyes glowed brighter and her
arousal deepened told him she felt every solid inch of him
and liked it.

It had been so long since he'd found comfort in a
female's arms. Needing a taste of her, he reasoned one kiss
wouldn't hurt. Swiftly, he lowered his mouth to her tempting
lips. Electricity zapped between their meshed lips and raced
through his blood stream like white lightning. It prodded
him and ruined his intention to share a simple kiss as his
need took over.

She melted into him and returned his fervor with equal
intensity, parting her lips in invitation. His tongue slid along
hers in a sensual glide mimicking what his errant cock
wanted to do to her heated core. The familiarity of her was
both comforting and confusing to his mindless desire.

Her responding moan as their lips moved frantically
elicited one from him. He needed her. Needed to be inside
her as she screamed her satisfaction. He settled for holder
her closer. She fisted his hair and tilted her head to take
more of his mouth. It wasn't an elegant or sweet kiss by any
means. Their teeth clashed and she bit his lip speaking to
his animalistic instincts.

Their animals drove them forward. Never had a kiss
been so raw for him. No female had ever enticed so much of
his beast. More often, a female appealed to his physical
needs, but this female summoned his leopard to take over.

His hand roved over her backside, squeezing the firm

globe while his heart beat out the truth. "*Mine*," his leopard growled in his head.

Hearing that was like being doused with ice water. Immediately, Orlando pushed her away despite the fact his ardor had yet to abate. This had been the most honest, truthful moment he'd ever shared with another being in his life. All his desire had been laid bare and she'd responded in kind, which scared the shit out of him. He had no idea how to deal with this sort of thing.

He was completely out of his depths, but what had him hyperventilating and sweat beading on his upper lip was the fact that he wanted more.

"I shouldn't have done that," Orlando blurted and instantly wanted to kick his own ass when he saw the light leave Ember's eyes.

Her gaze hardened and she hit his shoulder, "Put me down, asshole," she demanded.

He wanted to go back several seconds and have her writhing against him. The words he said were true, but the winter air didn't cause the cold that crept in the moment their bodies separated. His chest ached at the look of hate he saw on her lovely features, as well as, the need to flee from him.

"That's strike two. You won't get a third chance. For the record, I'm not the one that kissed you. You kissed me. I don't get you. Why would you kiss someone who clearly disgusts you?" she snarled.

Orlando took a step toward her wanting to comfort her and explain himself, but she put her palm up, stopping his movement. "Don't you dare come any closer to me. I don't want your pity," she spat as she held her hand up, placing a barrier between them.

"You deserve better, Ember, and I told myself to leave you alone, but for some fucking reason I can't," he admitted.

Clearly it wasn't what she was expecting because her mouth dropped open and she gaped at him. "What?"

Orlando put more space between them so her sweet frangipani wasn't toying with his mind quite so much. "For too long I have fallen for the wrong female and been hurt over and over because of it. I don't what else to say, but I don't have anything left to give. And then there's Brantley. I now have an infant to raise. I wish it were different, but it's not."

"Whatever Orlando. We've all fallen for the wrong person or been hurt in love, but that doesn't mean you give up. You pick your shit up and move on. You are choosing to allow this to dictate your future. I didn't think you were a coward. Clearly I was wrong," she replied with a shrug as if her words weren't daggers to his heart.

"You have no idea what I've been through," he retorted.

"I'm just making an observation. And, I have a pretty damn good idea what you've been through. Difference is that I refuse to allow it to control the rest of my life," she said with a dismissive wave. "Regardless, I'm done trying and I need to see Hayden about these demons," she interjected before he could respond.

Her words bothered him more than he'd been prepared for. He should be elated. After all, he was the one who broke the kiss and said it was a mistake, but hearing her say she was done cut him to the bone and had his leopard howling inside his skull. He suddenly couldn't breathe and wanted to claw his chest open.

There was no way she was going to listen to him after he'd clearly hurt her. He may wish he could make it better, but that was not going to happen.

She was so beautiful as she pushed her glasses up her nose and held something to the light. It was then that he realized she was clutching a blue feather. "You really think there are two of them?" he asked, curious why she felt this was proof of that.

"Yep, I do. This feather is not like the one we picked up at the club. See here," she shared as she pointed to something at the base of the item. "Aside from being a different shade of blue, these striations are different from the other one. Plus, this one has a black quill where the other one was light gray."

"How can you be so sure?" He couldn't hide the doubt from his tone, but he barely remembered the shade of blue of the demon.

"Because I kept the feather, dumbass," she snapped. "And, I'm a stickler for details. It's what makes me the best at what I do," she boasted.

"You'll get no argument from me on that," he agreed, trying to lighten the mood between them. He didn't like her angry. He far preferred her passion to her ire. "Your reputation is legendary. I concede to you on this one."

She snorted at his comment and even that was sexy as sin. "Okay, now you're laying it on too thick, Warrior. I doubt there's anything else of use in this mess. I need to get this to Hayden."

"I have a proposal, Wildcat. What if you let me take both feathers back to Zeum with me? And before you curse me..." he jumped in before she could chew him a new asshole. "...the Rowan sisters can use them to scry for the locations of these demons. We could attack them when they least expect it and gain an upper hand in this war," he finished, hoping this was the needed break for them. He wanted these archdemons out of the picture. They were far too dangerous to humans and the realm.

Surprisingly, she stopped and considered his suggestion. After several silent seconds staring at him, he realized his desire for her hadn't lessened. Neither the cold rain nor the somber scene could dampen his arousal and he was walking to her before he could stop himself.

"Sure, I'll agree to that," she said, taking a step to the side to avoid contact with him. "I want these bitches dead for what they did to our people, but I'm calling Hayden and having him join you there. I have patrol in twenty or I'd be there, too," she replied as she handed him the feather before turning and walking away.

He was glad to have the demons to focus on because his mind was a fucking mess where this female was concerned. One second he wanted her and was practically shredding her clothes from her body and the next he was pushing her away and wanted nothing to do with her. She had every right to be pissed at him and he had no idea if he could make things right between them. The term certifiably bipolar came to mind as a groan escaped him watching her sweet backside sashay to her vehicle.

CHAPTER 10

Zeum was a far cry from what it had been two short years ago, Orlando mused. There had been no mates then and no *stripling*, but in the intervening time over half of his fellow Dark Warriors had been mated and now as they prepared for one of the Rowan sister's rituals there were four *stripling*.

Donovan, the oldest child and Isis's stepson, was eating strawberry ice cream with Izzy in the corner of the ballroom.

"Mine," Izzy murmured as she pointed at Donovan's treat. It was a familiar argument between the two. Izzy believed anything he had belonged to her and Donovan graciously catered to her every whim. Elsie had been trying to teach the young cambion he needed to tell Izzy no. The queen feared her daughter was going to become a spoiled princess and she didn't like the idea one bit.

As Orlando watched, he chortled when Donovan handed the ice cream to Izzy with a smile. If Orlando didn't know better he'd say the young cambion's innate sexual powers were already at play. That boy's inner demon would never go hungry if he continued treating females in that manner.

A hard smack to the jaw brought his attention down to the small male in his arms. Apparently, Brantley was finished with his bottle and had thrown it at Orlando's head.

"Damn, we're going to make a warrior out of you yet. You've got a great arm," he cooed at the infant as he lifted him to a shoulder and patted his back.

"You have got to stop telling him that, O. He's going to grow up thinking the only acceptable job is to become a Dark Warrior," Elsie chastised.

"Hey, if the shoe fits," Orlando indicated with a shrug. The baby made a noise next to Orlando's ear that had him chuckling and lifting Brantley up. "Good one, buddy. I bet you feel better now. Want to check out the females?" he asked as he turned the infant to face the room.

"Look at that hot witch over there," he whispered loudly to Brantley as he pointed to Pema's baby sleeping in a cradle nearby.

"She could be a bear, too," Ronan interjected. "We don't know if she can shift or not." That surprised Orlando into looking away from the pink bundle and at her father.

Ronan was a huge bear shifter with shoulders that filled the room. He was all muscle and a formidable fighter, which benefitted his job as a bouncer for Confetti Too. The male had become an invaluable ally in many battles over the past year, using his muscle for more than tossing around drunks.

"How's that possible? I thought one parent's genes domi-nated in children, not both," Orlando said referring to the fact that there had not been a being born with more than one set of genes.

"The first thing Aria did when she was born was shift into the cutest little cub I've ever seen, but she changed back and hasn't done it again. We can sense her power so we know she is a witch, we just don't know if she is more," Pema added as she wrapped her arm around her mate's waist.

Pulling her close, Ronan placed a kiss on the attractive blonde's forehead. The female was dressed in tight jeans and a low-cut blouse. You'd never know she had a baby less than a month before.

"Shifter babies usually go back and forth between their animal and human form with little control but since she hasn't shifted again it could've been a fluke. Suvi believes Aria is the first of a new era," Ronan continued.

Suvi sauntered over in her impossibly high heels. Orlando usually appreciated the way her shoes made her legs look a mile long but today all it did was remind him of Ember's long legs. He wanted his limbs entwined with Ember's as he sank into her silken depths.

"Of course my niece is the beginning of a new era," Suvi announced, distracting Orlando before he went too far down that path.

"Alright, we're ready," Pema interjected. "Place your candles to north and east, Suvi, and put yours to the south and west, Isis," Pema instructed.

The three sisters had been born within minutes of each other and carried the same amount of power, but Pema was the undisputed leader of the trio and it worked well for them.

While her sisters did as she instructed, Pema accepted the familiar silver bowl from her mate. After setting the bowl on the coffee table that Nate had brought in as their makeshift altar, Pema grabbed a bottle of water from her diaper bag and filled the bowl.

Having been through the same ceremony numerous times over the past couple years the atmosphere in the room was surprisingly relaxed considering what they were doing. Before the room was silent as the witches worked, but now Izzy and Donovan were laughing and Brantley and Aria were happily cooing while the adults talked. It said a lot about how drastically things had changed in the compound.

"You guys doing this sky-clad?" Rhys asked on a laugh. Then again, some things never changed, Orlando thought.

Orlando couldn't help but glance at Rhys's Fated Mate, Illianna, to see her roll her eyes as the room erupted collectively, "Fucking Rhys."

"What? Don't tell me I'm the only one thinking it. I know you were, Dante," Rhys teased his cambion lord.

Rhys was happily mated but was always going to be the same old Rhys. Everyone, including Illianna, knew he couldn't help himself, it was just who he was. It was comforting to Orlando to know that his friends, for the most part, were the same despite being mated now.

Fated Mate blessings had swept through the realm like wildfire and Zeum had been caught up in the fervor. After going nearly seven centuries without a single mate blessing, it left many reeling from the effects. Many families had been irrevocably changed by the recent matings and not everyone was coming out happy.

The Rowan triplet's father was a perfect example. Until recently, he had been bitter and depressed over losing their mother to her Fated Mate. Luckily, Rachel came along and filled the emptiness in his heart, but there were countless Greg Rowan stories to be told. Many had been left devastated by recent change.

Glancing back to the witches, Orlando watched as they proceeded to pull incense from their bag. Lotus, jasmine and hyacinth filled the room as they lit the slender sticks.

"What are those for?" Tori, Santiago's mate, asked.

The female was a Valkyrie assassin and Orlando had worried how the other females of the house would react to her, but they had come to love her and she was now a part of the gang.

Everyone, Orlando included, had gone out of their way to help her while Santi was locked in the dungeons. It wasn't easy on the couple to be apart so soon after their mating, but Santi was paying the price for eschewing the rules. Orlando easily sensed Tori's pride in her mate and knew her love for his best friend was deep and abiding.

"These flowers are connected to water, which is the best medium for scrying and location spells," Isis explained as she worked.

"And this demon won't know you're looking for her?" Tori asked as she reached for Pema's baby but winced and lowered her arm.

It was easy to forget that Tori had suffered a debilitating injury at Lady Angelica's hands and no longer had much use of her right arm. The female hid the injury well and it was only when she over-exerted herself that you noticed.

"No. We've sealed the circle and nothing can enter or exit until we break it," Pema explained.

"What if Ember is right and there are two different demons?" Orlando asked, curious if that would confuse the scrying.

"Then we will see more than one location," Suvi said as she laid the feathers side by side in front of the bowl.

Orlando could now see the subtle difference in the two feathers that Ember had described, indicating they could be facing not one, but two, new demons. No one had wanted to talk about what that meant for them. They'd faced numerous archdemons at once before, but none had taken the risks these two did.

The room finally went silent as the sisters joined hands and their mates placed their hands on their shoulders. The glow from their palms filled the circle and the energy from their collective magic filled the room. Their power was staggering, reminding him they had powerful allies.

"*Doiteain*," the witches chanted together.

The candles and incense ignited and the witches knelt before the altar. Suvi and Isis grabbed Pema's waist as she reached into the bowl of water and invoked the element of water.

Relaxing into a meditative state, Pema plunged two fingers into the water and swirled in a clockwise motion. Repeating this four times, the sisters began chanting in unison, "Let the water reveal to me the location of the owner of these feathers. Let the water show me where they are. So mote it be."

On completion of the fourth round, the lights in the room flickered and the water misted over then cleared to reveal a familiar forest. Ember and one of Hayden's Lieutenants were patrolling pack land. And, it seemed they were oblivious to the demons watching them. Orlando saw the female demon situated in a tree as she watched the pair on the ground.

Orlando's heart raced in his chest as Hayden jumped forward and snarled at the sight. "Is this happening right now?" Hayden barked as Orlando handed Brantley to Cailyn and checked for his weapons.

Right before the scene changed a swarm of skirm attacked the unsuspecting couple. Fangs were bared and Ember didn't hesitate to grab her weapon and spring into action. Orlando raced from the room, not waiting to see what happened next. Ember was in danger and his mind fractured at the thought of losing her.

ORLANDO THREW his car into park and jumped out into the frigid air. Light snow fell against the windshield and immediately melted on the warm surface. To his relief, Hayden pulled up in his truck and he and Santi hopped out. Elsie had called his cell phone to explain the other demon was attacking humans at a popular restaurant near Pike Street Market so he was glad to see the shifters were there to help him.

The rest of the Dark Warriors were needed where innocent humans were being targeted. Orlando understood, but it would have been nice to have the cavalry at his back.

Hayden shifted into his bear form without bothering to remove his clothes. Orlando heard sounds of fighting close by and the smell of blood and brimstone permeated the air. As Hayden let out a loud roar, Orlando's leopard leapt beneath his skin to respond to his Omega's call. It was his concern for Ember that had him holding back. He needed to remain in human form so he could ash the skirm.

Hayden looked back at him and Orlando held up his titanium *sgian dubh*. Weapons made from titanium were the only ones capable of turning the skirm to ash. With a nod of his head the bear took off into the woods and Santi's wolf followed suit with Orlando on their heels.

The fight hadn't moved from the location he'd seen in the scrying water. The ground was covered in bodies, both shifter and skirm, and black blood had turned the foliage to shriveled black husks. Even the trees were beginning to be affected as brown needles fell from the sky like rain amidst the snow flurries. Frantically searching the area, Orlando was suddenly caught off guard and fell forward.

Landing on something soft, he was relieved to hear the

grunt from a fellow pack member. He was injured badly, but Orlando didn't have time to stop and help. Bouncing to his feet while trying to avoid the injured shifter beneath was impossible so Orlando gave up and focused on killing the skirm that had attacked from behind.

"You assed out motherfucker," Orlando snarled one of Bhric's favorite taunts as he slashed the skirm's chest.

The mindless minion let out an ear-piercing wail before Orlando ended the matter quickly. Waving the ash away, he quickly scanned the area for Ember. She was nowhere to be seen. The archdemon was still perched on her the same branch smiling maniacally. He expected an evil cackle to leave her lips any second.

"You and your partner won't win," Orlando called up to her as ashed another skirm charging towards him.

"Ha, guess you're not as dumb as you look. No matter, you'll still lose. Lucifer will be free soon," the demoness informed Orlando before tossing a spell from her hand.

Orlando was prepared when the Dark magic came his way. He waited, making the demon think he was as stupid as she insinuated. At the last second he swiveled to the side. A nearby skirm screamed and threw its head back when the magic hit its chest.

That evil laugh echoed above him, pissing Orlando off. What the fuck was so funny? An uneasy feeling settled in his gut, but he didn't have time to ask any further questions.

Surrounded by three skirm, Orlando surprised them by taking the offensive and charging two of them. He pushed them to the outer rim of the circle of bodies where he could move freely. Stabbing out, he ashed one and then another in rapid succession. He heard Ember's curse and his heart settled at the sound.

Unfortunately, her expletive was followed by a cry of

pain. Rushing to the sound of her voice, Orlando stumbled as he saw the skirm that had been hit with the Dark magic transform into a grotesque cross between a pus demon and a human. He caught sight of a skirm lifting Ember off the ground by her throat before burying its fangs in her shoulder. A river of red flowed from the wound as Ember thrashed against his hold.

Palming another weapon from the sheath at his lower back, Orlando pushed off a nearby tree and launched himself at the skirm. He hit and the three of them went sailing toward the ground. There was no way for Orlando to block Ember from a hard landing so he focused on killing the creature. His blade sank into flesh that oozed green pus.

At first, nothing happened and Orlando thought he'd have to hack its head off. Pushing the weapon deeper, he felt when it popped through the outer wall surrounding the heart and the demon fell on top of Ember as a rotten stench filled the air and overpowered the purity of new-fallen snow.

"Are you okay?" he asked as he lifted off the delectable female.

No answer came as he stared at her closed eyes. His leopard howled in his head. He couldn't lose another female. Forcing himself to take a deep breath and calm down, he took stock of the situation. Reaching over, he felt a faint pulse at her neck and was relieved to know she was breathing. Gently picking her up to carry her to Jesaray house, he noted the fight around him was winding down.

The pack healer didn't have Jace's natural ability to heal wounds and illness, but he could save her. He had the anti-venom injection and needed to get it into her pronto. The flesh around her shoulder was already turning necrotic and rotting and she was losing so much blood. The only explanation he could come up with was it had to be the Dark magic in the air around them. Skirm bites didn't cause this much destruction.

He had to remind himself Ember was a shifter and tough to kill. If Ember were human she'd be dead. Surely, Fate wasn't so cruel that she would take another female just because Orlando was attracted to her. He was beginning to feel cursed. Grimly, his mind whispered he might have an enchantment on him. The idea wasn't so ridiculous as he recalled the centuries Jace lived under the evil spell of Angelica without knowing it.

He silently prayed to the Goddess to spare Ember's life. If she did he would walk away and leave her to find happiness with another. He owed her that.

CHAPTER 11

"Goddess," Ember groaned beneath her breath.

The attempt at blinking her eyes open sent them wide as her whole body went taught on instinct. A scream trapped in her throat as razors sliced her insides. She'd never felt such pain. Everything hurt, even her hair, but the worst was her shoulder. Her vision was blurry but she knew it had more to do with the fact she wasn't wearing her glasses.

It took a minute to recall why she hurt so badly and when she did she immediately panicked. Surely the issue resolved in their favor. She doubted demons would stitch up a wound and put her in a comfortable bed much less allow her Omega to add his healing powers.

The comforter beneath her fingers was soft and inviting. Slowly moving her eyes, she noticed it was dark blue and the furniture in the room was large and sturdy mahogany. She was in Jesaray house. Her heart raced when she realized how close she'd come to dying.

For Hayden to have added his healing energy, her injury

must be severe. She'd never forget the feeling of acid burning her flesh as teeth imbedded in her left shoulder. It had raced toward her heart so rapidly that she wondered if it would kill her, or worse, change her into something else.

She'd heard the stories about how all kinds of females, both supernatural and human, were transformed into a demon crossbreed after being bitten. If memory served, one of the Dark Warriors was mated to a vampire that had been changed by the previous archdemon.

She felt like herself, she thought, as she did a mental inventory. Her cougar was resting in the back of her mind, soaking up Hayden's energy as she healed. Aside from the pervasive pain, she was hale and whole, albeit battered and bruised.

Low murmurs brought her out of the dreamlike state. Hayden and Zeke were close to whatever room she was in. She acknowledged she'd never been in any rooms except the large family room and kitchen at Jesaray house.

Listening closely, she caught Hayden's annoyed voice. "I have agreed with the edict of remaining hidden from the humans until this point," the Omega snapped.

Ember imagined him standing with his arms crossed and the muscle along his jaw jumping as he clenched his teeth.

"And, we have the most to lose if the humans learn of us," Zeke objected. His masculine timber was familiar and comforting, but no longer affected her like it used to. "The humans will throw us in their labs and test whatever random bullshit they see fit on us. We would be a boon to their scientists."

"You don't need to remind me," Hayden barked. "I know with our human qualities we would be the perfect combination for them, but we are stronger than them. We can over-power them. These new demons have changed the game. Ember is brilliant for discovering that were two archdemons and probably saved many lives tonight because of it." Ember preened at hearing the praise from her Omega.

"They have not hesitated to bring the humans into this war, and, I for one, think we should use them and their weapons of mass destruction to eliminate the enemy. Think about it. They would call in their military and aide us in keeping the rest of the humans safe. This is too much for us to do on our own. The Dark Warriors are taxed and we can't help them this time. It would leave the pack too vulnerable," Hayden mused.

Ember's mind was reeling from what she heard. She had to do something. The only one that came to mind was Orlando. She quickly sat up on the side of the bed and hung her head until the world stopped spinning. The t-shirt someone had put on her was huge and smelled like Hayden. Surely, he didn't change her out of her bloodied clothes. She glanced to the side table to see if her glasses were there but didn't see them. Lifting a hand, she ran a hand through her hair only to discover it was a knotted mess.

Needles shot through her feet when she stood then turned to hot coals after she took a few steps. A quick glance out the window told her she was on the first floor of the house. Searching the room, she found her boots at the end of the bed. Her feet objected to the mere idea of being shoved into the steel-toed monstrosities. However, the sticks, stones, and pinecones that littered the forest floor would be even worse.

Unhappy with her options, she elected to sneak out and shift then run home and change into comfy shoes before heading out to find Orlando. He'd most likely be out patrolling, but she'd stop by Zeum first. Nate seemed to like her. Maybe she could schmooze him into sharing Orlando's patrol schedule. It was either that or drive around the city sniffing out the window for his scent. She'd rather search for the proverbial needle in a haystack than try the latter.

The sash lifted soundlessly and she pushed the screen from the frame before she slid out and landed on the rough dirt.

"Shitmotherfuckerdammittohell," she rambled in agony as pain wracked her body.

The cold night air stole the breath from her lungs. Taking a moment to gather her strength, she listened to see if the males had heard her curses. Thankfully, Zeke and Hayden continued discussing the merits of coming out to the humans.

Ember agreed with Hayden. Not that she minded protecting humans, but supernaturals were engineered in ways they were not. Hayden was right. Humans had weapons that could help in this battle. A small part of Ember's conscious nagged at her that the humans would just as easily turn the weapons against them. Shoving that thought away, Ember resolved to seek the help Hayden needed to come out to the humans. Supernaturals were dying alongside the humans because of the demons. Surely, Orlando would see the wisdom in Hayden's idea.

White light enveloped Ember as she called her cougar. Welcoming the Goddess's magic into every cell greatly lessened the agony. The shift always healed injuries and this time was no different. Taking off into a quick lope, Ember skirted the heavier populated areas, not wanting to stop and discuss what had happened with anyone she might run into.

A familiar masculine musk reached her nostrils and she stopped in her tracks several feet from her small cottage.

Cocking her head, she called the change back to her human form. What the hell was Orlando doing in her house?

Intent on finding the answer to that question, she rushed inside then shut the door behind her. No lights were on but she could see flames dancing in the fireplace next to the sofa. She walked further inside the living room and saw him sprawled across the adjacent sofa, sleeping peacefully. He must be exhausted if he didn't hear her enter the house.

Glancing down, she remembered she was naked and scurried to her bedroom to grab her robe. She winced a little as the garment slid over her shoulder, causing it to throb from the contact. Tying the silk sash, she grabbed her spare pair of glasses then walked back to the living room and sat on the floor next to where Orlando was sleeping.

He was gorgeous. She inhaled deeply, appreciating his masculine smell. His scent called to her primal nature and her mouth watered at the sight of his flawless features. Perfectly bronzed skin that she wanted to caress. And a muscular body that had her core weeping with need. She hated to admit it but she had never been so attracted to a male before. She reached over and ran a hand through his silky white hair.

"What the fuck?" Orlando shouted as he jumped and sat up, ready to attack.

"It's just me," she muttered as she rolled her shoulder and rubbed at the dull ache.

Surprisingly, it was feeling much better. His demeanor softened when he realized it was her.

"We gave you the anti-venom. It will take some time but you will heal," he explained.

She glanced up at him and her mind stuttered as the heat in his green eyes burned through her. As if answering a call, her body leaned closer towards him.

Shaking her head, she fisted her hands in her lap to keep from running them up the hard planes of his chest. "I heard the scientists finally mastered the antidote. That's got to be a huge relief for the warriors."

His pupils dilated and his eyes began glowing. "It's a major step in the right direction. Feels like it's the only progress we've made in the centuries fighting this war. Makes skirm bites almost as pleasant as the last vampire I dated."

He laid back down on the sofa and leaned on a bent arm, which put him at eye level with her. He reached over and removed her glasses and she felt naked and vulnerable. His gaze penetrated deep inside as his body heat scalded her.

Or it could've been the sudden flash of anger from the implication a vampire had sunk her fangs into him. Ember was territorial by nature and didn't like the thought of any other female laying a hand on the delectable male in front of her.

It didn't matter if he belonged to her or not. She wanted him and could tell he wanted her, too.

"You guys have to deal with that all the time," she mused aloud, changing the direction of her thoughts. "How do you continue going into battle knowing you could be bitten again? Speaking of, will I turn into another creature now?"

Orlando reached over and ran the back of his hand over her cheek, causing blood to flush her skin.

"No, you should be fine after the shot you received. We took a vow to serve the Goddess. We are all that stands between humanity and the demons, not to mention, the realm," he declared.

"About that," she began, seeing an opening. "Don't you

think its time to involve the humans in this battle? They aren't entirely helpless, you know."

"No they aren't, but we are just as likely to become their targets. Humans lose all sense when they become afraid and they lash out and attack before stopping to gather the information. History tells us exactly how dangerous their reactions can be. I know you were around for the burnings at the stake, the lynchings and Inquisition, among other atrocities. Most of those were committed against other humans, but supernaturals were involved, as well. Humans just didn't know it. What do you think they will do to a bunch of beings that are superior to them in every way?" he asked pointedly.

"I don't deny that history is not in our favor, but Hayden believes its time to come out of the dark and I happen to agree with him. Won't you even talk to Zander about it? The Vampire King, above all, should be more open to humans given that his mate used to be one," she acknowledged.

His hand trailed down her neck and when his finger traced the small tattoo a shiver ran down the length of her body.

"I don't know that I agree with Hayden on this one. If I look at the bigger picture I see it backfiring, but I will mention it to Zander," he offered as he continued rubbing her skin, distracting her thoughts.

"Thank you," she murmured. "Now, why are you in my house?"

A corner of his mouth lifted and a solemn look crossed his face. "When I saw how severe your injury was and how much blood you were losing, I thought I was going to... anyway...I couldn't leave until I knew you were okay. I started out patrolling the area in case the demon doubled back and ended up here," he said, his words fading away as he shrugged.

Tilting her head back, she watched his eyes become a bright shade of green, reminding her of springtime at the Grove. His lips parted slightly and he leaned close enough to where their mouths were scant inches apart. When she felt his hot breath against her face, all intentions of rejecting him or stopping his lips from touching hers flew out the window.

He had pushed her away but the memory of the explosive kiss they shared had her wanting more. And, she'd be damned if she allowed pride to get in the way of experiencing another moment with Orlando.

She moaned into his mouth when their lips touched. He tasted of beer and spicy food and her stomach rumbled with hunger, but when his tongue licked her lower lip, everything evaporated except her appetite for him.

She automatically opened her mouth and slid her tongue along his. They tangled wetly and he wrapped his hands around her waist, pulling her onto the sofa so she lay on top of him. One hand slid up the back of her leg and clutched her bare ass underneath the robe while the other tangled in her matted tresses. She didn't care that her hair was a mess. Her body had been on a slow burn since catching his scent and now it was a blazing inferno.

Clawing at his shirt, she broke the kiss, panting, "Take this off."

She moved just enough to where he had room to pull the lightweight sweater over his head then she sat up and straddled his hips. She untied the sash of her robe and slid the garment off her shoulders, enjoying the way his eyes drank in the sight of her nude body.

"You are so fucking sexy," he murmured as he pulled her flush against the hard line of his body.

Placing open-mouthed kisses along her cheek to her jaw, he squeezed her backside. She whimpered when she felt his fingers inch closer to her drenched core from behind and she lifted her ass, wanting him to touch her where she needed it most.

"Patience, Wildcat. All in good time," he murmured.

She was coming to love the sound of him calling her that. She would love nothing more than to introduce him to her animal.

"You aren't going to stop in the middle of this, are you?" she panted as she recalled how he'd pulled away and denied her.

It still stung that he'd rejected her, but her body's demand was in overdrive and she couldn't slow down.

"An attacking horde of demons couldn't stop me from fucking you. I could've lost you tonight," he growled against her throat then licked the sensitive area below her ear.

He may deny his feelings for her, but there was no denying he wanted her and that was good enough for now.

Her head fell back as he kissed between her breasts and her hands slid across the hard planes of his chest. His breath wafted over one of her nipples, heating the pert tip until her flesh burned from need. She was ready to shove the hard tip between his lips when he chuckled and sucked it into his mouth.

Her fingernails dug into the solid flesh of his pectorals earning a groan from him. Ember's breath caught as pleasure shot from her nipple to her clenching womb. She arched, pressing more flesh into his mouth. He squeezed her other breast as his tongue and teeth tortured her nipple. Her core rippled when his fingers went further and found her pool of wetness. A gasp left her throat as she lost her mind from the pleasure of him touching her sex.

Her hands roamed over his sweat-dampened skin, stilling over his flat nipples. Returning the favor, she tweaked his nipples as she claimed his full lips again. She sucked the bottom lip into her mouth gave it a quick nibble. He groaned and devoured her mouth like it was his last meal. She wrapped one leg across his waist and brought her aching center in alignment with the impressive bulge in his pants.

"Stay still," he rasped roughly. "My control is shaky, Em. Do not push me right now."

"I need, Orlando."

Her blood raced in her veins as her body cried out in hunger. She unbuttoned the closure of his jeans but struggled with the zipper.

"Goddess you smell good. Like a tropical beach," he whispered inhaling deeply.

"I can't seem to get these damn things off," she protested as she jerked the stiff fabric.

He sucked in a breath when she shoved her hand inside his underwear and her knuckles brushed the head of his cock. He grabbed her wrist and turned her palm, encouraging her to feel his girth, but stopped her movement when she firmly gripped his shaft and pumped. It was awkward with the zipper in the way, but she was determined to make him as lost to the lust as she was.

"Goddess, Wildcat," he groaned as he undid the zipper. Her eyes flared as his enormous erection sprang free and pressed against her stomach.

"You are so...big," she gushed as she once again reached for what she wanted.

He allowed her to encompass him with her small fist. He

pumped his hips, forcing his shaft through her tight hold while his fingers reached around and found purpose between her legs. She pumped and squeezed him as he slid between her wet folds, pressing down on her engorged nub. When he pinched her clit, she rubbed her sex against his hand. They writhed against each other as their mouths crashed together.

Lips, tongue and teeth came together urgently with their building need. She'd never been so close to the edge from so little foreplay. Some males called her a *tough nut to crack* or *ice queen* because it took a lot to arouse her and even more to bring her to climax. But this male had her wild with need from a single touch. Once she got going she *was* a wildcat, but she was not a female who enjoyed a male that wanted nothing more than to pound into her and be done in five minutes.

"Enough," he said with a growl as he pulled out of her grip.

He squirmed off the sofa and picked her up. She wrapped her legs around his waist in response. As he began walking she rubbed her wet slit over his cock and he faltered.

"I wanted to get to your bed where we would have more room," he growled as he pushed her against a wall in the hallway, "and take my time pleasuring you, but I can't wait," he confessed before shoving his jeans down and thrusting inside her with one hard stroke.

His shaft parted her flesh so suddenly that pain lanced through her and made her suck in a breath.

"I'm okay," she replied quickly at his look of concern. Sweat beaded his brow and covered his body with his effort of holding back.

The pain was gone almost as quickly as it began and

she nodded at him and lifting off his shaft before bouncing back down. He filled and stretched her in the most delicious way possible. Her chest sighed in contentment at finally having him seated inside her but at the same time it begged for more. Sharing this with him felt fundamentally right. Feeling a bit silly for the thought, but something told her she had been heading towards him her entire life.

Their sweat mingled as she deepened the kiss and he bucked wildly. "Don't want to hurt you...but can't...stop," he muttered against her lips.

"Feels so good," she panted, reveling in his frantic movements. He held her up with one arm under her ass and the other snaked between them and fingered her sex.

He brought his finger to his mouth and licked it clean. "I want to taste *all* your honey next time," he informed her.

She liked the sound of a next time but was enjoying this moment far too much to consider that it would end. She wanted it to last forever.

She nodded in agreement as his long fingers slid through her folds and pinched and tweaked her clit. Her nails dug into his shoulders as her muscles clenched.

"So close," she muttered as she had the urge to bite his hot flesh.

As if reading her mind, he leaned his head and bit down on her nipple. She detonated around him, milking his hard length as her orgasm barreled through her like a storm. Burying her head in his neck, she cried out his name as her muscles clenched tighter and her body shuddered with pleasure.

Her body prepared for another orgasm, but then blinding pain ripped through her upper arm. Her eyes flew open with all the competing sensations and she met his glowing green orbs. They were wide with shock as his face twisted in ecstasy.

When his cock jerked with its orgasm and her second one released, she realized several things.

First, pressure from a barb had extended from the base of his cock and embedded in her soft flesh, hitting her G-spot while it held him locked inside her. The barb only allowed short jabs for his thrusts and his pleasure washed through her right before his pain did.

Second, the pain they were feeling was a brand that was magically burning into the skin of their right biceps. The pain from that had her eyes watering while her body came down from the most intense orgasm she'd ever had. Everything clicked into place and she knew the look on her face matched the stunned one across his.

"Oh my Goddess. We're Fated Mates," Ember breathed as she cradled his face in her palms, joy spreading like wildfire.

Something deep clicked into place and everything in her world was suddenly right. She'd found her other half. This male carried part of her soul and was made for her. She could have been given any type of being as a mate and would have been happy, but the fact that the Goddess had given her a shifter was her wildest fantasy come true.

"I never thought I'd find a mate," he responded automatically, a furrow appearing between his eyes. He lifted her and separated their bodies after enough of the barb had retreated. "I'm afraid I'm dreaming. Nothing can feel that good."

"It can and it did," she assured him with a kiss to his lips.

"I don't know what to say to this. I need some time to think," he mumbled, making her wish she had a blanket or a baseball bat.

She wanted to cover her exposed body or hit him over the head. She wasn't sure which one took precedence. His words hurt more than she could've imagined. She'd always hoped her Fated Mate would fall at her feet from sheer elation when she found him. What she'd been given instead was a far cry from what she'd expected.

It sucked to go from the height of bliss to utter disappointment.

CHAPTER 12

Bubbles floated up the staircase as Orlando headed down to the dungeons. What the fuck was Santiago doing down there? Did Tori get permission for a conjugal visit and Zander forgot to tell him, Orlando wondered. The only reason Zander had given him permission was because he had told him about the mating so he highly doubted Tori was there. Orlando thought the king was going to force him to hash his shit out with him, but luckily he'd understood Orlando needed his best friend's advice on this.

A pink sparkler zipped past his head and he quickened his steps down the stairs. Laughter escaped him in a rush at the sight that greeted him. Some of the gnomes were busy redecorating Santiago's cell.

"Shut the fuck up," Santiago snarled. "I swear Zander is having them do this as part of my punishment," the warrior lamented with a shake of his head.

Orlando glanced around and caught Pepper's eye. The little gnome winked at him and continued changing Santiago's comforter. Orlando had no idea what prisoners were typically given but he doubted it was pink and sparkly. "Are those ruffles?" he asked, unable to stop laughing.

"Yes, they are. Izzy is rubbing off on these creatures," Santiago replied as he stood with his arms crossed over his chest.

"Oh, you know you begged them to paint that pretty unicorn on the wall," Orlando teased.

In the next moment, the bars to Santi's cell became a rainbow of color next and the bubbles thickened to where Orlando could barely see his friend. "Is Izzy's bubble machine in there?"

"No, the wonders of magic. Like I said, torture," Santiago muttered dryly. "Please tell me you're busting me out of this place."

Orlando met his friend's eyes and saw the stress lines, as well as, the pale color to his skin. Being imprisoned and given three squares a day didn't seem like much punishment until you considered that the warrior was newly mated.

Anyone of the Dark Warriors would struggle with confinement. They were accustomed to constant action and battle. For a shifter confinement was a particularly cruel sentence because their animals not only craved freedom and the outdoors, they needed it to survive or they could go insane.

When Orlando considered his own mating compulsion and his desire to seek out Ember and claim her in every way, he truly understood the full extent of Santiago's plight. Yes, Santiago had brought his situation on himself, but a newly mated male denied the comfort of his mate was unthinkable.

"Stop being a baby. You were out just last night," he teased the warrior, hoping to distract him from his dilemma.

Like a pin popping a balloon, Santiago slumped onto the pink bed and glitter flew around him in a thick cloud.

"My wolf howls constantly and I want to claw my skin off. It would have been easier to be beaten with a morning star daily, so long as I could return to Tori at night. It's her belief in me that keeps me holding on. That, and the fact that, I only have one week left," he said and Orlando could feel his relief over that fact.

Orlando thought of the affect a Fated Mate had on a male and wondered why Ember hadn't had the same impact on him. She'd been there when his world had been torn apart and Jaidis died, asking Orlando to care for her son. Fate seemed to have it out for him, he thought bitterly.

A voice in the back of his head reminded him that Ember did help calm him that night. That he'd been ready to tear Kenny's corpse and the entire house apart when her scent reached him. He'd been able to think clearly after that, even if it hadn't stopped all the pain.

"If you're not here to get me out, why are you here?" Santiago asked, changing the subject.

"I found my Fated Mate," Orlando blurted as he rubbed his shoulder where the mate brand burned like a hot coal.

Santiago jumped to his feet and crossed to where Orlando stood, a huge smile spreading across his face.

"No shit? Congrats, O. Damn, you work fast. I have no idea how you managed that after the brutal fight last night, but you deserve all the happiness she will bring you. Who is she, and, why the hell don't you look happy about it?" the warrior asked.

Orlando considered the question. Was he happy? He wanted to be happy. This is what most supernaturals dreamed of finding. He was happy, but it was overshadowed by all the other shit.

"I don't know what to think or feel right now. So much has happened in the past month that my mind is struggling to catch up. And, I haven't slept in weeks so that doesn't help," Orlando stated.

"Is this about Elsie?" Santiago narrowed his eyes and pinned Orlando to the spot.

The intense gaze had him shifting from foot to foot. "No. Yes. I don't really know," he answered honestly.

This was why he needed to come see Santiago. He needed help screwing his head on and his best friend was the perfect person for the job.

"First of all, you need to put that fucking crush behind you. Elsie has never belonged to you and she never will. You have found your other half. Bro, she carries part of your soul," Santi exclaimed.

"I know, and it's not really Elsie, per se. I'm fucked up, I know. First, I fell in love with a female that belonged to Zander and as soon as I got over her, I fell for another female that belonged to someone else. Shit, I barely knew her. I smelled her sweet scent..." he drifted off as he realized why he'd been so drawn to Jaidis.

She'd worn some perfume that smelled like a tropical flower, which was close to Ember's natural frangipani.

Dipple raced by Orlando's shins carrying a huge stuffed bear nearly as big as him. He and Santi watched, their conversation momentarily forgotten as the gnome attempted to stuff the animal through the bars. The little guys were entertaining, if nothing else.

Shaking his head at the sight, he refocused on Santiago who looked confused by Orlando's ramblings.

"To make a long story short, I met Jaidis. She was pregnant and had an abusive mate. I realize now that she smelled like my Fated Mate. Regardless of my initial pull to her, I was determined to save her and her unborn baby from the horrible situation they were in. Jaidis's mate attacked her and she ended up killing the sonovabitch then died giving birth to their son," Orlando explained.

Santiago leaned against a now purple stonewall shaking his head. "Only you, my friend. So, let me guess, your head is all caught up in the dead female and you can't get past that."

"Pretty much. Took a week for Ember to seduce me to her bed. I had been resisting the urges towards her, but after Crocell nearly killed her, emotions were high. The thought of losing her slammed home and I couldn't deny my attraction any longer," Orlando admitted.

Santiago nodded his understanding. "So, who is the lucky female? And, please tell me that you ended that blue bitch after I was taken back here."

"No, we didn't find her, or her twin. Ember Hawthorne is my mate. She's the feline shifter that fought with us last night and she is the one that discovered there were two demons. She saved countless lives last night." He couldn't help how his chest puffed with pride. Ember was intelligent, sexy, and passionate...and she belonged to him.

"Ember was the one you were so freaked out about. I thought it was because she was a female, but your reaction makes sense now. So, why aren't you still in her bed?" Santi asked matter-of-factly.

"Why do I keep falling for the wrong females?" Orlando countered.

"Wake the fuck up, bro. This isn't like the others. She belongs to you and you alone. She will never want another. You're so stuck in the past mistakes you've made that you aren't seeing what is right in front of you," Santi chastised.

Orlando hadn't stopped to think about that fact. It didn't

lessen the pain of losing Jaidis or his chagrin with how he'd fallen for Elsie, but Santi was right. Ember was his other half. His and his alone.

"You're right. But I have a baby now. There are so many issues I don't know if she will accept."

"I'm assuming the baby you're referring to is the one that belonged to Jaidis because we both know until your recent cherry-popping with Ember, you couldn't have gotten any female pregnant. By the way, the gnomes haven't stopped flapping their chops over how good Brantley is," the male added as he swatted at the bubbles wafting around his head.

Orlando recalled the feeling of his barb extending for the first time and had to agree that it was a lot like losing his virginity, but in the most pleasurable way. He'd never experienced anything like it and his body craved to feel it again.

"Yes, Brantley is Jaidis's son. She asked me to take care of him. It was her dying wish so there's no way I'm giving up that child for anything, or, anyone" he explained.

"Of course you did. I would expect nothing less from you. I can't wait to meet the little tyke. He will be a great addition to the family," Santiago replied with a smile. "But as your mate, Ember will welcome him. You don't need to worry about that."

"That's just it. She has never once asked about the baby. I'm not so sure she will like raising another female's child. Especially, knowing how I felt about Jaidis."

Santiago groaned and rubbed his goatee. "Don't tell me you told her how you felt about this other female."

"I didn't know she was my mate at the time," Orlando defended.

"I admit it's a fucked-up situation," Santi mumbled, "but you'll never know how she feels until you talk to her. And for the love of the Goddess, tell her how much she means to you. She's your mate, O. This is great news."

Orlando recalled what everyone had told him about finding a mate. They'd each been inescapably drawn to them and unable to deny their desire. And, after that first sexual experience they'd seemed so tight and inseparable.

Orlando couldn't relate to that. Yes, he was drawn to Ember, but they weren't a team. He couldn't help but wonder if they could ever function as one unit.

"Thanks. I guess I need to go see a certain female about a mating ceremony. I'm glad you'll be out soon so you can be there."

"It's not just the ceremony, Orlando. You need to get real and tell her how you really feel," Santi advised, his brown eyes sincere.

"When did you get so wise?" Orlando asked before he turned to head out.

"Through lots and lots of mistakes that I don't want to see my best friend make."

Orlando shook his head and climbed the stairs, tossing over his shoulder, "Thanks again."

His blood heated in anticipation. He had a cougar to hunt down.

EMBER SAT at her kitchen table glaring at her sexy mate. Her mate mark burned, she was horny, and he was blabbing about everything but the reason he walked out of her house after discovering they were mates.

She'd known he was less than enthused about the idea, but he sounded like he had a business proposal for her. She looked at the wood surface half-expecting to see a document in front of her outlining their future together.

"This isn't an arrangement, you know," she snapped as she pushed her glasses up on her face. "We are connected at the soul. Something we will never share with another being, but if you don't want this, then tell me now. I will figure out a way to deal with the repercussions."

"That's possible?" he asked entirely too interested in the thought. She had the urge to kick him off the spindly chair he was sitting on.

"I don't know, but I have no problem being the first in the realm to deny a mating. I have no desire to be tied to a male who doesn't want me. I'd rather live with constant pain from this mate mark," she informed him. Her bicep screamed and called her a liar.

The pain mainly felt like she had a bad sunburn, but at times, it sent sharp stabs straight to her soul and she knew it would be unbearable to go through the rest of her life with the constant reminder of a denied mating.

Orlando held up his hands and shook his head back and forth. "I am fucking this all up. That's not what I meant. This whole situation has taken me by surprise, but I want to mate with you. I'm trying to ask if you'd like to complete the mating with me," he suggested.

She'd always been particularly good at discerning lies and sensed he was being completely honest with her. It was the resounding declaration of love and devotion that was missing from his speech. She wanted, no needed, to have that with a mate. But truth was, they barely knew each other and it would take time to develop a relationship.

As she opened her mouth to respond he stopped her then added, "But, I need you to know something first. I have a child and if we mate he will be yours, too. Are you okay with that?"

"Is it that female's child? The one that died in your arms? I wondered what had happened to him," she observed.

She had admired his promise to look after the female's child and knew he could've chosen to do it from the sidelines. The fact that he had taken the child into his home told her he was loyal and protective. Both were qualities she wanted in her mate.

"Yes. His name is Brantley and I formally adopted him, so there is no going back on that score," he warned firmly.

There was a glimpse of the Dark Warrior in him and it made her shiver. She was blessed with one of the most powerful males in the Tehrex Realm and couldn't be more pleased with the Goddess's choice.

"I would be honored to help raise him. Things have been so crazy I hadn't had time to find out what had happened with him. How is he doing without his mom?" she asked, sympathy for the baby filling her chest. She wished he were there so she could wrap him in her arms and offer comfort.

"He's doing fine. Fits in with the rest of the house as if he was meant to be there," Orlando said with a smile as he reached over and pulled her into his lap. She went willingly soaking up his warmth.

His presence filled the entire kitchen, sucking all available air and she suddenly realized they'd have to add onto her home. One bedroom and a small main room weren't big enough for the three of them. She made a mental note to ask her grandfather and uncles to build additional rooms.

"I still can't believe I found you," he murmured, interrupting her thoughts, and kissed the pounding pulse at her neck.

She understood his disbelief. The past several hours seemed like a dream, but then her brand would flare, reminding her it was all too real. She wrapped her hands around the back of his neck and threaded her fingers in his short hair.

"You're mine," she declared.

His glowing eyes met hers and he chuckled. "So it seems, Wildcat. You know we never did make it to the bed last time," he said as he kissed his way across her collarbone.

"Screw the bed. This table is perfectly fine," she whispered in his ear and felt his body shudder.

"I like how you think, you naughty, naughty female," he responded lifting her shirt over her head.

CHAPTER 13

"Stop glaring at the Vampire Queen," Faith whispered in Ember's ear.

Ember turned to the female that had been by her side nearly her entire life. She loved Faith like a sister, but felt she was betraying the best friend oath.

"I know you aren't taking her side," Ember countered sharply.

They were in the park near the main dining hall along with the Zander and his precious Elsie, Orlando, Hayden, and Ember's sister, Emily, and their mother, Evelyn. She laughed to herself recalling how her father had called them his *three E's* referring to their common first initials. She couldn't help but miss her dad as she looked over the area where she would hold her mating ceremony. She was so glad Orlando hadn't put up an argument to mating at the Grove.

Santiago had been mated at Zeum so Ember had expected Orlando to follow suit, but he said it was her choice. It had always been her dream to claim her mate on sacred ground belonging to her people. To her, there was no other option.

"Never. You know that I'll always have your back. What's her deal anyway?" Faith asked, her voice a little louder this time.

"What's whose problem?" Emily asked and all eyes turned to them.

Faith jumped right in without hesitation. "Oh, you know. We're just trying to decide what Grandma Flo's going to cook for the ceremony," she quipped and ember gave her a grateful smile for saving her from an uncomfortable conversation about the vampire queen.

"You have to have her make her rack of lamb. She puts this crust on it..." Hayden said as he closed his eyes and a satisfied grin crossed his handsome face, "make you feel like you've died and gone to Annwyn," he finished and rubbed his stomach.

Ember couldn't recall having that specific dish, but Hayden would know best given that Grandma Flo was his blood relative.

Elsie screwed up her face and joined the conversation. "Orlando doesn't like rack of lamb. His favorite is Chicken Parmesan. I have the recipe if you'd like it," the queen offered.

Ember's fingers curled into a fist that itched to meet those clear blue eyes. How dare she speak for Orlando when he wasn't her mate? Unfortunately, it was one more reminder that she didn't know much about Orlando. They'd spent the past few days becoming more acquainted in the unlawful carnal knowledge department but not much else.

"Hell yeah. Your Chicken Parmesan is the best. I think I need to taste test it before we decide though," Orlando teased Elsie who returned his smile.

The fact that he so easily smiled with this female burned Ember and she was at his side before she realized she'd taken a step. He glanced down and his smile faded, but he reached out and grabbed her hand and interlaced their fingers. The connection zinged with electricity, warming her.

"Sure, I can make you some tonight if you're coming home," Elsie jabbed.

"Doona blame him, *a ghra*, he's a male in love," Zander interjected with a chuckle.

If only that were true, Ember thought. They hadn't even said the three little words that every female craved to hear. If she were honest, she wasn't ready to say them, either. No matter, they were building something true and lasting and she knew love would find its way into the equation.

Faith and Emily were at her side in the next heartbeat, a silent offer of support. They understood her better than anyone else. It was just another reason Ember loved belonging to a pack.

"So, is this where you will hold the ceremony?" Elsie asked as she glanced around the area.

Even in the dark of night, Ember could see the dissatisfied look on the female's face as she looked around. Izzy struggled in her mother's arms until she put her down then the little girl took off running to the nearby swing set. Luckily, there were plenty of lights from the nearby buildings, but Ember could see the queen's protectiveness for her daughter as Izzy squealed her delight.

Nothing about the pack was as fancy or stuffy as Zeum. The place screamed money and refinement whereas shifters connected with nature and lived simpler lives.

"It's so charming," Elsie continued, surprising Ember. "Did you and Zeke help make this replica of the amulet?"

the queen asked Hayden, referring to the intricate pattern made from various stones of different shapes and colors. It was a truly stunning work of art and Ember was proud to have been part of its construction.

"Yes, most of the pack was involved with its creation in some way. Whether picking up stones, clearing debris from the area or in the design itself. This spot has a purpose now and that gives the pack a peace it had been missing," Hayden explained.

The center of pack land was where the nursery, school, medical ward and dining hall were located. She, like most members, had crossed the image of the Triskele amulet over the years and not paid it much attention, but ever since the Goddess had began bestowing Fated Mate blessings everyone regarded the area with reverence.

"If you don't want my recipe, what can I help with?" Elsie asked. The offer seemed genuine, but Ember didn't trust it.

"I have my sister and Faith, not to mention, my mother and grandparents. What Grandma Flo can't do, they can," Ember told her flatly.

"I'm sure there's something Elsie and the other females can do," Orlando interjected.

If she didn't know better, Ember would say he was playing peacemaker and she took it as a clue to play nice.

"Them being here for you is enough," she told her mate as a sudden thought occurred to her. "Is your family coming? Do they live in the area?"

"No, they're in New York and they aren't coming," Orlando replied as his brows furrowed.

He hadn't said one word about his childhood and the look on his face told her it was a sore subject. She hoped he would eventually open up to her and talk about his family.

She wanted to know everything about her mate.

"Okay, so the inner circle will be my family with the rest of the guests will form the outer circles," Ember clarified.

"No. The Dark Warriors and their mates will be in the inner circle, as well. They are *my* family," Orlando added as he pulled his hand away from hers. Ember couldn't deny the bond between Orlando and this formidable group even if she wanted to.

"My mother asked to hold Brantley during the ceremony if that's alright," Ember offered, realizing he may have another plan for the baby. She had spent a few hours each day with the baby and was quickly falling in love. He was such a happy baby it was hard not to.

Orlando turned and gave her the biggest smile yet. "I hadn't even considered where he would be, but yes, I like that idea. Your mother will be perfect."

"If grandma doesn't steal him from her," Emily added with a chuckle. "She loves babies and Goddess knows we've had too few of those."

Izzy ran up to them at that moment and tugged on Ember's leg. Bending down, she met eyes identical to her father's. "I have a sparkly pink dress for your mating. You need sparkles, too. Can I have ice cream now?"

Laughing, Ember stood up and grabbed her hand. "Sure. Grandma Flo has the best homemade chocolate ice cream on the planet."

"I like strawberry," Izzy informed her as she scrunched her eyes.

"Her strawberry is even better," Faith chimed in.

Before they'd made it two steps from the group, a bloody arm sailed through the air.

∽

DISBELIEF SETTLED over Orlando as he saw the limb land in the middle of the group. It stood out like a sore thumb on the snow-covered ground. On alert, he scanned the area for the source.

"Shite!" Zander shouted as he pulled his weapons from their sheaths. "Elsie, take Izzy into the dining hall, now."

Elsie was in motion right before demons seemed to fall from the sky all around them. It was disorienting to see them drop out of thin air. Some writhed in pain, others landed in a crouch and attacked.

"She's teleporting demons in and tossing them through our protections," Hayden shouted with eyes trained towards the night sky.

"Fuck. Don't these bitches ever stop?" Orlando asked rhetorically. "I didn't realize that was even possible."

"Neither did I," Hayden growled. Clearly, none of them had considered this weakness to the protection wards.

Before Orlando knew it, they were surrounded. "Ember, go with Elsie. Get to safety," he called out. Every fiber of his being objected to having her so close to danger.

A pus demon cut off Elsie and Izzy and he saw Ember rush to help them. Suddenly, Orlando went sailing through the air and lost track of his mate. Felines always landed on their feet and the second he touched the ground, he was spinning to meet his attacker.

Claws scrabbled in the dirt and then the hellhound charged him. Orlando jumped at the last second and plunged his blade into its back as he sailed over the top of it. Using the handle as leverage, Orlando jumped and swung his legs over the large beast so that he straddled its back.

Like riding a bull, Orlando was bucked and tossed, but he managed to maintain his hold. He felt a pop and knew his shoulder had slipped out of its socket, but he ignored the pain and wrapped his arm around the hellhound's neck and twisted with all his might. A loud snap followed and the beast slumped to the ground.

A bright flash of white light momentarily blinded him before Ramiel appeared. "Do you ever stay out of trouble?" the angel asked Elsie and Izzy with a shake of his head as he placed himself in between the females and the demons.

Orlando marveled at Rami's enormous black wings. With a quick flare of the black appendages, several demons shrieked then heads went flying as black blood dripped from the razor-sharp tips of his wings. The male was lethal without even trying.

"Take Izzy and Elsie to safety," Zander ordered the angel, but Rami glared at the vampire king and continued to fight off the demons.

Ember stayed close to Elsie as Izzy disappeared from her mother's arms. "Where did she go?" came Ember's panicked question.

Orlando prayed the princess teleported to safety rather than a demon's arms. The little girl was very aware of her power to end a demon's existence with a touch of her hand, but no one wanted her taking such risks at her young age.

A second later she appeared in Rami's arms squirming and saying, "Play, play."

"Not now, Izzy. I'm a little busy with these demons. You stay with your mom and don't teleport anywhere. Do you hear me?" Rami ordered as he handed the child back to Elsie. Orlando marveled at the patience Rami showed Izzy when it was clear he wasn't a patient male.

Orlando punched a pus demon in the throat and felt his hand sink into the mushy smelly mess. Temporarily stunning the pus demon, Orlando risked a glance skyward. The blue-winged archdemons were nowhere to be seen, but he did see the faint shimmer of the protective wards and wondered if the presence of demons was making it do that.

Sensing movement to his right, he ducked and then checked before stabbing anything. They were fighting in close quarters and he didn't want to injure a friend. He was glad he took pause when he spotted Zeke charging the scene with reinforcements.

"Give us the Princess and we will leave," announced a Fury demon that was standing in the middle of the melee.

"Over my dead body," Ember spat, her breath coming out in an angry white cloud. He loved her courage, but he wished she'd shut her mouth and slink into the shadows where it was safer.

Hayden had shifted into a bear and swatted a Sheti demon aside as he tried to reach the mouthy Fury demon. In his fear for his mate, Orlando reached the enemy before Hayden and his leopard growled as it burst free right before the demon leaped for Ember.

Orlando didn't stop to think about what he was doing, just lunged. His canines sank into gray flesh and acid burned his tongue when he bit down. He thrashed his head and kept tight hold of the demon. His powerful jaws quickly tore through flesh, muscle and tendon as black blood sprayed in an arc. Ember cried out and clutched her arm while Orlando mentally called out to Zander to finish the bastard so his leopard could get to Ember's side.

Emily and Faith were standing together and shaking like leaves. With a hiss at Ember and a nudge of his head to her thigh, he tried to convey that she needed to stay with the females as he turned back to the battle. The snow was melting as the ground sizzled and the area turned black as the vegetation died. Rage surfaced that the site of his mating ceremony was being desecrated.

Too much had been taken from him and he was tired of it. His life had been one pile of shit after another, beginning with parents who favored his siblings to taking hit after hit in the female department and ultimately losing Jaidis to the demons destroying everything he cared about.

He'd been too wrapped up in his head to realize his mate was slowly gluing his pieces back together and he'd be damned if he allowed any demon to ruin his one chance at some happiness. She wanted to be mated on pack land and he owed her that. He had no idea how things would play out between them, but he looked forward to strengthening their bond and claiming her in every way.

With a growl, he leapt into action and tackled the hellhound, claws digging in before his jaws tore through its throat. The sound of battle waged around him and in the middle of it all he heard his mate curse, but he couldn't break away from the pus demon facing him. A hellhound paired up with the pus demon and the two swiped at Orlando, their efforts flaying Orlando's side. Blood poured from numerous wounds and he felt his body weakening.

The second his steps faltered a cougar let out a roar and pounced on the hellhounds back. Relief and panic warred as Orlando quickly attacked and killed the pus demon. Glancing sideways, he caught his first glimpse of his mate's animal. Ember had a gorgeous tan coat and was graceful in her lethality.

Watching her through predatory eyes, the mating compulsion blasted through him and heated his blood. He fought the urgent need to pin her down by the scruff of the neck and mount her. Shaking off those animalistic instincts, the next urge was to bend her over his knee and spank her for jumping into the fray.

Rami appeared next to them and the three of them worked together to eliminate all the demons near them. Orlando was grateful Rami was there. The angel didn't hesitate to come to Izzy's call and this time they had needed his help.

Orlando glanced around and saw Elsie holding Izzy in front of the dining hall where Emily and Faith had joined them. Wolves, leopards, lions, and a big ass bear stood in the clearing alongside Zander and Ramiel.

The demons were dead and the archdemon had disappeared. The playset was a pile of timber and the ground was littered with bodies where the demonic blood ate away at the foliage like acid. Shifting back to human form, Orlando grabbed a shirt from Faith and covered Ember as she shifted, as well.

"I told you to stay back with your sister and Faith," he growled at Ember, pissed that she seemed determined to put herself in harm's way.

"No you didn't. You growled at me and pushed my leg. You mated a warrior, Orlando. Hayden may not have made me his C.L.A.W. yet, but that is who I am at my core. You need to wrap your mind around that now. I will always fight by my pack's side," Ember declared with her hands on her hips.

She was so damn sexy when she became defiant he couldn't resist grabbing her into his arms and smashing his lips to hers, kissing her hard.

"My instinct as your mate is to protect you. I'm thinking of buying a box of bubble wrap to keep you safe," he teased as he assessed their losses. There were several injured shifters that were being treated, but thankfully, no casualties.

"They came after the Princess," Ember observed,

changing the subject. "Why is that? And, how did they know she was here?"

"Pile these bodies in the pit," Hayden ordered as he pulled on sweatpants and handed a pair to Orlando. Grateful, he slipped into the pants as Hayden explained, "Izzy isn't a normal stripling. She carries the magic of the Goddess."

"Aye, she became the Triskele amulet when she was born and has been a target of the demons ever since," Zander added.

"You mean she's been hunted her whole life?" Ember said, horror crossing her features.

"They began targeting her while she was still in Elsie's womb," Zander explained. "We didna think they would locate her during this short excursion. Plus, we thought the protections would keep her safe."

"She isn't safe anywhere," Elsie said through tearful eyes as she clutched Izzy close.

"She is safe with me," Rami promised.

"We will find a way to hide her from the demons, *a ghra*," Zander interjected as he rubbed his mate's back.

"We need to call in the witches to add to our protections," Hayden announced. "I will not have my pack so vulnerable and I refuse to place Isobel at risk during the mating ceremony."

Ember glanced around and Orlando watched her shoulders slump. The area had been dusted with snow, but now it was completely black. "How can we have the ceremony here? Their blood is killing the land," she pointed out and Orlando saw the disappointment in her eyes.

"The Rowan sisters can bring wood sprites and they can help heal the plants and soil," Hayden announced. "These demons will not take more from us. I promise this site will be healed by the time the ceremony comes around in two weeks," the male said and Orlando knew he was trying to reassure her.

"I hope so. I want our day to be perfect," Ember said.

"The triplets are the strongest witches in the realm and their sprites are eager to help. Have faith in the magic. Our mating ceremony will be nothing short of spectacular. Anyway, no more worrying about that. I have a treat for you," Orlando declared as he tilted her head up with his forefinger.

"Oh, are we going to christen another room?" she asked with a wink.

Chuckling, he kissed her lips then murmured, "Even better."

CHAPTER 14

Ember gazed out the window of Orlando's prized Mustang. She'd learned right away how attached he was to his vehicle. She saw the appeal of the muscle car, but she preferred her mate's muscles to a silly vehicle. Cars were more a practicality for her, a way to get from point A to point B.

Orlando had surprised her the past couple days and been far more affectionate towards her. Initially, she was wary and unsure of the reason, but decided to embrace it. He tried to hide his inner torment from her, but she sensed and saw that he still struggled with the idea of them being mates.

It was difficult to be upset over the complicated situation when she looked at Brantley. He was such a good baby and she missed him and Orlando when they weren't there. She couldn't wait to be mated so they could be a family in every way.

"What are we doing here?" she asked as she glanced out the window at the fancy restaurant.

She'd heard of Bouche à Bouche. Shifters owned it, but

they lived in the city rather than with the pack so she didn't know them all that well.

"Usually people eat when they go to restaurants," Orlando teased and winked.

He reached over and tweaked the end of her nose. He'd been more light-hearted lately. More like himself from what Hayden said. She was beginning to see the side of him she'd been told laughed easily and joked often.

"I wish you'd told me we were coming here. I'd have dressed better," she lamented as she ran her hand down her black dress slacks.

"You look absolutely ravishing. In fact, I'd rather eat you," he husked and reached over to pull her onto his lap.

The space was cramped in the car and she didn't get very far as her hip got stuck between the stick shift and console. Not the stick she wanted to be rubbing up against.

She started laughing as she squirmed and tried to get comfortable in the awkward position and her glasses slipped off and fell between the seat. Orlando reached down and fumbled for several moments before retrieving the object.

"Why do you need to wear these?" he asked as he slid them back on her face.

She realized she hadn't told him about the painful memory. Few knew the story. "My father was shot and killed by human hunters while in animal form. I was very young when it happened. Hayden came to our house to tell my family about the tragedy and I freaked out and fled into the woods. I ran as fast and far as I could until I realized I was lost. A mountain lion found me before my family did and attacked. I'm lucky I didn't lose the eye altogether, but the injury was severe enough to cause permanent damage to one eye. I know the glasses are dorky," she remarked as the loss of her father hit home again.

"I had no idea. I'm sorry to have brought up such a sad topic for you. I happen to think you're sexy as hell in glasses," he confessed as he reached over and caressed her cheek.

She looked deeply into his green eyes and melted when she saw genuine care and concern from her mate along with raw desire, causing blush to stain her cheeks.

"It's okay, you didn't know. I still miss him every day. I wish you could've met. He was quite the character, much like you," she said and smiled. "I think he would've approved of you," she added and leaned over to place a tender kiss on those full lips that were calling out to her.

That fast, the kiss heated as Orlando took her in his arms and passion erupted. It didn't take much from him before she was mindless with desire.

He ran his hand along her collarbone and unbuttoned the first few buttons on her silk shirt. His deft fingers slid beneath the fabric and inside her bra, brushing her nipple. Moaning, she wrapped her arms around his neck and mashed her lips against his. He palmed her breast and squeezed, eliciting a whimper from her as her core spasmed with need.

"You should buy a bigger car," she declared as she broke the kiss, panting, "because now you've got me all excited," she murmured as she sucked his bottom lip into her mouth.

His hot breath fell in puffs against her mouth and his eyes glowed brightly. "We will continue this after dinner, Wildcat" he promised as he fastened her buttons. The brush of his fingers against her flesh was torture.

"Cruel, cruel, male. Next time we take my vehicle," she told him as she climbed out of the car.

He hopped out and was at her side before she could shut

the passenger door and twined her fingers with his as they walked towards the restaurant. "What do you know about this place?" he asked.

"I know shifters own it and it's very expensive, but that's it. Why?"

"This is where Angel's Kiss was being manufactured and distributed," he informed as he kept his pace leisure and his body relaxed. She had no idea how he was so calm because she was taut as a drum and wanted to jump his bones in the parking lot.

"Why would you bring me here?" she asked incredulously. "Zeke told me the devastation that drug caused shifters. I saw Tobias when his family brought him back. He abandoned his mate and kids for that drug. Even now, months later, he's a shell of the male he used to be. He's lucky Santiago didn't give up on him. It was his persistence that got the bear into treatment."

Orlando stopped walking and gaped at her. "Tobias went into treatment?" he asked and she nodded. "Santi has no idea. He was certain the male had died. He will be pleased to hear that. He worked hardest of us all to deal with this drug."

"Well, he did a good job of it. The drug is gone and supes are on the mend. Zeke said shifters were hit hardest, so I'm glad someone had the balls to deal with this," she admitted and shivered.

Snow didn't fall in the city as often as it did on the east side where she lived and she was glad the night was clear, even if the breeze chilled her to the bone. The jacket she'd shrugged wasn't offering any warmth. It wasn't practical, but it sure was pretty and completed her outfit.

"Santi made many mistakes in his bid for justice and he is paying for them, but we owe him a lot. Because of his insistence and determination, Angel's Kiss was cut short."

"You say that like its not gone," she hedged as she stepped into his body heat.

"You're shivering. Come on, let's get you inside," Orlando prompted as he tugged her into motion. "There's rumors it's back."

"What? Steve never mentioned anything to me about any rumors."

Orlando held the door open and warm air blasted them. "They're new and there haven't been many. It's entirely possible he hasn't gotten wind yet. I haven't had time to dig deeper because of this new demon."

"Is that why we're really here?" she asked, unsure if she was okay snooping on another shifter.

"My treats never involve work, mate," he whispered coming in close to her body. She felt his erection against her stomach and her ache intensified. "I have my work cut out for me if you think I'd promise fun then ask you to work. I haven't forgotten that your seafood is your favorite. That's why we're here. All work and no play makes Orlando a dull male," he added as he leaned his head and ran his nose along her cheek, kissing behind her ear.

The male drove her wild with passion and she feared she wouldn't make it past the salad before she attacked him at the table.

"I don't know. Our last outing turned into a battle, after all. Far cry from dull if you ask me," she replied, nibbling on his ear as she pulled him closer.

A throat clearing interrupted their love play. "Can I help you," came a voice behind them. Chuckling, Orlando turned after he pecked her lightly on the lips.

"Reservation for Trovatelli," Orlando replied.

Ember had never felt so giddy on a date in her life. Her mate was an affectionate male and she couldn't wait to break through the rest of his reservations and see the real Orlando. She liked every piece that had been revealed so far.

Glancing around the restaurant, it was obvious something major had happened as the crystal chandeliers near the back hall were missing most of their crystals. The embroidered carpet was impeccable as were the white linen tablecloths, but to her sensitive nose, the smell of burned wood along with a faint whiff of rot lingered.

She held Orlando's hand as they followed the maître d' to their table. Orlando held out her chair then took his own. She slapped out when an unknown hand reached into her lap.

"What the hell are you doing? I'm here with my mate," she barked at the cambion who'd shown them to the table.

The male's eyes narrowed as Orlando snickered. "It's a courtesy to place your napkin in your lap."

"Well, he doesn't need to. I can do it myself," she replied, irritated and embarrassed that she'd made a fool of herself. She'd never eaten in a restaurant where they did things like place napkins on your lap.

She was in way over her head if these were the types of places her mate preferred to frequent. Her parents had a higher than average status among shifters, but they didn't take them to places like this. They believed in cooking meals at home and money was spent on trips or improving the communal areas.

"A bottle of Talaria Merlot, please," Orlando asked the maître d'.

"Very well. Stefan will be along shortly to take your order," the cambion said and walked off.

"I don't normally drink alcohol. It's always given he a headache," she informed him, hoping this wasn't going to be an issue between them.

Orlando waved his hand in the air. "That's because you're drinking the wrong wine. Just try it. If you don't like it, we will order something else."

"Deal, but I'm grumpy when I have a headache, just so you know," she warned.

"I think I can soothe any ache you may have," he replied with a waggle of his eyebrows. She knowingly grinned as a couple approached the table carrying a bottle of wine.

"Orlando, so good to see you," the female said as she took Orlando's hand.

He stood and embraced her briefly. Ember sensed they were wolf shifters, but she didn't recognize them as pack members. Maybe they were the owners.

"Good to see you, too, Mary. The place has come a long way," Orlando told the female before turning to the male. "John. Mary. This is my Fated Mate, Ember Hawthorne," Orlando introduced.

Flushing, Ember hurried to stand and came around the table to Orlando's side. "Its nice to meet you," she said, reaching out to shake their hands.

"Nice to meet you, as well. You have a great mate, here," John told her. "He helped us break Angelica's spell and get our restaurant back."

Ember looked up at her mate who was smiling easily. Orlando waved his hand and said, "I was only doing my job. I'm sorry we didn't figure things out sooner. We could have saved Charlie and his family."

"That vile woman had us by the balls, threatening to kill our families if we didn't do as she ordered. Thank the Goddess for Santiago," Mary added.

Ember thought Mary was beautiful, dressed to the nines in her designer clothes, high heels, and pearls. Ember's silk shirt and diamond stud earrings were decidedly lacking. This place was somewhere she could see the vampire royal family dining. It fit with their style that was for sure.

"Have you had any trouble since we vanquished Angelica?" Orlando asked.

The male couldn't help but work. It didn't bother Ember, though. In fact, she understood completely. With such a serious topic, she'd ask the questions, too, if she had the chance.

"The male that simpered after Angelica came around and tried to use a spell, but whatever the High Priestesses did to ward the building made his magic fizzle before it left his palm," John indicated.

"Did he say why he was here? Or what he was trying to do?" Orlando asked.

Ember could tell he was concerned with what they had told him as he leaned closer and listened intently to their words. The detective in him was coming out and it was just as sexy as everything else she'd seen.

"All he said was mongrels weren't going to get the best of his mistress. That everyone who'd harmed her would pay," Mary admitted.

"Do you have a name? Anything that may help us find him? Jace may know more if I can get a name and description," Orlando added.

"Don't know his name, but he was a tall, slender bald male with gray eyes. He had a tattoo of a raven on the back of his hand. Aside from dressing in expensive suits, that's all we can tell you," John finished.

"We won't take any more of your time, Orlando. So good to see you," Mary interjected. "Enjoy your meal."

When the couple was gone and they were sitting down, Ember couldn't help but tease her mate. "No work, huh?"

"Sorry," he said, sheepishly. "I have to get the information when I can. I guess you should know I'm never really *off* the clock. There will be times that battle will come up at the worst of times and I will have to respond. That's how life with a Dark Warrior is, but we know how to have a good time, as well. Granted, it seems those good times are always interrupted by demons," he relayed with a smirk and shake of his head.

"Demons are very inconsiderate," she joked. "It's like that with my job. I don't have regular work hours. I show up when needed. Once Hayden appoints me C.L.A.W. I will be gone as much as you."

"Then we will make the most of the time we have together. You're good at what you do. The realm needs you," he replied.

The waiter arrived to take their order before she could respond. She had no idea what she ordered. All she could think about was the warmth that spread through her knowing he supported her job. Her mother cautioned her that males would not want her in a role where she'd be in danger. She sent a silent prayer of thanks to the Goddess for picking the perfect mate for her. One that treated her as an equal.

Orlando was easy to talk to and her lobster and scallops were delicious, practically melting in her mouth. He had picked the perfect restaurant even if she initially felt outclassed. It didn't take long for her to relax and enjoy his attention. The conversation was natural, even though, wariness remained that she hoped dissolved soon.

"I can't believe you're a Trekkie. Don't tell me you're a

Chris Pine fan," he groaned with a shake of his head as he scooted his chair to sit beside her.

A decadent chocolate cake was set between them as she laughed. "Chris Pine is so much sexier than William Shatner. Of course I like him better. What female wouldn't?" she teased.

"I'll show you sexy when we get home. I can tell you right now by looking at him in those tights, I have a lot more to offer," he growled as he grabbed a fork and stuffed it into the cake, feeding her a heaping bite of the dessert.

Her eyes rolled back in her head. "Oh my Goddess. That is so decadent. You have to try it," she said on a moan.

Rather than take a bite, he leaned over and placed his lips over hers. He licked the chocolate from the corner of her mouth before his tongue delved past her parted lips. He stole her breath and kissed her until she was dizzy and craving way more than another bite of the dessert.

Moments later he broke the kiss and murmured. "Mmmm, best chocolate cake ever. Shall we take the rest to go?"

Nodding her head vigorously, she leaned over to whisper in his ear, "I'm going to spread chocolate frosting all over your hard cock and take my time licking every... last...drop."

Eyes wide, he raised his hand to signal the waiter. "Check."

CHAPTER 15

"Let's get these protections set so Rami can teleport Izzy in," Pema urged to the group standing in the clearing.

Orlando wiped his sweaty palms on his suit pants. It still seemed surreal that the ceremony they were preparing for was his mating ceremony. He had waited for this day for longer than he could remember. The Goddess had blessed him with the missing piece of his soul. They would finally be whole.

All they needed now was to make sure the demons didn't show up and wreck this ceremony, too.

He shook off the negativity of the demons ruining his day and focused on the bright spot that was Ember. He truly cared for Ember. She was beautiful, tenacious and the smartest female he'd ever met. She deserved so much better than his battered heart. She never asked for more than he could give and didn't push him. It was a relief to go at his own pace despite the many times he felt her exasperation.

Elsie stepped to his side bouncing from foot to foot. "You'd think this was your mating," he teased her.

Slapping his arm, she smiled at him. "I don't like being away from Izzy, but we weren't going to take any chances after last time. This is probably overkill," she responded.

"Nothing is overkill where she is concerned," Orlando assured as he watched the witches cast a cloaking spell.

They'd already added to the shield surrounding the Grove, along with Jace and Gerrick's assistance, so no demon should be able to get through the barrier now. But like Elsie had said, they weren't taking any chances.

Rami materialized with the exuberant little girl minutes later. Izzy ran up to Elsie blabbing nonstop about her sparkly dress then twirled to show it off. The princess's energy was infectious and even had Mack complimenting her girly dress.

Cloaking done, Hayden approached Orlando. "Ready?"

"More than ready," Orlando replied. The wood sprites had worked a miracle on the land surrounding the replicated Triskele Amulet. Even in the darkness of night, Orlando could see ferns and lush groundcover had replaced the blackened earth. The trees were still healing and would take longer, but white lights to distract from the damaged trunks surrounded the area.

Seeking Zander, Orlando couldn't help the pang that hit his chest when Hayden took his place as the ceremonial conductor. Orlando had been part of the Zeum family for centuries. These males and females fought by his side and shared in triumphs, as well as, failures. He'd made the concession with Ember that Hayden would be the only one performing the ceremony, and, while he wanted Hayden to be part of it, he was saddened that Zander would not be the one tying him to his future.

At least they would be in the inner circle, he reasoned. Each member of his Dark Warrior family was present, even

Santiago and Tori. The timing had worked perfectly with Santiago's release from the dungeons and his best friend was there to share in his special day.

Ember's mother caught his eye and nodded in his direction.

This was it. There was no turning back.

His life would never be the same after this night and he had no idea if he was ready. This signified so much change and a vulnerability he didn't know how to protect. He couldn't stifle her or lock her away. He was, however, certain that he wanted the pain of the mating brand to fade and planned on spending an uninterrupted week in bed with his sexy mate.

Taking in the setting, the area was dotted with tables and chairs off to one side while a path of rose petals led from Jesaray house to the natural arbor of two evergreens. The weather had warmed slightly and the snow was gone. As a being of earth, sun, and the wild, the outdoors was the perfect location for a shifter ceremony.

Orlando was surrounded by the energy of the pack and allowed that to feed his body and nurture his soul. He'd been gone so long that he'd forgotten what it felt like to be sustained by the pack on a regular basis, but since spending time with Ember, he felt more energized than he had in a long time. He received a similar jolt from the Dark Warriors, but it wasn't quite the same. His animalistic nature reveled in being here.

Grandma Flo exited the dining hall signaling to Orlando she'd finished preparations for the feast afterward. No shifter missed mating ceremonies mainly because they loved to eat and he had no doubt there was enough food to feed ten armies. He'd gone to Zeke's mating a while back and the pack had traveled to Zeum for Santiago when he'd mated a few months ago and both events had more food and drink than anything else.

There were several things common to everyone's ceremony and Orlando found those were the pieces he most looked forward to. The bonfire was at the top of his list. He'd made sure theirs was big enough to last throughout the night. He wanted his bond with Ember to be celebrated long after they left the ceremony to move onto his most anticipated portion of the night...the blood exchange.

Hayden adjusted his suit jacket and nearly dislodged his ceremonial cloak. Orlando got his first glimpse of the garment at Zeke's mating ceremony. It was comprised of the hides of every animal that lived inside the Omega.

It was rumored that the Goddess gave it to the first Omega and since then it had been passed down to subsequent leaders. Hayden wore it with pride. The sight was a major shift from the rugged attire of jeans and t-shirt the male usually wore. He'd even tied his hair back to complete the sophisticated look.

Adrenaline flooded Orlando's body as he waited for the event to begin. He wanted to howl to the night sky how honored he felt to be mating Ember. There were no words for the excitement he felt and that was buoyed by the emotions of everyone present.

"Oh my Goddess," Orlando breathed as Ember exited the back door of Jesaray house.

Stunning was his first thought, *mine* was his second. She was gorgeous in her cream-colored silk gown with a matching shawl over her shoulders. Her brown hair was pulled back and flowers adorned her head. His eyes locked with her amber gaze as she walked beside her best friend to his side and his knees weakened from the onslaught of her emotion. She was happier than he'd ever seen her and he vowed to make her smile like that every day for the rest of their lives.

Hayden chuckled and said, "Every time I do this the male wears the same goofy expression. I'm on the fence if it's a good thing or not."

"Very good," Orlando replied automatically.

The murmuring noise of the crowd evaporated when she reached his side. Nothing else mattered but her. He'd never understood the reason the males brought their females into their arms right away until now. It was because they were helpless to do any less. The second Ember was in his arms, desire coursed through him making him hard as stone. He kissed her rosy lips, not caring about the onlookers surrounding them. He had to taste her. The kiss quickly heated and his hands roamed down her back.

"I can see what you mean by good," Hayden teased, breaking into the moment. Ember was beaming when they parted lips and winked at Hayden.

Hayden directed them to the stone image of the Triskele Amulet inlaid in the dirt. While Orlando's blood, sweat and tears were in the amulet at Zeum, a piece of Ember's family lay in this replica and that made it just as meaningful.

"Friends and family, please form a circle around the couple," Hayden instructed.

As the embodiment of the amulet, Izzy strode to Hayden's side and grabbed his hand. The big male bent down and lifted her in his arms.

A loud cry interrupted the ceremony and Orlando jumped, realizing the cry came from his son. Brantley was in Evelyn's arms and wasn't happy about something. Ember's mother bounced the boy and turned him around to face Orlando and Ember. A smile immediately lit up his mate's face and the baby responded with a sweet laugh. Orlando waved and Brantley settled down.

Orlando loved Izzy, Aria and Donovan, but he hadn't been prepared for the unconditional love and devotion he felt toward the little guy. He hadn't expected such an all-consuming emotion given the indifference his parents had shown him. There wasn't anything he wouldn't do for Brantley and Ember felt the same way. He may not be their blood, but he belonged to them and he hoped Jaidis was looking down, pleased with her decision to ask Orlando to care for him.

He'd felt the tug of Fate the moment he'd met Jaidis and now he understood it was always about Brantley, not his mother.

"Someone doesn't want to be left out," Hayden chuckled as he looked to Brantley before he continued with the ceremony. "We have gathered here in this beautiful place, under the eye of the Sun and the glow of the Moon. Let the circle be blessed and consecrated with Fire and Water."

Faith and Emily stepped forward and lit the candles surrounding Orlando, Ember and Hayden. Whether from the magic of the night, Breslin's gift of fire, or the power of the Goddess, when the last candle was lit, fire rose from the earth to the heavens like shooting stars. And, as if guided by the same magic, water cascaded down in a sheer waterfall from the heavens back to the earth, extinguishing the fire.

"We call to the Goddess Morrigan, and invoke her to bless this mating," Hayden intoned.

Dozens of animals from deer to mountain lions to squirrels slowly approached the gathering. Owls and various other birds flocked to the nearby trees. Orlando knew it was the call of the Omega that drew them together and kept them from preying upon one another. The unity was felt between everyone and a sight to behold.

Hayden smiled at Ember before he placed the mating stone into her hand and gave her a squeeze. Orlando knew the two shared a deeper relationship than most and couldn't thank Hayden enough for being a father figure to Ember after her dad had been killed.

Orlando followed Ember's gaze to the ordinary-looking granite stone. The transformation it was about to undergo was one of the Goddess's most precious gifts. Orlando knew the mating stone protected different things for different couples and wondered what it would represent for them.

Orlando felt the electrical pulses that emanated from the stone. It crawled up his arm in a calming wave and he wondered how it felt to Ember. She was trembling as much as he was and their bond told him she was as awed as him.

Orlando laid his other palm over the top of Ember's. Power unlike anything he had ever experienced built beneath their hands. His heart raced and his soul stretched in his chest. His leopard prowled wanting in on the action, reminding Orlando the blood exchange would soon follow.

"We call upon the spirits of the East, of Air, Spring, and new beginnings. We call upon the spirits of the South and the inner Fire of the Sun, Summer, and personal will. We call upon the spirits of the West, of Water, Autumn, and healing and dreaming. We call upon the spirits of the North, of Earth, Winter, and the time of cleansing and renewal. Join us to bless this couple with your guidance and inspiration," Hayden chanted, his baritone voice carrying to the outer circles.

Ember placed her right hand over his heart and Orlando did the same, placing his right hand over her heart. "I bless this mating under the Sun and the Moon. This circle of love and honor is open and never broken, so may it be." Hayden's voice resonated with his blessing.

Heat built in the stone almost to an excruciating degree, but Ember's smile never wavered. Her joy and love shone through their bond. As he stared at his beautiful mate, Orlando was unprepared when he felt both souls leave his body to enter the stone. As brilliant light flashed between their fingers, Orlando's body filled with the magic. The connection he felt to Ember locked in place, and for the first time, he saw it as a gold chain that wrapped around his heart and ran to Ember's, entwining them. Ember stood taller when their souls surged back into their bodies.

Orlando had to take a small step backward. His transformed soul was foreign and slightly uncomfortable, but his chest was filled to bursting and the smile wouldn't leave his face. His soul was complete because of the stunning female in front of him. Ember was a part of him now and he could feel her in every cell of his body. She belonged to him and he belonged to her.

EMBER BEAMED up at her mate when the Goddess's magic settled around her like a fine mist.

"Mating stones protect and bless different aspects for different couples. You are a warrior at heart, Ember. You do your race proud, but you're stubborn. Your mating stone embodies compassion, courage and compromise. You will need all of them to face the battles ahead," a lyrical voice spoke in her head.

Ember glanced around. Orlando was smiling down at her and everyone else was clapping and cheering. Light shone between their clasped hands and she realized no one else had heard the Goddess speaking to her just now.

"I vow to keep this close to my heart and use it to beat the archdemons. I will not allow Lucifer into this world," Ember promised silently.

Tsking sounded in her head, making her flush with embarrassment. Apparently, that was the wrong response.

"This is about more than the demons. This concerns your future, your mate, the child you're raising, and your pack. You have the tools to face the trials and tribulations ahead and can conquer them all if you use the knowledge I've given you," the Goddess said before her presence vanished as quickly as it had appeared.

That cryptic warning settled like a weight in her gut, but she didn't have time to ponder it as Orlando lifted his hand to reveal an emerald the size of an egg. Their connection to the gem pulsed strongly through her body and its presence was comforting and settled her confused thoughts over the Goddess's words.

Orlando grabbed her into a tight embrace and his mouth crashed down on hers in the next moment. As always, their kiss fanned her desire and had her wanting more, but now wasn't the time as well-wishers descended on them.

Her mother handed a squirming Brantley to her. Orlando hadn't let go of her completely and the three of them stood together as the Dark Warriors congratulated them followed by the pack.

"Food is in the hall," Grandma Flo announced as she stood by the open doors of the dining hall.

Hungry shifters filed into the building in search of sustenance. The Dark Warriors held back as if uncertain. Orlando stood firmly by their side and she got another glimpse of the tight unit they represented.

"C'mon, let's grab some food," she urged her mate. "You're going to need your strength for what comes next."

Mack laughed and slapped Orlando on the back as she took the first step to the dining hall. Shifters drifted out with filled plates and wandered to the tables that were set up close to the bonfire.

"That's an understatement. Best part of the whole damn ceremony. Welcome to the family, Ember," Mack said as she and Kyran ducked inside.

Ember was unsure of the welcome she would receive from the females in the compound. Mack was the only one that had been friendly with her. She hadn't expected hugs and invitations to Girls' Night Out, but the cold shoulder she'd received from the queen was a bit much. Mack and Tori were the only ones that hadn't followed Elsie's lead.

The pretty Valkyrie had been consumed with missing her mate while he was in the dungeons and had withdrawn from everything. Seeing the female with Santiago, she saw a huge difference. It couldn't have been easy to immediately be separated after a mating. Seemed like torture to Ember.

"I think the little guy is hungry, too," Orlando observed as the others followed Mack and Kyran. Falling into step at her mate's urging she realized Brantley was sucking on his fist and fussy.

"My mom has his diaper bag with the bottles, I'll grab it from her," Ember said.

"I'll get food. You're going to need your strength, as well, Em," he said with a kiss.

Ember found her mom talking with Grandma Flo. "I need Brantley's bag. He's hungry," Ember said after greeting them both.

"Oh, yes. I'll grab it," her mother said and hurried away.

"Thank you for doing all this, Grandma Flo. You've

outdone yourself this time," Ember told the Omega's grandmother.

"I have missed these gatherings in the pack. We used to have ceremonies and feasts often and I forgot how much fun they were. They breathe new life into the pack and it's about damn time," Grandma Flo said as she brushed her blonde hair off her shoulder.

The tall female wore a sleek pantsuit and looked elegant. She didn't appear to be any older than Ember until you looked deeply into her warm brown eyes. They held the wisdom of her years and then some. "Give me that baby. You go find your mate and enjoy your Eve of Eternal Union," Grandma Flo stated with a wink.

Ember kissed Brantley's cheek and passed him over. "You're the best," Ember said as she hugged Grandma Flo and hurried off to find her sexy mate, tempted to forgo food and head straight to the mating cave.

CHAPTER 16

Orlando could see the candlelight flickering inside the cave from several feet away. "I'd heard about the mating cave. I thought that was a euphemism for a fancy room set up for couples to spend their Eve of Eternal Union," he muttered and tilted his head to look at his mate. "I didn't realize it was an actual cave."

Ember licked her lips and her tongue darted out across her bottom lip. He watched avidly. He could think of a lot of activities involving tongues. Through their bond he felt her heart racing but also her hesitance.

"Is that going to be a problem?" she asked.

"Baby, I don't care where we are so long as we're alone. It'll be uncomfortable if there aren't any blankets, but I imagine Hayden planned for that."

They entered the dimly lit cavern, but could easily see with enhanced vision. About fifty yards inside the cave stood a large four-poster bed with plush green covers. Candles sat in clusters every few feet and champagne with fresh fruit sat on a low table filled with various implements

Orlando was eager to try with his mate. The place was perfect.

He stopped her by the end of the bed and turned her to face him. She'd come into his life unexpectedly and he'd initially fought his instincts, but he was glad Fate won out. She was absolutely radiant and their bond strengthened by the minute. Hope flared that they could have an epic love like he saw between the rest of the mates at Zeum.

The soft whisper of her breathing sped up, inciting his leopard. He heard her heart racing and his immediately matched her pace. He ran the backs of his fingers across her cheek and pulled her hair free. Flowers fell to the ground as he threaded his fingers into the shoulder length tresses. It was soft as silk and her sweet scent filled the air.

Her hands landed on his chest and drove a groan from his throat. "Take off the dress, Em. I don't want to rip it to shreds and my leopard is close to breaking free," he informed her.

A spark flashed in her eyes and the corner of her mouth lifted as she continued running her hands over his torso. "You're highly mistaken if you think you're in charge," she stated.

His only response was a raised eyebrow. He wanted to see where his sexy little cougar was going with her boldness. They'd been together every chance they had and when Brantley wasn't crying, they were naked and pleasuring one another. She'd been content to let him control their love-making as they learned each other's body over the past weeks. This was a new side to her and he loved it.

"I need this gone," she demanded as she ripped his shirt open.

Buttons went flying and the heat between them became

an inferno as lips clashed and she shoved his jacket and shirt off. The fabric pooled on the floor and he slipped out of his shoes while she did the same, their mouths never parting.

Her hands were at his zipper and his pants and boxer briefs joined the rest of his clothes on the floor. She broke the kiss and stepped back to admire him.

"You are incredibly delicious and I'm starving," she confessed as amber eyes burned bright with her arousal.

"Feast away," he encouraged with a sly grin.

"I didn't tell you that you could speak," she chided him. Apparently, she was serious. His throat rumbled but he kept silent.

She stalked around him, running her hands over his chest and claws extended to rake across his flesh. His leopard jumped toward her teasing fingers. She palmed his ass then his hips and brushed over his shaft so quickly he jerked in response. It was exquisite torture. When her claw gently scraped his nipple, sweat broke out over his entire body.

Her eyes slit to that of her cougar when she looked up at him. His hands found the back of her dress and in the next moment the zipper gave way. She chuckled when the sound of ripping cloth filled the chamber.

"Someone anxious?" she asked seductively. She was uninhibited in a way he'd not seen from her and it was intoxicating.

"Yes," he managed to croak past a dry throat as her breasts were revealed to him.

The large globes had his cock jumping and her nipples pebbled in response. The silk of her dress in a pile, he laid his palms on her waist and lifted her against his body.

"You can take control after the blood exchange," he

informed as he kissed down the length of her throat. "I can't hold my leopard back for long."

"Then let him out to play," she challenged. "My cougar wants to be claimed."

His eyes flared wide. He'd never had sex in animal form but had always wanted to. The primal nature of mounting her called to his spirit.

"After I take your blood. I want to make you fully mine before letting our animals out," he replied as he took a breast into his mouth.

Arching her back, she forced more past his lips. She had no problems taking what she wanted from him and that was sexy as fuck. Once they got started it was always like this between them, a desperate rush to come together.

Crossing to the bed, he laid her down on the comforter and pulled her to the edge of the bed. She leveraged up on her elbows watching him as she placed her feet on the bed and spread her legs, giving him a spectacular view of her glistening sex.

"This is a beginning, Em. A fresh start with just the two of us, no history. We wipe the slate clean, right here, right now," he declared, putting it all out there so she would know how he felt. He'd never thought himself romantic, but he wanted to try and be the best mate possible. She deserved that.

Tears bloomed in her eyes and her smile blinded him. "I've been waiting to hear that," she admitted and he suddenly felt like crap for causing her any doubt.

Ready to start anew, he placed his hands on her knees and nudged them apart. The arousal coating her soft folds beckoned him. He ran a finger through her slit and enjoyed the shudder that ran through her body.

"Don't tease me," she ordered him.

"You aren't in charge anymore, Wildcat. Just lay back and enjoy this."

"Payback is a bitch," she warned. Her threat might have carried more weight if it was more than a pant. Her head flopped back onto the bed as Orlando kissed his way up her thigh.

He mentally shackled his leopard so it didn't break free. Knowing his mate was ready and willing to go animal with him made it hard to control. He glanced up and saw her struggling to control her cougar, as well.

"Patience," he whispered and ran his tongue through her folds.

"Ah!" she cried out and gripped the bed sheet as he lapped at her sweet nectar.

He was addicted to her honey. One taste and he couldn't stop until she was writhing beneath his mouth. One hand ran up her abdomen to her breast as his other teased her drenched opening.

Her pleasure reached him through their link and he didn't know how he was going to keep control with the dual sensations wracking his body. Allowing one finger to tease her opening, he licked and sucked her clit into his mouth. He'd known she enjoyed that, but didn't realize how much until now as he felt arousal rush through her veins that caused his cock to harden even more.

Their new bond was telling him how much she enjoyed each touch and caress. Inserting one finger, her muscles clamped down as she lifter her hips. Testing the waters, he swirled his tongue over her bundle of nerves and got a clear picture of the pleasure and torture that it caused her.

"Harder," she ordered on a moan. Her fingers grabbed hold of his short hair and she pulled him against her sex, forcing more pressure to the engorged nub.

His cock ached, needing to be inside his mate so he didn't fight her. He sucked her clit and plunged two fingers into her sex and within seconds she was bucking and crying his name.

EMBER PANTED as Orlando eased her down from the climax. She knew it was the first of many for the night and she tried to catch her breath. As he prowled up between her legs, she couldn't help but appreciate his feline grace. Her legs opened wide, inviting him to take her body.

His hard flesh was a flame against her skin. Seeing the smile on his lips and shine in his eyes as he lay on top of her was the pinnacle of the night. The pleasure and orgasms were incredible and she wanted more, but seeing his love and knowing it was directed at her was everything. He wasn't ready to profess his feelings, but she saw it in his eyes and that was all that mattered.

He meant it when he'd told her this was a new beginning for them. For the first time, she didn't feel the weight of his past between them. What she did feel was his erection resting against her thigh and she couldn't wait for him to be inside her.

She widened her legs and wrapped one around his hip, bringing his tip in line with her core. His lips crashed down on hers as she felt him release the tight tether he'd held on his need.

He rocked against her, coating his impressive length through her arousal. His hips moved as his lips devoured her mouth. Reaching back, she clawed his ass in silent urge to join their bodies.

She mewled in objection as he broke their kiss and lifted

his head from her mouth. Holding her gaze, he reached down and aligned his shaft. Before she could demand him to hurry and satiate her need, he plunged to the hilt in one tight stroke, stretching her to the point of pain.

It was a sense of homecoming as he entered her. They'd been made for each other and this was how it should always be between them. She used her thighs to press upward as Orlando came crashing down. He guided her movement with one hand as they came together. He lifted her calf over his shoulder, widening the angle so she could take more of him.

"Yes, Orlando. Give me more. I want it all," she demanded and he gladly obliged, pounding into her willing body.

They moved together, their bond keeping them in synch. Her body coiled as they came together over and over. Her need once again reaching that precipice, she met him thrust for thrust as they sought the edge and plunged over.

She knew what was coming as he broke the kiss and momentarily stopped moving. She'd never had the blood of another and was anxious to taste him.

"Do you want the athame for the exchange?" he asked wild-eyed as he trembled from stalling his movements.

"No... use canines," she panted as she swiveled her hips, encouraging him to move.

"Bite me when we cum, Em. I want your blood on my lips as you give me your body," he demanded as he began moving again.

Their movements became frantic and it didn't take much for her to feel the orgasm barreling down on her. Allowing a partial shift so her canines descended, she lifted her head and bit into his neck as her climax ripped her apart.

Stars danced in her vision as she drank his life's blood. She expected him to be coppery like the wild game she'd hunted, but he tasted like dark chocolate and she couldn't get enough.

A slight sting told her he'd bitten her, as well, and as his blood flowed into her body, their minds mingled as they reached for distant stars. They coalesced into one entity. She felt his hopes, needs and desires as his hot seed filled her womb and the barb extended, locking them together as their climaxes continued.

She couldn't agree more with him. They were lucky to have found their other half. Many dreamed of finding their Fated Mate. They'd been given this rare honor and nothing and no one would ever part them again. She'd seen love in his eyes and now she saw it in his heart.

It was a new love. One in its infancy, but with such great potential.

Pulling from her body he glanced down at her. "Are you okay?" he asked as he pushed the hair from her face.

"Never better," she assured him.

"My leopard wants his turn," he teased as he shifted in a bright flash of light.

His magnificent snow leopard stood over her and she marveled at its strength and power. She stroked a hand through its silky fur and heard a low rumble in its throat.

Giggling with excitement, she shifted. *"Come get me,"* she taunted into his mind and took off running.

Anticipation ignited a burst of speed as she sprinted from the cave into the cold night air. She couldn't wait for his leopard to catch her cougar.

CHAPTER 17

"**G**oddess, you're good with your tongue," Ember groaned as her mate coaxed her exhausted body to life.

She'd been on cloud nine for the past three days as she and Orlando holed up in the mating cave exploring each other. The nights were even more exhilarating as their animals became acquainted with one another.

Ember had discovered that his leopard had to dominate her in every way and her cougar loved it. Her animal was a pussy in every way when it came to his beast. It was a little annoying to Ember, but so long as Orlando understood she wasn't as submissive as her animal, they would be fine. Regardless, she reveled in the bliss of their mating.

The Goddess had given Ember the best gift yet in Orlando. The small peeks at his sense of humor were even more prevalent now and she realized that was the real him. The bitter, guarded image he'd carried around was a bi-product of the loss he'd experienced, in addition to his childhood issues he still carried. It was surprising to her to hear how his parents had largely ignored him. It went against the shifter way. As a species, they were the most touchy-feely of the Goddess's creatures.

"I'm the king, baby. I'll expect proper genuflection after I'm done," he said with a chuckle.

"The king, huh? And, here I thought I mated a warrior," she murmured and squealed when he tickled her sides until she was begging for mercy.

"Don't. Stop. Uncle, uncle," she cried out, unable to suppress her laughter.

A loud chime echoed throughout the cave, halting their sex play. "I'd like to pretend that didn't happen, but it could be about the demons, or, more importantly, it could be about Brantley," Orlando huffed in exasperation.

Ember didn't want reality intruding on their little bubble, either. They hadn't bothered to put clothes on since shedding them the night of their mating. Various pack members brought food and left it near the cave opening. She'd never had more orgasms in her life than she had the past few days and wanted to stay in their corner nook of the world and ignore the responsibilities of life a little longer. Unfortunately, that wasn't possible.

Orlando rolled over and reached for his phone on the low table. The ripple of his muscles as he stretched had her mouth watering and her lips seeking the back of his neck. She shamelessly draped herself over his back and kissed and nibbled his neck and earlobe.

A masculine moan made her smile. "You're playing with fire, Wildcat. That was Elsie," he murmured as she urged him to his back.

The way her breasts smashed against the hard planes of his chest sent a shiver through her body. His cock sprang to life near her hip.

"Brantley just crawled. Look," he said holding up his

phone as his eyes drifted closed when she gripped his hard length.

Ember adjusted her position so she was sitting astride her mate with his shaft nestled in her slick slit. He shoved the phone at her, forcing her to take it. Brantley was indeed crawling. Stripling grew too fast, she thought. In just a couple months, he had gone from newborn to an infant in no time and would be walking before they knew it.

"One more time," she pleaded as she set the phone down and wiggled against his pulsing cock. Her body needed him again and she wouldn't be denied.

Orlando sat up and wrapped his arms around her middle and pulled her close. "We have time for another round...maybe two, then we have to go to him. I want us to share in this moment with him."

He swallowed her response as he took her mouth. His lips moved over hers, his tongue slid through her parted lips and stroked the length of her tongue. Crawling stripling, demons and everything else flew from her brain as her mate pulled her into an erotic hurricane.

"THE PROTECTIONS around the Grove feel the same as they do here now," Ember observed as they crossed the boundary onto Zeum property.

She and Orlando were running a few minutes later than expected. After making love in the shower at her house, they dressed then undressed for one more round before finally getting in his car to head to Zeum. She hadn't wanted to leave their love nest in the cave, but she had to admit, she was anxious to see Brantley, too.

"Yep. When Hayden called in the Rowan sisters and the

sorcerers, he added the extra layers we've always had at Zeum. I think it should be much safer now," Orlando replied as they neared the front door.

"The Grove has never been targeted before now. We have always kept our own safe. How will this affect the pack hunts? Will we need to lift the spell during those? Can we even do that?" she asked as he parked his Mustang.

"The spell is designed to allow pack and invited guests through. Anyone can cross the boundaries during the hunts, but they will not be protected outside the bubble of magic. I wouldn't lift the protections for any reason. That'll be tempting to the demons," Orlando explained as they approached the house.

"I can't wait to have you by my side during the next hunt," Ember admitted as they entered the opulent foyer. "I still can't get over this place. It's so ostentatious and huge compared to our little cabin. Zander has expensive taste."

The brown marble floors had been buffed to a high sheen. The chandelier reflected off the surface despite the faint lighting. The crystals on the chandelier were bigger than her fists and had to have cost a fortune. In fact, she'd bet everything she owned that the chandelier alone cost more than her whole place, including the furnishings.

"Don't worry, you'll get used to it. And, we all had a hand in building Zeum. There's a piece of each of us here," Orlando shared, surprising her.

"You mean to tell me that the vampire royal family helped build this place? They didn't hire someone to do it?"

She had this image of spoiled princes and princesses being pampered and telling everyone what they wanted and how they wanted it done. Looking at all the craftsmanship around her, she couldn't deny the skill and talent it had taken to create the masterpiece. Knowing they'd poured so much of themselves into the building placed it in a new light for her. This wasn't a display of their wealth, but pride in their family and heritage. From the marble and hardwood floors to the ornate shutters, it was obvious they'd picked materials that would maximize their protection while still being exquisite.

"I have to admit I'm impressed. Brownie points for my mate on knowing how to build a house," she teased as she shook her head. "Will wonders never cease? One day you can add onto our cabin for us."

"Orlando, you're home. Welcome back," came a feminine voice a second later.

Ember turned her head and noticed the vampire queen rushing down the massive staircase. Seeing the female's reaction hinted at the intimate level of the living arrangements in the Dark Warrior compound.

She wondered just how close everyone's rooms were to each other. In Jesaray house they were right next to each other, with the exception, of Hayden who occupied one whole wing. It helped that the walls in Jesaray house were reinforced for maximum privacy, but she preferred having private space. It was why she moved out of her family's house and into her cottage.

It was one thing to live close to others and share meals in the main dining hall, but another to live in the same house with your sleeping quarters right next to someone. She wondered if Orlando always slept naked. He did when he was in her bed, but that could be because they were always having sex.

She didn't like the thought of Santiago bursting into Orlando's room while they were going at to grab him for a mission. That was the type of intimacy she imagined these warriors shared and it had her wondering how her mate was going to handle it when things changed.

Orlando let go of her hand and embraced Elsie, which had Ember gritting her teeth. *You're not jealous. He's yours and will never want another female,* she mentally chided, but couldn't stop the jealousy over the queen holding her mate so tightly. And why was he still hugging her? It wasn't like it had been that long since he'd seen her.

Shoving her reaction away, Ember blamed it on the fact that the queen had been standoffish to her from the beginning. They didn't get along and would never be best friends, but Ember didn't care. You couldn't win them all, she conceded.

"Where's Brantley?" he asked after they broke apart. Ember calmed slightly when he was stepped back at her side.

"He's in the kitchen with Cailyn. You guys are just in time. We're making dinner," Elsie said then led them down the hall.

"Fantastic, I'm famished. We haven't had a lot of time for food," Orlando said with a wink in Ember's direction.

Ember socked his arm as she blushed to her roots. Elsie turned around and waggled her eyebrows with a small laugh to Orlando.

He turned to Ember and muttered, "Speaking of being too busy, there's a rule around Zeum. Never walk into the kitchen without knocking first. Elsie and Zander like to do more than cook in there," he shared. The mirth in his voice was infectious and had Ember smiling along with him.

"Really? I never would've guessed," Ember replied, unable to imagine the snotty-nosed queen being so uninhibited. She imagined her demanding Zander to shower before having sex.

"Apparently, Elsie is the twisted kinky one in the family. We all thought it was Kyran, but his whips and ball-gags have nothing on our queen in the kitchen," Orlando joked.

"You're so full of it, O. I am not the kinky one in this house, and, if I was, you'd be the last to know," Elsie retorted as she pushed through a door that said Elsie's Throne Room. Now that seemed fitting, Ember thought, as she followed Orlando into the kitchen.

Once inside the massive room, she tried to contain her awe. Much like the rest of the house it was large and held the finest appliances and marble countertops. Where she felt the other areas of the house were formal and removed, this room invited her in and made her wish she knew how to cook better. She'd not felt welcome in the home until walking into the kitchen. It was full of people, including Brantley, who began squirming and reaching for them as soon as they walked in.

Rushing to his side, Orlando picked up the baby and lifted him into the air. "Hey, buddy. I missed you," her mate cooed as he cuddled the infant close.

Ember joined them and laid her hand on Orlando's hip, needing the contact to soothe her cougar and calm her jealousy. Brantley reached for her and Ember took him from Orlando's arms.

"You always show up for the food," Nate observed as he came through a side door with several pots and pans in hand.

"That's because my timing is impeccable," Orlando retorted as he reached over and snagged a carrot from a pile of vegetables on a chopping block.

"No, my sister is just always cooking," Cailyn added from her position with Jace.

Ember recalled the night she'd met the healer when

Brantley's mother had died. The healer was a quiet male and Cailyn was a lucky female. The predator beneath was proficient and she had no doubt Jace was one of the best among the Dark Warriors. She didn't need to fight beside the male to know that. It was evident in everything he did, including his healing.

"That's true," Elsie agreed. "Looks like you guys have had a great celebration," Elsie commented with a smile to Orlando. Ember barely held her snarl back. Their intimacy was none of Elsie's business.

"It's been the best," Orlando shared as he wrapped his arms around her from behind. She preened with his attention and loved it. She didn't realize it, but this had been missing in her life. Having a partner at her side, sharing life, and supporting her.

"I wished it could have lasted longer," Orlando finished. Ember had to agree with her mate. Forever would suit her just fine.

"I'd be willing to move into that cave with you and Brantley," she teased with a shake to her hips.

A growl left his throat as he grabbed her hips and stilled her movements. Leaning over he nipped her earlobe and whispered, "I'm going to spank your ass when I get you alone."

"Promises, promises," she replied as her insides danced. She'd take any spanking her mate wanted to dish out. He was playful in bed and didn't mind her taking the lead when she felt the urge.

"So, what did we miss?" Orlando asked Jace as he turned his attention to the warrior.

Ember listened as Jace filled them in on the latest from the demons. It appeared that the new archdemons were content to attack the humans in smaller settings. Thankfully, they hadn't attacked another large event like the candlelight vigil.

Ember knew Hayden wanted to come out to the humans, and she supported him, but couldn't deny that Orlando had made some good points as to why they shouldn't. She'd seen the cruelty humans instigated against animals everyday and had no doubt as a shifter her species would be treated the worst.

"Brantley's diaper needs to be changed," she interrupted, unsure if she should ask Nate to show her to Orlando's room. She had no idea where anything was in the house and didn't see a diaper bag nearby.

"Sorry, Em. Didn't mean to get caught up in work. Let's go change him. I can show you to our room," Orlando replied easily.

"Stop looking at my ass," Ember said over her shoulder as they ascended the stairs to his suite.

His stomach knotted the closer they got to his room. It was now *their* room and he wondered what she would think of it. He'd never taken a female back to his suite, unwilling to share that space with anyone other than his Fated Mate. None of them ever believed they'd be blessed a mate after the seven-hundred-year mating curse, but Zander was the one who never gave up and set the example. Each of the Dark Warriors had followed suit, and now, he couldn't be more grateful.

This was a privilege reserved for his other half and he was eager to share it with Ember.

"Then stop shaking it in my face. Don't think I missed that extra swing, Wildcat," he teased as he ran after her.

Brantley squealed, sensing the game and clapped in Ember's arms while she took off down the hall.

"I wasn't swinging anything," she denied with a snort. "Come on, Brant, we need to get away from daddy," she murmured, bringing their son into the fun.

Her words warmed his soul. No one had called him daddy yet. He'd been taking care of Brantley and considered the baby his, but no one had used that term. Hearing it felt right. He *was* this child's father. Happy in a way he didn't fully understand, he chased his mate. Catching up to her, he grabbed her around the waist and brought them both to his chest. After placing a brief kiss to her lips, he met Brantley's gaze.

"Don't even think about going against the male dominance. We're Team OB," he said kissing the top of the baby's head.

"More like BO because he stinks," Ember replied with a laugh as she pinched her nose.

Smiling, Orlando led them into his room. "Should we let mommy in the club with us?" he asked as he took him from Ember. Leading them through the living room to the bedroom, he watched as Ember soaked in her surroundings.

"I never would have pictured you as the modern type," she said a minute later.

He took in the room from her perspective. He'd never thought about his style, but he supposed the black leather and glass tables were more modern, especially in comparison to her rustic décor.

"I like the clean look of things, but we can change anything you want," he offered.

Her head snapped up at that. "I like the furniture in my house. I hope that's not a problem," she replied.

"Not at all. We can keep anything you want. Like I said, I

like the clean look, but the females have told me I will need to baby-proof soon," he admitted as he laid Brantley on the changing table.

"You haven't packed yet," Ember remarked. Orlando's head tilted her way and he noticed her turning in circles.

"No. Packed for what? We can't take a trip right now with the demons on the loose," he hedged.

She'd stopped circling and faced him. As she pushed her glasses up her nose, he marveled at her beauty. Her amber eyes were alight with joy and she had the biggest smile on her face. She was the sexiest female he'd ever seen.

And, she was *his*.

Brantley squeaked, reminding Orlando of his task. He broke eye contact and went back to changing his son's diaper.

"Packed to move in with me, silly."

Her statement was teasing and light, but his gut tightened and his heart raced. They hadn't had a conversation about living arrangements before they'd mated. It had honestly never entered his mind.

"I assumed we were going to live here. All the mates live here," he explained as dread filled his stomach.

Fire flashed in her amber eyes then turned black with anger. "In case you haven't noticed, I'm not like all the other mates. We don't belong here. We belong at the Grove, protecting the others," she snapped.

Brantley began crying and Orlando finished fastening the diaper then picked him up. "Em, I'm a Dark Warrior. I need to be here," he tried to explain, but his heart and head were spinning out of control as sweat broke across his back.

"I know you're a Dark Warrior, but that doesn't mean you have to live here. I belong with the pack Orlando. I don't fit in with the females here. Hell, Elsie can't stand me and the feeling is mutual. Plus, my family is on pack land. That's where we need to be," she explained to him.

Her words stung. How could she spew such venom towards Elsie? He had sensed there was no love lost between them, but he didn't realize how intense the animosity was between them. He wondered if it was one-sided on Ember's part.

"I think you're over-exaggerating about Elsie. She's really great once you get to know her. Plus, I can't leave. *My* family is here. I need to be here for them. You've seen how battles come up unexpectedly," he implored, wanting her to understand.

"How can you defend her?" Ember shouted as she flailed her arms wildly. "I'm supposed to be your family now, Orlando. Does that not matter to you?"

"Of course it matters. But can't you see it from my perspective?" he implored, wanting to resolve this before it exploded in his face.

"No, Orlando. I won't live here and you won't leave, so now what do we do?"

"You haven't given it a try here," he accused. His mind was whirling and his anger rising at her stubbornness.

This was not how a mating was supposed to be. Each one of the couples at Zeum had dealt with one fucked up situation or another and managed to work through it. He and Ember were supposed to work through their bullshit and come out stronger afterwards. That was the purpose of the mating bond. Nothing should come between them. Ever.

"And, you haven't given the Grove a try. I won't live here," she flat-out refused. His breath left him on a whoosh while pain engulfed his heart and he nearly dropped Brantley.

His eyebrows drew together and his eyes narrowed. He couldn't leave his colleagues in a lurch at such a dangerous time. Duty forbade it. "My leaving is impossible, Ember. This is bigger than you and me. I have an obligation to the Goddess. Innocents will die if I shirk that responsibility."

"Well, it looks like we're at an impasse. I should have known things were going too good for us. The Goddess warned me I had struggles ahead. Seems we will be the first mated couple to live apart. You know where to find me if you need me," she gritted then walked over to Brantley and kissed his cheek. "Love you, Brant. Mommy will see you soon," she stated before she turned and walked out the door.

What the fuck was happening? How could she be saying this? Orlando stood in the middle of his room, unable to utter one word to stop her while his heart shattered into a million pieces.

And she'd been the one to mend the damn thing.

CHAPTER 18

"Good luck. Let us know if we can help with anything else," Pema said as Angus embraced her. He was ecstatic that the piece of fabric they'd found in the cave was successful in the witches locating Keira.

"You and your sisters have done more than enough. You've given me hope and that is something I haven't had for a thousand years. I know my Keira is alive. I will find her," he promised.

"Of course we will," Lorne agreed. "Are you certain it's safe to shift and take off in the middle of a city like this? Figures I'd get naked when the only females around to appreciate my prowess are mated."

"We might be mated, but we aren't dead," Isis teased playfully and earned a growl from her mate. "You're good to go, we've got you covered until you reach a higher altitude and then the night will protect you," she informed them as she wrapped her arms around Braeden's waist, calming his possessive nature.

"You're welcome in Khoth anytime," Angus offered as he shucked his clothing and allowed his dragon to take over.

Before the change overtook him completely, he heard Suvi, the youngest of the triplets, say, "Damn, did you know the majordomo was so ripped? I knew he was good-looking, but I've never seen him out of a suit and had no idea he was built like that."

"I'm right here, mate," Caine growled, nearly causing Angus to lose the shift with his amusement.

Mated males were highly territorial and didn't like other males ogling their mates, much less, their females admiring others, especially naked.

Suvi placed her palm over Caine's heart and rubbed circles. "No one compares to you, baby. You rock my world. I just had no idea Angus was so muscular." Mollified, Caine pressed a kiss to Suvi's lips.

"Hello, dragon shifter, Suvi. He's a brick house, for Goddess sake," Pema added with a roll of her eyes. "We want to be there when you get hitched to Keira," Pema insisted.

The female's mate stood behind her holding their newborn baby. The infant looked even smaller in her father's large hands, but fatherhood suited the male, Angus mused.

The witches hadn't lived at Zeum, but they'd become part of the new family he loved. He was beyond grateful that he'd gotten over his isolation and found these supernaturals. They had enriched his life and he could never pay them back for what they'd given him and continued giving him. The monster he'd become in those early days was frightening and he hated to wonder what state this world would have been in if not for Zander and the others.

He hated to admit that he was the reason for the myth

surrounding dragons that ran rampant on earth. He'd terrorized villages, hunted humans and accepted sacrifices offered to him. He wasn't proud of his actions, but he hadn't been in his right mind.

Having always lived the life of an aristocrat where his every move had been scrutinized and corrected, it wasn't difficult under the circumstances to shed his civility shortly after he crossed to earth.

After his grief ebbed and his mind settled, he realized how lonely he was. He may not have known how to find Keira, but in his heart, he'd known she existed somewhere and she would never love the male he had become. He had no inkling how to survive in these foreign lands so finding Zander and the Dark Warriors had given him a new purpose in life.

Returning to Khoth without his new friends was difficult, but his people needed him. His kind was suffering. Without him there to perform the *Civappu*, dragonette birthrate had dropped to dangerous levels. If he didn't return his kind would become extinct. They needed new *Tuya* identified to mate with and it was his duty to conduct the ceremony.

He had one last task before returning to his homeland and that was to find Keira. As his shift completed, he shook out his wings. The thought of taking flight to find Keira was invigorating and his blood raced through his system.

Lorne shifted, as well, and the two of them took up the entire space in the Rowan Sister's backyard. Braeden, Isis's mate, approached them with two duffle bags that he secured to their backs.

On Khoth they had harnesses that magically adjusted with their shifting, but Lorne and Nate hadn't brought any of their weapons or the straps, so Braeden had to tie the bags to them. They would need the money and clothing inside when they arrived at their destination. A naked male wandering the streets would garner as much attention as a dragon.

"Don't forget to wear the amulets we made you. It's the only way to shield your presence," Pema reminded them.

Angus had been so relieved when they'd told him they could make something to mask his presence. He had no fucking doubt the Unseelie King was behind this whole mess and the reason he was always five minutes too late and couldn't find Keira. The bastard was powerful and kept moving whenever he sensed them coming. The only way Angus was going to be able to get close was if Cyril couldn't sense them.

"We owe you much. Thank you for your assistance," Angus mentally replied.

"We want the best rooms in the castle when we visit," Pema said and the group waved them goodbye.

"The best room's at my place," Lorne teased before the two of them inclined their large reptilian heads and took to the skies.

Anticipation urged Angus on. He was so close to being reunited with Keira. It had been so long since he'd seen her, but he hadn't stopped loving her for one minute.

He recalled the first time he'd seen her. As a sea dragon, she lived in the oceans of Khoth. Taking a break from the monotony of life at the palace, Angus often went to the beach. The sea called to him in a way he hadn't understood until the day Keira stepped from the waves.

His mouth went dry remembering the way her curves glistened in the sun, her lush breasts on full display. He didn't realize she was one of the Stoorworm, let alone the Stoorworm King's only daughter. Her long green hair should have been his first clue, but all he could see was the way her aura called to him.

She had this energy about her that livened every cell in his body. Her raspy voice had been at odds with her delicate appearance. When she'd greeted him, she stumbled in her attempt to walk and that was when he'd finally realized what she was. Keira had never let him forget how he'd lost his mind that day, practically drooling all over her from his attraction.

Keira was much like the females at Zeum. She had a fire that ignited his ardor and set him in his place at the same time. She spoke her mind and stood her ground, regardless, if she was wrong. But, she was happy, always smiling, and forever teasing him. Her aqua eyes would sparkle with mirth when she gave him shit about mundane things.

His heart lurched in his chest as his mind envisioned her beautiful face. He missed her beyond words and his world had literally come down around him after losing her. All hope had been gone for so long that it was difficult to accept that she was now within reach.

He glanced over and saw Lorne flying close, his slate gray hide barely visible in the dark sky. Angus could only see his green eyes as the male looked over. He swore the Máahes was smiling. Lorne was frustrated and wanted to go home, but it was obvious the male had a renewed energy for their quest after the witches located Keira. Determination had Angus putting on a burst of speed as they neared the Gulf of Mexico.

Angus gestured to the deserted beach below and they both landed gracefully in the sand. Angus shifted back quickly and removed the pack from his back. He'd worn expensive suits for so long that it was still odd for him to don the rough jeans. They weren't the softest material, but he wanted to blend in as much as possible so he'd left his suits behind for Nate.

"Ready?" he asked Lorne who was pulling a t-shirt over his head.

The warm, salty air tasted of his beloved sea serpent and had him more eager to find her.

"Ready as I'll ever be. We will have her back by morning," Lorne promised.

"Och, do you really think it will be that easy?" Angus asked.

"We can't afford to think otherwise," the male amended and patted Angus on the shoulder, offering support.

Angus slung the bag over his shoulder and began his trek towards the nearby mountainside. He was tempted to grab the weapons and have them at the ready, but he didn't want to frighten Keira. She'd always hated violence or anything to do with fighting or harming of another.

That thought had his mind stalling on another. Had she been kept in that cave the entire time she'd been missing? On the heels of that, he wondered what she'd been put through. Had Cyril harmed her? He'd kill the bastard if he dared lay one finger on her.

They made their way up the rocky cliff and into the small town. The second they entered the bar, it was clear to him that, once again, they were too late. Her magical signature was faint, but definitely Keira's.

"Fuck!" Angus exploded so frustrated he nearly lost control of his dragon. His beast wanted to rain fire down around the earth. It wanted its queen as much as Angus did. Keira had once again slipped through their hands.

"I thought for sure we had her this time," Lorne growled.

"Aye, so did I. Cyril is too bluidy smart. He keeps her moving and 'tis impossible to get a read on them. They are always one step ahead of us, but the Rowan sisters gave me proof that she is alive and I willna stop until I have her back," Angus vowed.

Cyril hadn't covered his tracks as thoroughly as he should have because Angus picked up traces of his Unseelie magic. The bastard would pay with his life for keeping Keira from him.

~

"Do you have a minute?" Illianna asked as she knocked on the doorjamb.

Orlando looked to the open doorway and saw Rhys's mate standing with a plate of food in her hand. He cursed himself for not being at dinner, but he hadn't been in the mood to be around the many loving couples. Hearing them laugh and chase each other through the hallway near his rooms was bad enough.

"Sure, come on in," he whispered as he looked down to a sleeping Brantley on the couch beside him.

Illianna glided gracefully into the room. He was still awed by the angel's gold wings as she easily maneuvered into his quarters and sat on the adjacent loveseat. Her presence was always soothing and comforting and it eased the ache in his chest. He missed Ember with a fervency he didn't think possible. It had only been two days, but it seemed like an eternity.

"I noticed you weren't at dinner and brought you a plate," she murmured and held out the plate of food. Looked like Elsie's enchiladas. Typically, he inhaled several servings of the tasty dish, but he didn't have an appetite.

"Thank you," he replied as he accepted the plate and set it on the coffee table in front of him.

"Where's Ember?" Illianna asked as she looked around the suite.

Orlando couldn't hide his wince. This was why he'd been playing hermit in his room. "I assume she's at her house, but I honestly don't know."

"Oh, I see. Do you want to talk about it?"

Orlando waved his arm dismissively, pasting a smile on his face. He hoped it wasn't as brittle as it felt. It was difficult to maintain his composure in the angel's presence. He barely held back the urge to punch his fist through the wall. If the angel entered his bedroom, she'd see how often he'd given into that impulse.

"What's there to say? I found my mate and then she left me. So much for that infamous mating compulsion. Ember seemed to have no problem walking away from me," he said meeting her striking silver eyes.

Rhys's mate held a world of compassion in those silver eyes and it hit that Rhys was one lucky sonovabitch for finding this female who offset his hedonism so perfectly.

"The mating compulsion doesn't erase a person's will. It is merely a guide. You still have freedom of choice. Why did she leave? Did you two have a fight?" she asked with concern.

"You could say that. She refuses to live here with me. Said she belonged at the Grove and that the females living here don't like her," he relayed, shocked that he was telling her so much, but it just poured out of him. "I tried to talk to her, but she became unreasonable and stormed out."

"And, have you gone after her?" Illianna asked then reached over and ran her palm over Brantley's blond head while she spoke.

Her soft-spoken words hit Orlando like bullets as he admitted to himself he hadn't even tried calling Ember.

Truth was, it was killing him and he needed to hear her voice and be close to her.

"No, I haven't. I don't think she wants me around. I can sense her anger and frustration," he replied.

Countless emotions were bombarding him. He usually put up barriers to block sensations around him, but he was such a wreck, the walls were crumbling and it was difficult to pinpoint Ember's feelings from his own, but the fact that she was still pissed came across loud and clear.

"But, how do you feel? What is it that you want?" she asked.

"I want my mate...more than anything," he admitted, "but I can't leave the compound with this new demon on the loose. We are all needed and me being gone is out of the question."

"I can understand your dilemma. I went through a similar choice when I met Rhys," she shared.

Orlando had heard a little about what had gone down and knew that Rhys had died and Illianna made the choice to save him. He recalled her early days in the compound when she didn't have her wings.

"You gave up your wings for him," he recalled.

"I did. Angel's aren't blessed with a Fated Mate like your kind and I fought Rhys's claim on me every step of the way in Hell. I knew that accepting and mating with him would mean I had to give up my job and my home in Heaven."

Orlando had never equated Illianna being an angel as her job, but that was her job just as much as him being a Dark Warrior. Her duty was to bring joy and happiness like his duty was to protect innocents from the demons. She had sacrificed everything for Rhys. He really was a lucky bastard.

"After being a prisoner in the Underworld and suffering their cruel torture, I wanted nothing more than to get back to my brethren and heal. When I watched Rhys be slain, I realized I couldn't survive unless he was by my side. He had healed me by showing me over and over how much he loved me. And you know what? Rhys was going to let me go so I could be happy. He didn't care what it did to him so long as I was fulfilled. Taught me, bearer of joy and happiness, a thing or two about giving *true* joy and happiness."

"To see you now I never would have guessed it. You two are a perfect match. It seems like every couple in the compound is the perfect couple and I don't think I will ever have that with Ember. None of you have this insane jealousy between the females. It's a real barrier for my mate."

"You only see half of what goes on, Orlando. Each one of us has had our issues. I am reminded every day that my mate has slept with nearly every female on the planet," she said with a laugh, "and I don't even have peace in my own home. The Rowan triplets step foot through our door and I constantly remind myself that they are mated and happy, as are Rhys and I. I may be an angel, but that doesn't mean I don't have an urge to slaughter all those that came before me. But I deal with it and soak up my mate's love every chance I get. It's a choice I make," she admitted, shocking Orlando with her candor.

"I never considered how Rhys's history would affect you. You hide it very well. I never sense anything but respect and devotion between you two."

The pretty blonde sat quietly for a minute and Orlando felt her angelic power at work and he allowed it to flow through his battered soul.

"I'm going to leave you with your thoughts, but remember it takes two to make this work. Consider what you might do to make this an easier transition for her," Illianna murmured before she got up and left the room.

Orlando watched Brantley sleep peacefully while his mind churned. He missed Ember, his body ached to have her and his head was stuck up his ass. How the fuck was he supposed to make sense of anything under these conditions?

CHAPTER 19

The stars were bright in the sky, the bonfire was ready to be lit, and the pack was gathered around. All but the most important person, that is, Ember mused. Her stomach fluttered and she thought she might hurl as she stood there facing her family and friends. They were so excited for her with beaming smiles on their faces and pride shining in their eyes. She imagined her father was watching from *Annwyn*, as well. She was making history and her mate was not there to share the moment with her.

"Ember, we can't wait any longer. We have to begin," Hayden informed her.

Ember looked around the clearing and saw six tiki torches burning, as well as, the table set for the ceremony, but didn't see Orlando's white blond head anywhere. The bond she shared with her mate told her he was still wallowing like he had been for the past week, but he was nowhere near.

He wasn't coming.

"Yes, Sire. I understand." The ache in her chest twisted, stealing her breath.

"I haven't seen Orlando in several days. What's going on with you guys? You have excelled in your patrols and earned your position as one of my C.L.A.W.s but he isn't here for you." The words were more of an accusation and she didn't miss the threat in Hayden's tone.

"We had a disagreement. It's nothing to worry about. It will not affect my performance." She couldn't allow her personal life to jeopardize her new position. She had wanted it for too long and had worked her ass off to get where she was.

"I'm not worried about your performance, Em. I'm worried about your heart. I have half a mind to string him up by his hide," Hayden growled.

"No, don't do that. He's been busy with the new demon threat. It will be worked out," she promised even as she doubted her own words.

"It better be. I will not tolerate this treatment of you," Hayden told her. The defense warmed her heart and echoed what her grandfather had told her, as well.

"Pack, we are gathered here to witness history," Hayden boomed to the gathered crowd. "Ember Hawthorne has worked hard and earned the title of the first female Lieutenant in the C.L.A.W.'s history. Tonight, I am proud to bring her into the fold."

Hayden turned to Ember, a huge smile on his face with his hair blowing around his brown eyes. His pride was evident and broke through some of her melancholy over not having Orlando by her side for the ceremony. Her heart kicked up when she realized the goal she had been fighting to achieve for decades was finally here.

Wiping her sweaty palms on her black dress pants, she folded them in front of her and kneeled in front of her Omega when he gave the order. From her position, Hayden was larger than life. He had on dark denim jeans and a button up white shirt that made him look regal. Shifters were far more casual in their ceremonies, with the mating ceremony being the exception.

"As we celebrate this day, we must remember that no one becomes a C.L.A.W. without passing trials and proving themselves worthy. Ember has displayed great skills in battle and stepped up in defense of the pack regardless of the danger to herself. We have never had a female work harder to prove their worth. You honor the pack and your family. Are you ready to take your vows and join the fold, Ember?" Hayden boomed.

Ember shook off her nervousness and cleared her throat as she nodded her head and began reciting her oath of fealty.

"I hereby declare on pack land that I absolutely and entirely pledge my allegiance and fidelity to my fellow brethren," she vowed and sliced open her palm on the sword Hayden was holding. The cut wasn't deep, but blood immediately leaked from the laceration.

Zeke stepped forward and picked up the nearest tiki torch. He tossed the torch onto the bonfire then walked to stand in front of Hayden and cut his palm on the same sword then clasped Ember's palm, sealing their brother-hood. He stepped away and took his place among the other C.L.A.W.s.

"I will support and defend against all enemies," she swore before Grant stepped forward and tossed his torch then walked to the sword and cut his palm. Grant winked at her when they clasped hands and a smile spread across Ember's face for the first time in a week. Grant was a good friend and having him as her brethren was such an honor.

"I will wield my sword on behalf of my pack," she

promised before Scott stepped forward and repeated the same process then shook her hand. She glanced to the fire, expecting a roaring inferno, but it seemed content to remain around each torch.

"I will perform all duties necessary to protect the safety and integrity of the pack," she pledged and then accepted Beau's handshake. With the mingling of their blood on the blade, she heard a hum begin in the metal as if being tempered by the combined fluids.

"I take this obligation freely without reservation or malice," she declared and clasped hands with Don. Don's firm handshake and warm smile welcomed her into their fold. In fact, each of the males had accepted her without hesitation.

"May the Goddess bless my journey," she concluded and stood up. Hayden cut his palm and they clasped hands before he wrapped his arms around her, hugging her tight. He grabbed the last torch and tossed into the fire. Suddenly, an inferno erupted and flames shot to the sky.

"Welcome to the C.L.A.W.," Hayden boomed and handed the sword to her with a flourish.

A gasp escaped as she glanced down in awe. Bastien, the pack swordsmith, handcrafted the weapon. He used natural resources found at the Grove. Ember's eyes clouded over as she marveled at the tiger's eye stone set into the pommel that was shaped like a claw. It was by far the most elegant sword ever created. Bastien had captured the importance of the occasion perfectly, she thought.

Looking to her palm, she noticed the six cuts were already healing. The significance of the ceremony caught up to her and tears welled in her eyes. She wanted to see the pride in Orlando's eyes. Her friends and family weren't enough. The post-celebration began and she should be ecstatic to join in the drinking and eating, but she couldn't stand there and put on a happy face. She was a millisecond from having a meltdown and all she could do was flee. As soon as she hit the forest, the waterfall of tears broke through.

"HE SHOULD HAVE BEEN THERE FAITH," Ember snapped as she paced her friend's living room.

She'd made pack history, becoming the first female C.L.A.W. Her entire family had been there to celebrate her achievement, but Orlando had been a no-show and she had fled like a heartbroken *stripling*. And, what an embarrassment to lose her Fated Mate three days after mating when they should still be in the throes of passion. Some Lieutenant she was turning out to be. Couldn't hold her emotions in check to share one damn drink with her pack.

Where the hell was her mate anyway? And why didn't he give a shit that she was making pack history? Her fists clenched as she realized Orlando hadn't seen the significance of her big day or felt it important enough to take time away from his precious Elsie and the others. It still burned that he considered Elsie's feelings over hers.

"You're right, Em, but it's not that simple," Faith replied. Ember loved her best friend to pieces and appreciated that she never told Ember what she *wanted* to hear, but what she *needed* to hear.

"First off, did you even tell him about the induction?" Faith persisted.

Ember turned around and leveled a glare at the female who stared back completely unfazed by Ember's irritation.

"That's not the point," Ember snapped.

"How is that not the point? Unless you can read each other's minds, how was he supposed to know about today?" Faith stated and cocked her head as her long blonde hair fell over her shoulder. The challenge was unmistakable and pissed Ember off even more.

"No, we can't read each other's mind," Ember denied.

There had been a connection between her and Orlando from the moment they'd laid eyes on each other which intensified after the mating was completed. There would be a point when they could communicate telepathically, but they weren't there yet. She'd been told it varied with each couple and for some took years to develop.

What she did feel was Orlando's emotions as clearly as if they were her own. Wherever he was, he was upset and felt abandoned. She couldn't believe *he* felt abandoned after everything he'd put her through.

She had no idea why he thought they would live at Zeum. She'd never once given him any indication she would move in with him. Hell, they'd never spent any time there. It should've been crystal clear to him where she wanted to be and he should be there with her now.

"He doesn't need to read my mind to know I wanted him there for the ceremony," Ember continued.

Faith stood up and walked to the kitchen, grabbing two energy drinks from the fridge then handed one to Ember. Cracking open the can, Faith met her gaze. "He needed to know about the induction to be there, Em. You can't be mad at him if he had no idea it happened."

Ember's jaw tensed as she realized she hadn't considered that. Hayden wouldn't have called to tell him, assuming Ember would. For that matter, none of the C.L.A.W.s would have contacted him. There would be no way for Orlando to have known about it.

Ember sank into the couch and held up her drink, "I think this needs tequila."

"Done," Faith replied and slipped back into the kitchen and quickly returned, carrying a pitcher of margaritas and two glasses. She loved that her friend always had the cocktail on hand, especially at times like this.

Joining her on the couch, Faith poured her a glass and Ember mixed in the energy drink. "I'll take that to mean you didn't talk to him about it," her best friend pointed out.

"I haven't talked to him since I left last week. He should call me. I shouldn't have to call him."

"How's that working out for you?" Faith asked.

"I'm sitting on your couch drinking with you instead of celebrating with my mate. How do you think it's working?" Ember retorted.

Faith set her drink aside and swiped up a set of cards from the coffee table. She lived with her parents and two siblings in a large cabin not far from Ember. Shuffling the cards, Faith murmured, "Why is he the only one responsible for reaching out? From what I know of the male, he's been through hell lately and shortly after he finds his Fated Mate, she leaves him standing in the middle of a room holding their infant son."

It irked Ember that her friend was always right. She wanted to hold onto her righteous indignation, but never could with Faith around. Ember hadn't considered anything aside from her own anger. She had walked out and left him with Brantley. It didn't matter that Brantley wasn't their blood, he was their son and she had adopted him the moment she mated Orlando.

"I really fucked this up, didn't I?" Ember blurted as she took a gulp of her drink.

Faith dealt each of them seven cards before she

responded. "If I know you, I'm certain you were a stubborn bitch when he asked you to move to Zeum."

Ember snorted at her best friend's way of saying she had really screwed the pooch this time. "I'm not saying what I did was right, but he should have come to me by now. Instead, he is still living in the queen's home and not even talking to me."

"I'm not saying you're completely wrong about Elsie, but what you need to focus on is why he should come to you. You weren't willing to discuss it with him so you guys could come up with a compromise," Faith countered.

Ember couldn't focus on her cards as her friend's words rang in her ears. The Goddess had mentioned compromise. But, did that mean she had to do all the work? She wanted him to show her he wanted her and truly loved her. Ember knew he'd had feelings for Jaidis and she was past that, but Elsie was an entirely different situation.

"Ugh," she snarled and admitted, "The Goddess said something to me about courage, compromise and compassion. You suck, you know that?" She took a drink as tears swam in her eyes. "This is actually really good."

"It is. You could always get a job as a bartender if nothing else. So what are you going to do about all this?" Faith asked. They were both holding their cards, but had yet to play their hands.

"I have no idea. I need to know he wants me as much as I want him. I feel like the consolation prize. I guess I need him to show me that's not true," Ember admitted as the tears fell. Ember wasn't an overly emotional female, but she couldn't stop when she considered Orlando might not try to get her back.

Faith tossed the cards on the table and pulled Ember into her arms. "You aren't a consolation prize. That male adores you and you know it. He may have needed time to really embrace what the Goddess gave him, but once he did, you became his entire world."

"You really think so?" Ember hated her insecurity. She wasn't a weak-willed female that needed constant reassurance, but, in this instance, she needed her mate to extend the first olive branch.

"Have I ever blown smoke up your ass? I'd never hurt you like that. You need to pull your head out and meet him halfway, Em. It will never work if one of you doesn't swallow your pride."

"When did you get so wise?" she asked with a laugh as she brushed her tears away. She didn't know if she would make the first move or not, but she missed her mate more than anything and would give anything to see him again.

CHAPTER 20

"Steeeve," Ember called out when she saw O'Haire. "Good to see you again. What the heck is going on?" she asked as she glanced around the scene.

There was yellow tape sealing off a large area in a supermarket parking lot. It was a chain store that focused on health foods and was in the same shopping center as a realm restaurant. She'd eaten there before and loved their wings and burgers.

She was surprised to see a large group of humans being cordoned and monitored by SPD officers. Each one carried haunted looks and their fear was thick as smoke. She saw why when she noticed the countless white sheets draped over what she guessed were dead bodies.

Officers shouted and gave directions as they snapped pictures and their CSI unit gathered evidence. The human authorities had a huge number of people working the scene. She'd noticed it at the club scene, as well, and hadn't given it a second thought. Seeing it again she wondered why they needed so many. Some of it she could see was for crowd control, but the rest seemed redundant and unnecessary.

Surprisingly, they worked quickly despite the cold temperatures.

"Why did you call me to a human crime scene? Was this the demons again?" she asked.

Steve's broad shoulders ruffled in obvious irritation. The huge bear shifter was garnering looks. With his larger than normal stature, he stood out in the crowd. The humans would never believe he was a big teddy bear given the menace he radiated.

"I didn't know this involved humans. We got an emergency call about an attack involving sorcerers. We didn't get much more information as the caller was suddenly cut off so I called you on my way out here. I can't get more information because these yahoos won't let me through. Please tell me that your mate is on his way. He has connections to the human officers. By the way, congratulations on your mating. Sorry I missed the ceremony," Steve said.

Ember winced at the mention of Orlando. She still hadn't spoken to him and Faith's words from the night before rang through her head. She'd finally worked up the nerve to call him but then received the call from Steve and used it as an excuse to put the conversation off even longer.

"Thank you, it was an amazing ceremony," she said, focusing on the positive. "I have no idea where Orlando is or if he has been called in. Is that a Harpy?" she asked and changed the subject when she noticed a human lifting the arm of a victim and black wings poked from underneath the sheet.

Nerves had her itching to get to the body and take custody of it. Her feet shifted and she bounced as she watched humans investigate bodies that were proof of the existence of supernaturals.

"Oh shit. This is bad," she murmured. Pushing her

glasses up her nose, she contemplated calling Orlando. This could blow up in a major way.

Steve glanced over at her question and proceeded to curse. "How the hell are we going to cover this up? Look at all these humans video-taping with their cell phones. Goddamn technology. I miss the old days when disguising situations was easy," he cursed.

"I usually appreciate modern conveniences, but not today," she retorted as she shifted her bag higher on her shoulder.

Of course, the scene was in the middle of a well-lit area of the parking lot giving the humans a perfect view of the mess around them. They might as well have a huge spotlight shining down on everything. They weren't lucky enough to have it be closer to the burger joint where the streetlights in the parking lot were busted.

"I'd give anything to go back home and crawl back in bed with Stacy," O'Haire admitted.

She laughed and punched his arm. "You're dating that human?"

Steve's cheeks turned pink and he rubbed the back of his neck. "I don't think you'd call it dating. She's fun for the time being," he remarked as his eyes shifted over her shoulder.

"Thank fuck your mate is here," Steve blurted before she could harass him more.

The change of topic made Ember's heart gallop and sweat broke out over her body, despite the fact, it was so cold she could see her breath. Beads trickled down her back, making her silk shirt stick to her skin as she turned to face the parking lot.

Orlando climbed out of his car and locked eyes with her. She saw Santiago exit the other side of the car but she was too busy drinking in the sight of her mate. He was sex walking in his tight leather pants and charcoal gray shirt. His leather jacket completed the look and had her panting for him as her chest constricted the next second.

She missed him terribly and wanted to jump his bones.

Her ache was intensified when she sensed his pain through their bond. Tears misted in her eyes. She regretted acting so rashly and she wanted to make things right with him, but she didn't know how. He refused to live with her and she refused to leave the Grove. She was a C.L.A.W. now and had to be nearby for Hayden.

Orlando and Santi stopped two feet from her and an awkward silence descended between the four of them. She could see Steve gawking from the corner of her eye while Santiago watched his friend. Ignoring them, she focused on Orlando.

"Okaaay. This is uncomfortable," Steve muttered. "I'm going to go over there and blend in with the locals. Call me if you need me."

"I'll go check in with the lead," Santiago added. "Good to see you, Ember."

"Good to see you, too, Santi," she replied. She hated how her voice wavered. She was strong female, dammit. A member of the C.L.A.W. for fuck's sake. *Get it together,* she scolded herself.

Ember watched the males walk away. Santiago ducked under the tape and headed into the middle of the action and Steve veered to the left. The sight of O'Haire standing there with his arms crossed over his chest while he rocked on his feet was comical. The male stood out like a sore thumb among the humans while Santiago managed to blend in. They were both cops, but the difference was remarkable in this setting.

Once alone, she couldn't ignore how much her heart

hurt standing so close to her mate. Orlando was the one being in the universe she should be most comfortable with and it felt unnatural.

"Ember," Orlando murmured, drawing her attention. She gave him a watery smile and had to bite her lip to keep the emotion at bay. "I didn't know you were going to be here."

How did they get to the point where their interactions were so cold and clinical, she thought, as her heart fractured? Could they resolve this and bridge the ever-widening gap between them?

"O'Haire called me in. I had no idea this involved so many humans. What can you tell me about what happened?" she asked.

He seemed cool as a cucumber while she was an emotional wreck, nervously smoothing her hair and shuffling her feet. If she didn't sense his turmoil through their mating bond, she'd say he wasn't bothered in the slightest over their situation.

When she looked close enough, the golden chain connecting them appeared tarnished and that was the most telling. There was a massive wedge between them that needed to be dealt with. Problem was, she had no idea where to begin.

Orlando took several steps closer to her, taunting her body with his heat. She greedily soaked up his masculine scent and leaned toward him, losing track of all thought except wanting to kiss the breath out of him.

"That's not how this is going to be between us," he practically snarled.

Her eyes flew wide at his words and the anger behind them. His determination was palpable. Was he about to deny their mating? She didn't think she could live through it if he did. He had become her whole world and she wasn't complete without him.

Before she could ask his meaning, he grabbed hold of her upper arm and she found herself smashed against his hard chest. "I need to talk to you where there are no ears," he told her.

She closed her eyes as his breath fell against her lips. All it would take was her going to tiptoes and her lips would be pressed against his. Self-recriminations flew through her mind along with every curse word she knew. This male had the power to destroy her world and it seemed she barely affected him.

"What about the crime scene? I'm pretty sure I saw a harpy being examined a second ago," she muttered. His eyes glowed bright green and were ablaze. If he wasn't careful a human could catch it on videotape, but she was relieved to his passion hadn't died.

"Fuck the scene. You are far more important that the humans or this case. Besides, Santiago is for damage control. Come with me," he ordered and tugged her alongside him as he began walking toward the side of the building, away from the crowd.

Stumbling, she struggled to keep up with him for several steps before she found her stride. She was normally as graceful as her cougar and it was a sign how far off her game she was. He had her all discombobulated and she shook off her reaction, trying to clear her head.

"Orlando," she started when they reached an empty alley. There were several large dumpsters, along with broken down cardboard boxes, and wood palettes littered the walkway, but they had privacy everywhere.

"You're beautiful," he murmured pulling her into his arms. As his body surrounded hers, the knot in her gut unfurled the tiniest bit. It was difficult to hold back the hope that wanted to burst forth.

"I don't even know where to begin," he said. "I really fucked things. Even worse, I've been a stubborn ass and let it keep me from you."

The truth of his admission was confirmed through their connection, as well as, his affection for her. It was the first glimpse she'd gotten of anything aside from anger and frustration from him in over a week and it meant everything to her.

"I didn't call you, either. We're both guilty of allowing our pride to come between us," she admitted.

"I wasn't fair to you. I assumed you'd move in with me without asking what you wanted and that was wrong," he said as he placed a kiss on the top of her head and ran his hand up and down her back.

Arching into him, her cougar settled for the first time since she had walked out on him. "I didn't tell you about needing to stay on pack land, either. I'm new at this and have no idea how to be in a relationship," she admitted. She'd dated before, but Zeke was the closest she'd come to a serious relationship and that didn't count for much.

He chuckled as he laid his hands on her hips. "I don't want to hear about you being with other males. In my head, you were a virgin when we met," he growled then leaned in and nipped her lower lip.

"We were both virgins. And, you never slept with Elsie, just pined after her," she murmured unable to keep from mentioning her jealousy. "Anyway, me running off didn't help matters. Faith has told me the folly of my ways."

"Elsie is a good friend, but that is it. She is important to the Dark Warriors, but she doesn't come before you. I wanted what she and Zander had more than I ever wanted her and I realized that when I lost you. You are all I want," he declared as he held her close. "And you should listen to Faith, she's a very wise female," he teased and placed his finger under her chin. He tilted her head back and looked deep in her eyes.

"I know that I'm a difficult person to live with. I can't promise I will ever be perfect, but I promise to try," Orlando promised.

"I've missed you," she admitted as joy broke through, despite her reservations. She wanted to tell him she wasn't leaving the Grove and make him agree to move in with her, but she kept her mouth shut. They hadn't exactly reached a truce and she refused to upset the delicate balance they were striving for.

"I missed you more," he murmured. He held her gaze for several seconds then blurted, "Ah, fuck it," and his mouth crashed down on hers.

His fingers threaded through her hair while his tongue licked at the seam of her mouth. Her heart raced for an altogether different reason and her stomach clenched with need.

She lifted one leg and wrapped it around his hip as she deepened the kiss. His responding groan was music to her ears. The fact that he lost himself so completely in his desire for her brought a smile against his mouth.

Breaking the kiss, his mouth moved along her jaw and he grabbed onto her ass with both hands, lifting her. She immediately wrapped both legs around his waist and a moan escaped her throat at the feel of his erection pressed between her thighs. Shifting her position, she aligned their bodies so he was pushing on her clit.

"Ember. I need to fuck you, but this is not the time or place," he lamented.

She didn't give a shit where they were. She needed him. Grinding her hips, she rubbed against his shaft and laughed when he stumbled.

"Mate," he growled then nipped her ear.

"I can't help it. It's been too long," she complained.

Removing her legs, he set her down but held onto her shoulders until she was steady. She knew her eyes were glowing from her arousal, but she didn't care.

"We aren't finished. We will continue this after we're done here," he promised.

Grabbing her hand, he began walking back to the scene at the front of the building. "You are my everything, Wildcat. We will work this out somehow," he promised as he adjusted his shaft.

A smile broke out across her face at hearing his words and she prayed to the Goddess to give her the courage, compassion and compromise needed to make it happen.

"Good, because Hayden made me a C.L.A.W. and I need your support. I could use your training, too," she said and looked over to see his reaction to her news.

He stopped walking and stared at her with his mouth open. "When?" he asked, clearly surprised.

"I was inducted last night," she admitted, uncertainty creeping back in. Was he upset that she accepted the position? Did he think females weren't fit to be a C.L.A.W.? She'd never asked him and suddenly his support was more important than anything else.

"I was a stubborn jackass and missed the most important night of your life. How do you not hate me?" he asked with a self-deprecating smile.

"The most important night of my life was the night we got mated. I won't lie I was hurt that you weren't there, but all that matters to me is having your support."

His large hand cupped her cheek and he placed a kiss to her lips. "I had no idea it had happened, but I am so proud of you. That's such an accomplishment and I couldn't be happier for you. Next time something this important happens, I want to be there. That means you need to tell me shit," he ordered her.

"Deal," she agreed readily. "Now, what can you tell me about what happened here?" she asked returning to the task at hand as they approached the scene.

"All I know is that a blue angel attacked a group of humans in front of this store and other monsters joined in, according to witnesses," he replied. Orlando waved Steve over and flashed his badge, guiding them under the barrier.

"Monsters?" she asked as she got a closer look at the covered bodies. "None of these seem big enough to be a demon."

"It seems the archdemons and a handful of skirm attacked. From what I can tell, the monsters they're referring to are supernaturals," O'Haire interjected.

They'd made their way to Santiago's side as the male added, "O'Haire is right. There were no lower level demons, but plenty of skirm and a handful of supes. This is a cluster-fuck. We need to call Zander and let him know what happened."

"And, I'll call Hayden," Ember replied.

Orlando stood with his arm around her while she updated Hayden. The Omega cursed so loud she had to hold her phone away from her ear. He growled he was on his way then the connection ended.

"What about all the camera phones?" Steve asked.

"Yeah, this is getting out of hand," she exclaimed. "We might not be able to contain this. Who knows if they've already posted their videos to the Internet or not? Zander may not have any choice in the matter this time."

Orlando cursed and Santiago slapped his back. "Don't worry, brother. I've already confiscated phones for our investigation and the witnesses are being held for questioning. This is a mess, but it's contained for the moment," Santiago shared.

Ember had been torn about coming out to the humans. She supported her Omega, but couldn't ignore the way her gut twisted over the idea. It was difficult to erase over two hundred years of hearing you'd be killed if the humans discovered your existence.

Glancing over at her mate, she realized telling the humans wasn't her biggest fear. Were she and her Fated Mate about to be on opposite sides once again? They'd just begun to make amends and another fight threatened to break them apart.

She had to ask herself who was more important...her mate, or, her pack.

CHAPTER 21

Orlando thanked the Goddess for intervening and forcing him and Ember together. He'd been worried about the wrong things. Being with his mate was what mattered and just having her close again settled his agitation. He'd do whatever it took to be with her. If that meant living with her then so be it. He was useless without her anyway.

He grabbed her hand, needing the contact. "Pick up anything else?" he asked knowing she'd been cataloguing the scene and deciphering all the evidence. He loved the way her mind worked. She was brilliant, sexy, and confident. And she was his.

"These humans have trampled through the scene so much that it's washed out some of the scents and has made it tough to tell exactly what happened. But, my best guess is that either Crocell or her twin brought skirm here to feed. There are several victims drained of blood, while others have been maimed. I'd guess that some of the supes eating across the way caught sight and rushed over to help. Why the hell would they attack at a grocery store? It makes no sense," she murmured as she shook her head.

"They want to create chaos. They're keeping us so busy we barely know which way is up anymore," Orlando observed.

Zander and Elsie were worried about the threat to Izzy and with good reason. The demon's real target was the princess and they were determined to succeed.

"Reyes, Trovatelli," Captain Rowley barked as he approached them.

Orlando groaned. Having their captain there was the last thing they needed to deal with. Turning, Orlando stuck out his hand and shook Rowley's hand. The male had a cigar in the corner of his mouth and a scowl on his face.

"Good to see you, sir," Orlando replied. Santiago greeted the captain and introduced Ember and O'Haire as their consultants.

"What do you make of this crazy shit? That body right there has fucking wings. And, the ME said it's not a goddamn costume," Rowley barked.

"I've seen some crazy fucking shit out there. But sewing wings onto your back is going a bit far if you ask me," Orlando replied easily, putting as much disgust and disbelief into his tone as possible. "I mean it's one thing to wear freaky contacts and file your teeth down or insert horns under your skin, but wings?" he ended with a shake of his head.

Rowley went to the sheet and lifted it and scowled at the dead harpy. "Could have fooled me. Those wings look real to me. If I didn't know better, I'd say this was a giant-ass fairy. If this is a new cult, they're taking it to the extreme. And, attacking in my city. Find them and stop this shit," Rowley ordered as he pointed at Orlando and Santiago.

"Yes, sir," they echoed to their captain who shook his head and stalked off. Orlando watched him go to the front of the building where blood was splattered across the brick and glass.

"I can't believe he believes that BS you just spouted," Ember murmured.

He looked down at her and saw the adorable wrinkle between her eyes as she concentrated. "He's human, Wildcat. They don't want to believe what's right in front of them. I think it's a defense mechanism. The truth is a lot harder to accept. It's easier to believe monsters are myth. They take the easy explanation every time, even when evidence is staring them in the face like now," Orlando explained.

"Problem is we can't keep covering it up. There are some who believe in supes and will spread the word. SOVA is a perfect example. If enough listen to them, then humans will start killing supernaturals, just like Elsie and Mack used to do," Santiago interjected.

"But they killed skirm," Ember reasoned. "Not us. They couldn't take us down," she insisted.

"Don't underestimate humans. They can be cruel and vicious. Their weapons of mass destruction are proof of that. All it would take is a trigger-happy human," Santi added.

Orlando could tell his feisty mate hadn't considered that. She'd been sheltered within the pack. She may have encountered demons, but she was naïve when it came the species, believing they weren't a threat.

Orlando's phone chimed a second later, drawing his attention. Pulling it out of his pocket, he saw it was a text message from Zander.

"Zander and the others are here. Do you see them?" he asked as he scanned the crowd. Orlando had been around his share of crime scenes, but his anxiety had never been this high seeing so many humans with recording devices in their hands.

"Over there," Santi said as he pointed to Orlando's left. As a group, they made their way to the grim-looking vampire king.

By the time they reached his side, the other Dark Warriors surrounded Zander and Hayden was coming up behind him. Orlando's SPD colleagues watched him approach the group of intimidating males. Some of them shrank back and others turned away. Humans always sensed the danger they posed, even if they didn't understand it.

"Give me the headcount. What are we looking at?" Zander demanded with a wave of his hand.

"The demons were gone when we got here. We have a dozen skirm dead and black blood all over the place, but we also have dead supes. The harpy is garnering more attention than the black blood. Santi had witnesses detained and confiscated phones," Orlando summarized.

"A dead harpy. Couldna get much fucking worse," Zander mused. Zander's phone was at his ear the next second. "Kill, I need your computer skills ASAP. The demons attacked humans and supes in a store parking lot. There's a dead harpy on display and I have no doubt some of these yahoos caught footage. Och, make sure nothing has been posted."

Orlando should have thought of calling Killian sooner. The Dark Alliance council member was the best and if there were anything on the Internet he'd find it. The guy owned the most popular nightclub in the realm and was one of the sharpest males Orlando knew.

"Why bother?" Hayden chimed in before Zander had a chance to hang up.

Orlando tensed and took a step closer to Zander, pulling Ember with him. She tugged at his hand and shook her head, refusing to budge. He understood her loyalty to the Omega, but he was torn. Hayden was his leader, but Zander had earned his devotion. He owed them both, but on this, he agreed with Zander.

He had no desire for the humans to know of their existence. The Goddess had ordered them to keep it secret and he would do that until the day he died. Even now, the thought of a human dissecting Ember had his blood running cold and only reinforced her edict in his mind.

"Because the humans have seen too much," Zander countered with narrowed eyes.

"I disagree," Hayden snarled. "Look around you. Several of their kind is dead. They will be pissed about this and wanting revenge. We can use them to help us fight the demons. We don't have the resources to keep the humans safe while trying to stop the demons. Not with them intentionally targeting the innocents. We have our own to take care of."

"Doona lecture me aboot protecting our own," Zander growled as he clenched his fists and his eyes turned black.

Orlando had never seen the council members argue to this degree. They'd been friends forever and together had formed the Dark Alliance council. They'd always supported each other. Hell, the council was the backbone of the Tehrex Realm and the stability everyone relied on. Orlando's gut knotted as he watched the two most powerful beings in the realm hash out their differences. If they couldn't come to an agreement, this could destroy more than a friendship.

He wasn't certain the council would survive something this big between its founders. Not to mention, it would force many to choose sides. Orlando felt the tug within his mind between the two men that owned his allegiance.

"My entire life is aboot protecting the realm and the humans. It's my family that's in danger. My daughter that is being hunted to the point she canna leave our house. So I understand better than most what the fuck this is aboot. It would be far easier to let the humans know and wash my hands of everything so I can focus on protecting my mate and child, but the Goddess has forbid that," Zander continued, his Scottish brogue thickening with every word.

"Maybe its time to stand up to the Goddess and tell her we're done protecting everyone else. We focus on our own and the rest do the same," Hayden suggested.

"Next time the demons attack your land, I will remember you said that. I hope your fucking C.L.A.W.s can battle two archdemons and whatever else they may rain doon on you," Zander spat as he took several steps forward.

This was about to explode if someone didn't walk away, Orlando thought. Trembling raced up his arm and he looked over at his mate and noted how shaken she was. Words weren't all that was flying around. Zander's power was like pea soup while Hayden's surrounded everybody, threatening to suffocate. Every supernatural present was affected and even the humans were rubbing their chests and looking around.

"*Brathair*," Kyran rumbled as he placed his hand on Zander's shoulder. "Calm doon. You're drawing unwanted attention. Doona create more trouble for us," the male added.

Orlando had always known Kyran was a sadist, but the male must really enjoy pain to approach Zander when he was this upset. The last time Orlando had seen Zander this out of control, he destroyed the war room. It had been the night Elsie was kidnapped by the archdemon Kadir and it had taken months to repair the damage Zander had done in a matter of minutes.

Zander glared at his brother for several moments then Orlando felt the king's wrath subside. "Too much is at stake, old friend," Zander told Hayden after taking a few deep breaths. "We canna let the demons divide us. Working together, we will succeed."

"You're right Zander. Too much *is* at stake. I'm not willing to lose anymore of my shifters to these bitches. I'll do what's necessary to protect mine. You do what you need to. But, mark my word. The day is coming when the humans must be told," Hayden growled before he turned on his heel and walked away.

"Doona do this Hayden. I doona want you as an enemy," Zander called out to his retreating back.

Everyone stood in silence. Had Zander just declared war with the shifters? Orlando was a shifter and had no desire to become the enemy of the Dark Warriors. He'd dedicated his life to them. They'd taken him in and given his life meaning and purpose. He gladly dedicated his life to fighting the evil that lurked in the night and didn't want to give it up. The entire realm would suffer if there were a division.

"Are you coming, Ember," Hayden asked, ignoring Zander's comments.

Orlando looked to his mate. The dilemma on Ember's beautiful face said everything Orlando had just been thinking. Not only was he torn, but also his mate had been pulled into it, as well, and was agonizing over this rift between the leaders.

Orlando wanted to pound some sense into both males. Their disagreement was already pulling the realm apart and Orlando feared how far this would go.

Cupping Ember's cheek, Orlando leaned down and lightly kissed her lips.

"You're his C.L.A.W. You need to go, but my job is here right now. Can I come see you later? We have unfinished business," Orlando told his mate.

He refused to allow anything else to come between them. He would do whatever he needed to have his mate in his life. Duty and pack had always come first, but this time their mating would come before everything else.

Nodding her head, she kissed him one more time before heading to Hayden's side.

A large palm landed hard on his shoulder. "Och, that didn't go verra well," Zander murmured.

"That's an understatement, Liege. I'm with you, but if it's a choice between you and my mate, I will pick her every time," he told the male that had been his most important mentor.

"Shite," Zander cursed and raked a hand through his black hair. "Let's hope it doesna come to that, O. I doona want to lose any of you, especially no' one of my closest friends."

As they split into small groups to begin erasing the human's memories, Orlando couldn't help thinking a loss was inevitable.

CHAPTER 22

Pacing the large family room in Jesaray House, Ember couldn't settle her raging thoughts. Her stomach was twisted in a knot and her chest ached. The mating bond, she decided, was both a curse and a blessing. She had purposefully been blocking it off the previous week, but seeing Orlando again had removed the shroud.

Immediately, she'd been overwhelmed by Orlando's desire for her. That she understood because she felt the exact same way and it wasn't difficult to embrace those emotions. But, in the past half hour his thoughts had changed. Whatever he was contemplating had him torn.

She had an idea of what he was debating. Living with her, or leaving her and staying at Zeum. How could she compete with warriors he'd spent centuries with? They weren't mere colleagues to him. He considered them family.

It wasn't long before she sensed his resolve, but he wasn't relieved like she'd expected. What did that mean? Was he leaving her? Biting her nail, she continued her circuit around the overstuffed furniture.

"You joining us, Ember?" Hayden barked. His deep voice startled her and stopped her in her tracks.

"Yes. Sorry, Sire. Just thinking," she replied as she lowered her head in submission.

"I want us patrolling in pairs at all times, more when possible. And, Zeke has redrawn the territories. You will notice each of you has a smaller domain to cover. Nothing will slip past us," the Omega relayed. "I'm considering recalling every shifter from the Dark Warrior ranks."

Ember's heart ached for what that would mean for her mate. Being a Dark Warrior was everything for Orlando. She recalled the way he had told her that Zander had given his life meaning when he'd recruited him for the Dark Warriors. There was no love lost between Orlando and his birth family. Her mate hadn't even invited his family to their mating ceremony. That told her everything she needed to know about how much being a Dark Warrior meant to him.

Squaring her shoulders, she jumped into the conversation without thought. "May I say something about this?"

"Please," Hayden said with a sweep of his hand.

"Well," she began and swallowed the lump in her throat as she felt all eyes on her. "I don't recommend burning that bridge with Zander and the Dark Warriors, let alone, the rest of the Dark Alliance Council. Consider the help we've needed from them this past month. Several times, they've dropped everything and come to our aid when the demons were attacking. I have faith in each and every one of you," she motioned to the other C.L.A.W.s, but what we have been facing is beyond our capability to deal with alone The one lesson you taught me early on, Hayden, is that we need to work together to beat the demons. Divided, the demons will find their way in and beat us all. I think that's why they are targeting us."

Hayden crossed his beefy arms across his chest. She understood why he was upset. His pride wouldn't allow him to back down from Zander. Plus, he believed that the humans needed to take care of their own. She understood why he was tired of protecting them. The humans weren't incapable, but they were volatile and temperamental.

She was still on the fence about whether she agreed with Hayden on that topic. She'd recalled pictures of animals being tested in laboratories. The blistered, hairless, bleeding creatures had been taken to the brink of death and sometimes beyond in the attempt of improving their lives. The thought alone caused her cougar to revolt within.

"Your point is valid. I will not place the pack at risk over my pride. But, I want everyone sticking as close to home as possible. My gut tells me these demons aren't done with us yet. Dismissed," Hayden replied.

Ember watched the Omega approach his second in command and her heart went out to Hayden. She couldn't forget that he was at odds with one of his best friends and that had to be difficult. She couldn't imagine being at odds with Faith and not having her support during the past weeks.

Ember stepped out into the cold night air and her breath left her. Orlando was leaning against his car in front of Jesaray house.

"Hi," she murmured as she rushed to his side.

"Hi, yourself," he replied. He'd changed into dark jeans and a green shirt that sculpted his muscular chest and had her mouth salivating to shed his clothes.

"I wasn't sure if you'd come," she admitted and met his eyes as her insecurity surfaced. This was the one person, aside from Faith, that she could show her vulnerabilities to and not have them discounted or taken advantage of.

"I will always come for you, Em. I'm sorry I made you believe anything less. I'm a stubborn fool and have lost count of the mistakes I've made regarding you. I will no doubt make more, but never doubt how much you mean to me," he replied as he wrapped his arms around her waist and pulled her tight against his body.

"This whole situation is messed up," she lamented and laid her head against his chest.

"Is that a bonfire I smell?"

"It is. Hayden canceled the hunt this month because of the demon attacks and danger, but the bonfire ritual won't ever be denied."

"Come on. Aside from our mating, I haven't been back for a bonfire in ages. Does Joe still break out his home brew?" Orlando asked. Grabbing her hand, he started walking with her in tow.

"Yeah, we can always count on Joe for a good beer. I swear he works all month creating a new masterpiece. Last month he made a stout with cinnamon. Not my favorite," Ember relayed as she shuddered in revulsion.

Ember kept in step with him as they made their way around the house to the clearing where the pack held their gatherings. The flowers and ground cover the sprites created for their mating ceremony were still bright and vibrant despite the lingering cold in the air.

"Doesn't sound too bad. I like cinnamon," Orlando added.

"Ugh. I can't believe you'd say that. I like it too, but not in my beer," Ember laughed.

"Orlando," Hayden boomed when he caught sight of them. "We missed you at Ember's ceremony. Glad you're here now," he said pointedly.

Ember wondered if the Omega was fishing for information. He had questioned her about him and she had brushed him off. She still didn't want to discuss the topic and snuggled close to Orlando's side, letting everyone know that things were fine between them.

Saying things were fine might be an overstatement, but damned if it was anyone else's business. She knew they hadn't acted like every other mated couple in history, but she didn't care. Their path was different and had challenges in store for them. The Goddess had told her it would require a lot of effort to have a successful mating and that was what she was working on.

"Not half as sorry as I am for missing it. How are the pups handling the canceled hunt?" Orlando asked as they watched the activity around them.

Ember saw the striplings roughhousing in their animal forms while the adults played washers and drank beer and kept them corralled to close quarters. The energy of family and pack suffused the air, rejuvenating her cougar. This was what she didn't think she could live without and hoped it was a reminder for Orlando.

"The pups are restless, as you can see. Constantly testing the boundaries, but they understand the reason. It's those just past transition that use the hunts to release their pent-up aggressions. As you know, they need the hunt the most," Hayden explained. "You two enjoy and take care of my Lieu-tenant," the Omega ordered more than suggested before walking away.

"Wanna grab a beer and sit for a bit?" she asked not wanting to take him back to her house just yet. She knew what would happen the second they were alone and she wanted to hash some things out before the mating heat took over. There would be no talking after that.

"Only if there's cinnamon involved," he teased.

"If that's the case, you can have mine," she assured him.

A few strides later, they were standing in front of Joe and his keg. "Joe, it's good to see you again," Orlando said by way of greeting. The males clasped arms and did that half-hug males did.

"Good to have you back. Santiago with you?" Joe asked.

"Nah, he's back at home with his mate. He said he'd try and make the next hunt," Orlando shared. Ember's heart twisted hearing him call Zeum home.

"What's on tap tonight?" she asked Joe, interrupting their conversation. "I told Orlando about your cinnamon beer last month."

"Don't look so disgusted, Em. You're in the minority. Most loved it. This month I kept it simple with an American IPA. You'll like it, Em. It's super hoppy," Joe explained with a broad smile. The male lived and breathed beer and was proud to share his creations.

"Sounds, perfect. Thanks, Joe," she murmured and gave the male a hug before accepting her mug.

Orlando grabbed his beer and told Joe they'd catch up later then led her to the side of the gathering, close to the bonfire. He took a seat on a lounge chair close to the blazing inferno and pulled her down in front of him.

She sighed happily and snuggled against his chest. "This is nice. I'm usually sitting with Faith getting drunk during these get-togethers," she admitted.

Running his hand over her hip, he whispered in her ear, "Get as drunk as you want. That'll make taking advantage much easier," he teased.

"As if you need me intoxicated to be at your mercy. You own me heart and soul and you know it," she countered with a chuckle.

He tensed at her back and his fingers dug into her hip. "So I haven't fucked it up beyond repair?"

"No, Orlando. It's not all your fault. I walked away and shut you out. Can you forgive me?" she asked, needing absolution more than anything.

"No need to forgive when you did nothing wrong. I was callous and didn't consider your feelings. I feel terrible for my behavior and want to make it up to you," he admitted.

She took a sip of her beer, savoring the bracing bitterness. Some didn't care for the hoppy beverage, but she loved it. Bring on the bitter beer face, she thought with a chuckle. "I know how you can make it up to me. It's poking me in the back."

She squealed when he tickled her with one hand and squirmed, trying not to spill her drink. "Soon," he promised huskily, "but first, I have a proposition for you."

She pushed her glasses up her nose and sat up at the seriousness in his tone. "Okay. I'm listening."

As if needing contact as much as she did, he scooted so their bodies remained touching. "I want to move in with you. Brantley and I, that is. I know it will be cramped in your one bedroom cottage, but I will add on as time permits. What do you say?"

"What do I say?" she echoed as shock gave way to elation. "I say about damn time, Trovatelli! Are you sure though? I know how much the Dark Warriors mean to you."

He pressed his finger over her mouth, stopping her words. "They mean a lot to me, yes. But, they aren't my everything. You are, Em and I'm I made you doubt that. I love you and I can't live another day without you by my side."

Joy burst free and she tossed her mug aside before wrapping her arms around his neck and straddling his waist. A dull thunk told her his mug met the same fate as hers. "I love you, too. And, I can't wait to bring Brantley home. I promise you won't regret it for a second," she murmured then placed a kiss to his lips that turned passionate in seconds.

His tongue tangled with hers, igniting her need to a fever pitch. Hearing him say he loved her was everything she'd ever wanted. And, the fact he was willing to move in with her was icing on the cake.

"Let's go home before we go pick up Brantley," she said against his mouth, not willing to break the connection completely.

He stood up, still holding her and she automatically wrapped her legs around his waist. "Best idea I've heard all night," he agreed and began walking.

They ignored the catcalls and whoops from the pack as he quickly took them to their small cottage.

ORLANDO PECKED Ember's lips before he jumped out of the car. If he didn't get inside and pack their stuff he'd never make it home. Home was no longer the mansion he was gazing up at. The thought made his chest ache, but he meant what he'd told Ember. She was his world now and he needed to place her needs above his own, even if that meant sacrificing a piece of his happiness.

He was certain they'd find a new kind of peace and happiness in time. Seeing the smile on her face and being the recipient of her gratitude made up for leaving the family he'd come to love. It wasn't like he would never see them again, he reminded himself. Taking a deep breath, he steeled his nerves for what he faced next.

With his hand at the small of her back, he led Ember to the front doors. For a brief second, Orlando missed Angus. The dragon shifter would have been outside greeting them the second they'd pulled up. Anytime one of the females came home or a visitor showed up, Angus made a point to greet them outside. Nate, Angus's replacement, didn't bother with those types of niceties. If you got past the gate, he figured you were supposed to be there.

Orlando could hear the activity throughout the house as soon as they entered. He headed straight for his room with Ember in tow, not ready to tell anyone what was happening yet.

"It's not as impersonal as I originally thought," Ember remarked as they made their way up the grand staircase. He hadn't been aware she saw the home as cold and unwelcoming. He felt just the opposite when he walked through Zeum's doors.

"I've always felt at home here. Like I belonged in this family. In fact, this was the first place I felt like I belonged," he admitted to her, wanting her to understand what this place meant to him.

"I know. Which is what makes your sacrifice mean so much to me," she admitted and squeezed his hand.

They made their way to his room without encountering anyone and he hurriedly began grabbing suitcases and throwing clothes in them. "Can you take this bag and pack Brantley's clothes?" he asked Ember.

Lost in rehearsing what he was going to tell Zander, he didn't hear Elsie come in until her voice echoed throughout the room. "What's going on? Are you guys taking a trip?" Elsie asked. Brantley was cradled in her arms and immediately perked up when he saw Orlando and Ember.

Walking over to his son, he took him from Elsie's arms as

Ember stilled by his side. "No, we aren't," Orlando, admitted. "I'm moving out."

"What?" Elsie practically screeched. "What do you mean you're moving out? You can't."

"Calm down, El, it's okay. I'm moving in with Ember in her cottage. I won't be far," he replied, hating the sheen of tears he saw form in the queen's eyes. She meant a lot to him too. He saw their relationship for what it was now. They were friends with a closeness that he didn't share with any of the other females in the house, but nothing more. That didn't mean the thought of leaving her and the other didn't hurt.

"What's going on?" Zander asked as he stepped inside the room. No doubt the commotion had drawn him to the room.

Santiago and Tori weren't far behind Zander and Orlando heard several others gathering in the hall asking what was going on. "Orlando's leaving us," Elsie told her mate. Her expression saying she was clearly unable to believe what she was hearing. "Don't go, Orlando, we need you. You're a Dark Warrior."

"Shite, you're really leaving? Why didna you tell me?" Zander asked, his anger and hurt clear in his deep blue eyes.

"I'm not leaving the warriors. I'm moving into Ember's house with her. She's one of Hayden's C.L.A.W.s now and needs to be there. It's really not a big deal. I'm only a phone call away."

"Fuck," Zander blurted and ran his hand through his hair.

At the same time Elsie blurted, "This isn't about being a Dark Warrior, Orlando. This is about being part of our family."

Orlando glanced from Zander to Elsie and noticed she

was glaring at Ember who had fisted her hands at her sides. "Why are you doing this?" Elsie continued. "Why are you splitting us up? How selfish are you that you're taking him from his only family?"

"I'm not splitting anyone up, your *Highness*," Ember said, spatting the title. "Orlando is *my* Fated Mate. That means he's mine, not yours. You have your mate and daughter. And, don't forget Orlando is a shifter, in addition, to being a Dark Warrior. He belongs with pack just as much as I do."

Orlando saw Ember's claws extend followed by Elsie's fangs.

"Shite," Zander groaned.

Orlando and Zander were in motion in the next heartbeat. Orlando wrapped his free arm around Ember while Zander pulled Elsie from the room before blood was shed. This was not at all how Orlando had envisioned this going.

He heard Elsie cursing at Zander, demanding to be let go. Orlando was torn. He hated seeing Elsie upset, but ultimately it was Ember's unhappiness that had him handing her Brantley and asking her to hold him while he finished packing.

Santiago joined him and pitched in to pack up the clothes. "Well, that was fun. I thought we were going to witness a cat fight for a minute," Santi chuckled.

""That's not funny, Santi. This is serious. I've never seen Elsie like that," Tori chided. "Ember, she's really a good person, but she's like the mother hen of the house and protects those she loves with a ferocity I've never seen. Orlando means a lot to everyone here, but I understand how difficult it is to give up your life and move here. I have chosen to see it as not giving up my old life, but adding new dimension."

"I'm sorry," Ember said to Tori. "I hadn't stopped to

consider that this was difficult for any of you. I assumed you all embraced it and came willingly."

"We did come here willingly. We love our mates, but we each left something behind. But, I didn't lose it all. I still have my family home and we have Santiago's loft. We take a day away from here as often as we can," Tori confessed.

Orlando could see the wheels turning in Ember's head. Before the situation escalated again, Orlando zipped his suitcase and turned to Santiago. "Tell, Zander I meant what I said. I'm still a Dark Warrior. I will see you for our shift tomorrow morning, and, in the meantime, if anything comes up and you guys need me, just call. I'm twenty minutes away."

"Will do," Santiago agreed then hefted the baby's suitcase and followed Orlando down the stairs.

As they climbed into the car, Orlando gazed into Ember's amber eyes and saw her love and devotion. This was why he was moving out. He wanted to deserve her adoration and give her what happiness he could. Apparently, at the expense of his own, because driving off with Zeum in his rearview mirror was one of the hardest things he'd ever done.

CHAPTER 23

"Come on, buddy. Grandma is waiting to see you," Orlando told Brantley as they walked to the main dining hall. They'd been at Ember's house for a couple weeks and had settled into a routine.

Brantley missed Zeum, it seemed, but being with Ember's parents or in the nursery made up for it. Orlando continued to work days with Santiago at SPD, but his patrols with the Dark Warriors had been cut in half.

Concerned that he was being shut out because he'd moved, Orlando paid a visit to Zeum and confronted Zander. Zander had assured him that wasn't the case and that he was giving Orlando time to bond with his mate. As much as he appreciated the sentiment, he still worried he was slowly being shut out.

It had been odd to be back at Zeum. Elsie refused to speak to him. She hadn't even offered him any of the Paella she was cooking. It smelled delicious and in his attempt to thaw the prickly female, he'd snuck bites from her pot while it was cooking, but even that received a cold shoulder. The others had been cordial, but it was clearly not the same anymore and that hurt worst of all.

Izzy had been the only one that had missed him and treated him the same. The princess had run up with sticky hands telling him she loved him before placing a slobbery kiss on his cheek.

He felt like he was losing the only true family he'd ever known. Ember worked hard to make their home something special, but he missed Zeum and his friends. He wanted to take Ember home and have her become part of *his* family. As it was, a brick wall that he didn't know how to knock down separated the two halves of his life.

"You okay, baby?" Ember asked, breaking into his ruminations.

Shaking off his morose thoughts, he pasted on a smile and bussed her lips. "Fantastic. Smells like Grandma Flo is making fried chicken tonight. You want to try some fried chicken?" he asked Brantley and tickled his tummy. The baby cooed and laughed.

"He's not a shifter, Orlando. He can't eat chicken yet," Ember chastised.

"Is that a problem?" he asked curiously. More than once over the past few weeks he'd wondered if she had a problem with their son not being a shifter. To Ember, everything shifter was superior. He'd never met a more loyal pack member, but it did make him wonder where others stood in her mind.

"Is what a problem? Him not being a shifter?" she asked incredulously.

Her tone told Orlando he'd offended her. He felt bad for upsetting her, but he was tired of keeping his mouth shut. He'd been walking on eggshells some days because he wasn't certain about her feelings on certain topics.

"Yeah. I know how much pack means to you and I wonder if you have room for anything else?"

Her eyes flew wide and she stopped him with a hand on his arm. "Yes, pack means a lot to me, but it's not everything. I love Brantley as if he were my own which is why I don't want you feeding him chicken when he's too young. Someday you will get to corrupt him all you want, but not while I can still protect him."

He threw his head back and laughed. That was the thing he loved most about Ember. She didn't beat around the bush or waste time on inconsequential details. "You hear that, Brant. Guess you can't have that beer if mommy is watching. Someday though. Now let's go find your grandma," he encouraged and they continued walking.

The main dining hall was so different from Zeum. The warriors were growing by leaps and bounds, but it was still small compared to the throng that filled Flo's.

He and Ember made their way through the crowd to the table where her family always sat. Brantley practically jumped into Evelyn's arms and Emily and Faith immediately bombarded Ember with plans for a girl's night.

Orlando filled his plate from the large platters scattered in the middle of the table. Grandma Flo served meals family style saying it was easier than manning a buffet or having servers. He had to agree as he heaped portions onto his plate. Joe plopped down next to him and handed him a beer.

Hayden and Zeke joined the group, along with Tia, Zeke's exotic mate. The room reacted to the Omega's presence and the atmosphere tensed as the group measured his mood. Hayden rarely graced the pack with his presence because he was so busy. Orlando understood the apprehension. He was right there with them wondering if something had happened to bring the Omega to dinner.

Hayden greeted everyone at the table before turning to Orlando. "It's been great having you around the Grove. I've noticed you haven't had many nightly patrols. You think it's possible that the demons returned to the Underworld?" he asked.

Orlando took a bite of mashed potatoes, savoring the rich, buttery taste before responding. "I have no idea what game they're playing. They've continued to attack humans in small groups. Given the big splash they initially made, I expected them to escalate much quicker. Ember said there haven't been any more attacks here."

"No, the protections seem to be holding, thank the Goddess," Hayden said as he filled his plate and kissed his grandmother's cheek when she approached the table.

The Omega dwarfed most people, but his grandmother looked like a sprite compared to him. His hand spanned her back as he hugged her, but Orlando knew the power she wielded over the formidable male. She was likely the only being on the planet that could put Hayden in his place.

"Are they trying to find a way in? Ember didn't mention anything," Orlando asked as the thought occurred to him that the demons were waiting for their guard to fall.

"No doubt they are testing the border, but it's nothing so obvious right now. You might be right. Good thing we won't be letting our protections down anytime soon," Hayden replied.

"One thing I've learned as a Dark Warrior is that the demons never give up. You can't get comfortable because the second you do, they will retaliate," Orlando shared.

Hayden joked with him about finally leaving the Dark

Warriors to become a C.L.A.W. like his mate. Orlando wouldn't even consider it. He was a Dark Warrior to his core and that would never change.

"SURE. MOVIE NEXT WEEKEND SOUNDS GREAT," Ember replied to Faith as she watched Orlando from the corner of her eye. Her mate was absolutely miserable and it was all her fault.

"You know I thought things would change after you mated, but they haven't really. You're still here for meals like usual, and, while you do moon over your mate, you're not obnoxious about it," Faith teased. "I'm glad we can still do girl's night."

That brought Ember's head around. Faith was right. Nothing had changed in her life except she now had Brantley and Orlando living with her. Orlando, on the other hand, had his entire life turned upside down. He'd given up his friends for her.

The Goddess's words echoed in her head. Somehow, Ember doubted the Goddess meant for Orlando to do all the compromising. She loved him even more for the dedication he'd shown.

"We will always have girl time, no matter what happens. You're my best friend and nothing will ever come between us," Ember promised and reached over to hug Faith.

Orlando's laughter drew her attention back to him. Whatever was said might have been funny, but it didn't touch Orlando, not really. The smile on his face didn't reach his eyes. Or maybe it was that she sensed his unhappiness through their bond. She'd known it would be difficult for him, but she hadn't grasped the depth of the bond he had with those at Zeum.

While she loved having him around, she knew he felt pushed out of the Dark Warriors. Initially, she thought maybe he'd taken some time to settle with her and Brantley, but she'd overheard a phone call with Santiago and discovered that wasn't the case. He hadn't patrolled more than half a dozen times in the past weeks and it was clearly getting to him.

The pack should replace the warriors. Pack is what differentiated shifters from other supernaturals and what made them stronger. She knew Orlando was energized by the pack, but it did nothing for his emotional wellbeing. She hated to admit it, but her mate wasn't happy.

That acknowledgement was like a hot poker through her chest. The selfish part of her wanted to be his entire world and everything he needed, but that was wrong of her to even entertain. After all, he wasn't her entire world. She'd just vowed to Faith that nothing would come between them.

She made a mental note to call Santiago and have him talk to Zander. She didn't want Orlando excluded because of her. He needed to patrol on a regular basis. If she suddenly lost her duties as a C.L.A.W., she would be miserable, too. She would make sure he was back on patrol, and then, she reasoned, he would adjust and be happier.

"COME BACK HERE, Brant. Don't make me chase you," Ember called out from their bed and Orlando couldn't help but laugh.

He ran a hand over his mate's back. "You know he isn't

going to listen. Ever since he learned to crawl, he refuses to stay put."

"Yeah, I know, but I'm tired. Someone wore me out while he was napping," she murmured in a husky voice before lifting her head and nipping his lower lip.

His body stirred to life and he growled playfully. He heard Brantley in the living room playing with the small drum set Santiago had given him. Ember giggled and scrambled away from him to the other side of the bed. On hands and knees, he prowled to her, a low growl rumbling up his throat.

"Hmm, is the big leopard going to eat me?" she taunted.

"Hell yes, I'm famished," he murmured.

Just as he lunged and tackled Ember on the bed, Brantley made his way back down the hall. Orlando lifted his head and saw Brantley sitting in the doorway with a smile on his face. When their eyes met, Brantley began clapping. "Dada," he squealed.

Ember shot out from under him and was scooping up Brantley in the next second. "Did he just say his first word?"

"Yes, he did. And, it seems he loves me more, Wildcat," he teased.

"In your dreams, warrior. He loves his mama, don't you?" she cooed at the baby. Brantley giggled and grabbed her face and kissed her before squirming to be let down.

"We might as well follow him," Orlando advised. "If we stay in here I'll end up calling your mom or Faith to come get him so I can have my dessert."

Ember playfully slapped his arm and headed out the door. "As soon as the little rug rat is down I will let you feast all you want," she promised with a sway to her hips.

Orlando watched her sexy ass walk down the hall and groaned. He adjusted his erection and followed suit.

"So, what do you think of the plans I drew up for the addition?" he asked, needing to focus on anything but her delectable body.

He missed being at Zeum and there was a piece of his life missing, but there was no doubt how happy his mate made him and how much he craved her.

Orlando had come to appreciate the rustic décor of Ember's house. It wasn't the glass tables or black leather furniture in his rooms at Zeum, but he liked the raw edge wood tables and suede sofas in their cottage.

"I loved what you drew up, but you left out your man cave. I was certain you'd want space where you could escape everything," Ember replied as she got a bottle of juice for Brantley. She handed it to him and he bounced on his bottom, happily slurping the drink.

"A man cave is a great idea. One with a locked door and a bench I can bend you over," he suggested.

His voice dropped an octave and his nostrils flared as his mate's arousal enveloped him. Sweet frangipani had his mouth watering and his hormones threatening to take over.

"Should I call my mom?" she asked seductively.

A plastic drum stick sailed through the air, telling him that Brantley wanted their attention. As much as he wanted to tell her yes and indulge in her lush body, their son needed them. They worked long hours and were away from him more than Orlando liked. Their days off needed to be focused on him.

"Let's save that fun for later," he said with a wink as he sat down on the floor next to Brantley and started banging the drum. "Besides, I want to hear him say dada again. You can do it Brant. Say, *dada*," Orlando encouraged.

Brantley threw down the cup and giggled again. Orlando loved how happy their son was, especially considering how he came into the world. It meant Orlando and Ember were doing their jobs.

"I haven't seen you with your switch blade lately," Ember remarked as she joined them on the floor.

"That's a habit I resort to under extreme stress, but I'm trying to break it. The last thing I need to be doing is flipping a sharp blade around Brantley," he said with a shrug. When he'd initially met Ember, he had the damn thing in his hand all the time, but since life had settled into something much calmer, it had been easier to give up.

He missed her reply as he swayed and nearly fell face-first from the force of Zander punching into his mind. It had been a while since his Liege had reached out telepathically to him. Orlando's heart raced, knowing there was an emergency at Zeum.

Before his mind went down the rabbit hole, Zander barked, *"Get your arse to Zeum right now. We're under attack and half of us can't go ootside. We need you."*

Orlando recalled the last time the compound had been under attack during the day. Elsie and Zander both risked sun exposure to help in the fight and suffered terrible burns.

"I'll be there in ten, Liege," Orlando responded already in motion.

Brantley cried out, but he didn't have time to stop and comfort his son. Grabbing his weapons from the gun safe, Orlando was rushing towards the door in the next second.

"Zeum is under attack! I have to go. I just hope I'm not too late," Orlando informed Ember.

"I called my mom. I'm going with you," she insisted.

"I don't have time to wait and I don't want you in danger," Orlando replied. The thought of her facing the demons had his blood turning to ice in his veins.

Ember's mother ran inside before she had a chance to

respond. Without saying a word or arguing further, the two of them raced to his car and jumped in.

Orlando floored the accelerator and said a prayer to the Goddess that no one was lost. Regardless of where he lived, those at Zeum were his family and he loved each and every one of them.

CHAPTER 24

"What the hell are those?" Ember blurted as soon as the gates to Zeum came into view. Her eyes went wide and her mouth gaped open as she stared at creatures she'd never seen before.

"Those are Sheti demons," Orlando responded. "The offspring of humans and fallen angels. They're tough as fuck to kill and we almost lost Jace to them not long ago," he gritted and she felt a wave of rage pulsed through their bond.

She understood his anger and wasn't looking forward to facing them. Even from a distance, she caught glimpse of lethal claws and large fangs that looked like knives. Anything able to injure a Dark Warrior like that was not to be taken lightly. She was a capable fighter, but she wasn't as skilled as the warriors. The likelihood that she might die in this fight crossed her mind, but she refused to back down now.

She sensed her mate's fear and frustration at not being there earlier, along with, his determination to help his family.

"Good thing I grabbed my sword," she remarked, letting him know she was by his side. "How did they get through the protections? I thought they were impenetrable."

"Nothing is impenetrable. Last time they got through using Dark magic. For all I know, they've been eroding the spell for the past few weeks. I haven't been here so I'm not really sure," Orlando shared with her.

Ember heard the self-recrimination and guilt stabbed her heart. It was her fault he hadn't been there. Gritting her teeth, she reminded herself there was no way to change the past. Before she could respond, they cleared the gates and Orlando slammed on the brakes. Between one blink and the next they were out of his Mustang and smack dab in the middle of the chaos.

Countless lizard demons were fighting a handful of Dark Warriors. They were greatly outnumbered and she swallowed, trying to convince herself she could do this. She'd never seen so many demons in one place.

The first warrior she spotted was Gerrick. He was vicious in his attack. She caught a glimpse of his light blue eyes and a shiver ran down her spine. He was cold as ice and lethal as hell. And, he never missed his target, she acknowledged, as she watched demon after demon slump to the ground.

The demons were surprisingly small up close. She guessed about five feet tall, but evil seeped from their pores like tar and the sharp spikes running down their backs had her palms sweating. Then the stench hit her. She was nearly knocked out by the scent of brimstone, slightly sulfuric and rancid, mixed with the odor of dead fish.

"I forgot how nasty these fuckers smell," Orlando remarked. "Stay alive, Wildcat. I need you," he murmured then kissed her hard before he ran and joined the melee.

Taking several deep breaths, she decided on the stealth approach. So far she hadn't been seen and wanted to use that to her advantage and sneak up on the creatures. Ducking behind a large bush, she crept around and got a close look at the mini-Godzillas with dark green skin that was scaly and thick. She glanced down at her sword praying it was sharp enough to pierce their hide.

The sound of snarls and weapons clashed, piercing her ears. She jumped out and had her sword swinging before the nearest creature knew what was happening. His head rolled and stopped in front of another Sheti who hissed and lunged toward her.

She ducked, but wasn't quick enough. The Sheti caught her shoulder with its claws and ripped her leather jacket and broke through her skin. She'd forgotten to ask if they had the same venom as skirm, recalling how their bite had burned like acid. Expecting to feel her blood blaze through her veins, she was relieved when it hurt like hell, but nothing more.

Seeking a brief reprieve, Ember stayed close to the shrub and got the lay of the land before she attacked again. Ten yards in front of her, Orlando fought with four Sheti at once. He was a thing of beauty in action. He ducked and kicked out, knocking one on its back. Before it had a chance to get up, Orlando stabbed it through the heart and gave a rapid twist to his blade while at the same time plunging his other blade in the thigh of another.

From somewhere close to the house she heard a deep male voice yell, "You fucked up, taking me away from my luscious angel." The male's long hair swirled around his head as he twisted then sliced through the enemy.

She thought it was Rhys given the comment, but couldn't

be certain because she hadn't spent enough time around Orlando's friends.

Her gut twisted and her chest tightened when she realized Orlando had happily spent time with her friends and family over the past weeks yet she hadn't done the same for him. She had shut out that part of his life completely and that wasn't fair to her mate.

Her mate's curse brought her head around and snapped her back into focus. Good thing, too. She couldn't afford to be distracted in the middle of one of the worst battles she'd ever been in.

Four Sheti surrounded Orlando, but he shifted in the next second, momentarily blinding the demons. He'd barely completed his shift when Santi's wolf joined him, and together, their claws imbedded into two Sheti while their canines ripped out the throats of two more. It happened so fast she was hardly able to track his movements. Black blood sprayed and Orlando's leopard roared when the gooey substance coated its fur.

Something hit her back and Ember was airborne before she knew what was happening. She cursed, her hiding spot had been discovered and a Sheti managed to catch her off guard. She went into battle mode and gripped her sword with both hands.

She swung and missed the first time, but followed the momentum, adding an extra push and caught the demon on the turn. Its arm fell to the ground and the demon crumpled as black blood spurted across her face and coated her glasses.

With a snarl, Ember cut through its throat and raced on as she swiped an arm, clearing the thick liquid before she was totally blind. She understood why Orlando had roared.

Their claws and fangs weren't venomous, but their blood was like acid to the skin.

The sun was setting and as she ran, she tripped over one of the twins. She couldn't tell if it was Cade or Caell. His leg was hanging by a thread and his skin was blistered and bloody. If he hadn't blinked, she'd have thought him dead.

Frantic, she glanced around and noticed Jace in the throes of battle. His war cry pierced the air as he took out three enemies surrounding him. The warrior was busy fighting and Ember knew he wouldn't be able to help the vampire. She wasn't far from the house and noticed Elsie and her sister standing on the other side of a large window. They were frantically waving their arms, urging Ember to get the vampire inside.

Taking a chance, she lifted the injured male and tried to drag him to safety. He weighed a ton and she didn't get very far before she was attacked again. She fought the Sheti and wanted to shift but knew she couldn't help the vampire if she did. Stabbing her blade through the Sheti's chest, she pinned it to the rapidly dying grass.

Back at the male's side, she lifted again, wincing at his groan of pain. Dirt and blood matted to his wounded leg. She didn't see how they were going to save the limb. Her heart raced and she strained, throwing all her power into getting him to safety.

She'd barely made it to the carport when strong hands joined hers. She glanced up to see Zander standing there, no worse for wear. He was blistered from the sun, but not nearly as bad off as the vampire at their feet.

"I've got him. Shite, he's verra bad off. He took off before we could stop him and I lost track of him. Thank you for helping for him," the vampire king murmured.

"Will he live?" she asked, worried.

"I doona know, but we will do everything. I'll take him to Cailyn. She can heal him. Get back to the others. Nate has things under control oot back. He'll be up here to help as soon as his beast is done snacking on the demons," Zander said as he hefted the injured vampire over his shoulder while keeping hold of the injured leg. The male cried out, but they were inside the house within seconds.

What was Nate doing in the back? Wasn't that their majordomo? Did they let him fight in battles because he was a shifter? She hoped they had trained him to fight and didn't just throw him at the demons because the vampires couldn't be out in the daytime.

The hits just kept coming, she thought wryly, facing yet another piece of evidence about how she knew next to nothing about Orlando's friends and family. Ember was convinced the Goddess was trying to prove a point.

She turned and rushed back into the fray while, at the same time, Kyran, Bhric, and Breslin took position under the portico where it was safest. It was a relief to see they had two strong warriors for their last line of defense.

Her sword clanged and made her arms shake when it met the spiked back of one of the Sheti. It rattled her and made the pain in her shoulder flare. Note to self...don't attack their backs. Ice went flying by her head and slammed into the demon, freezing his legs and torso into a solid block of ice. Startled, she looked around and saw Bhric laughing maniacally.

"Feel the freeze, arsehole," the vampire prince cursed as more ice left his palm.

In the next moment, fire shot past Ember's head and a group of Sheti burst into flames. Breslin had her arms outstretched, unleashing her fiery inferno. The combination of the blues and whites added to the reds and oranges was mesmerizing. Ember couldn't help but be awed by their gifts of fire and ice.

Those were badass powers to have. Seeing it, she understood why the Tarakesh family had been leading the vampires for centuries. She imagined Zander and Kyran had equally impressive powers.

She lifted her blade, ignoring the agony that came with the effort and was preparing to slice the Sheti's head off when Bhric stopped her. "Nay. Wait, lass. Kyran has this one. Go help the others."

Before she could ask his meaning, Kyran appeared with an enormous sword clutched in his hands and the demons head was rolling to her feet. Immediately, Kyran disappeared. When she looked around, he reappeared next to Bhric again. Powerful family, indeed.

Shaking her head, she took off and headed for her mate. He was surrounded, but that didn't deter his vicious claws. He sliced and tore through everything in front of him. Ember joined the fight, a new surge of adrenaline giving her renewed strength as she cut through Sheti.

The ground shuddered and had her stumbling. Panic quickly followed. Her fight-or-flight instinct kicked in and told her to get the hell out of there. Whatever was causing tremors that substantial was going to swallow her whole.

"Bout damn time, Nate," Mack shouted so close Ember's head whipped around. She hadn't been there a second ago. Obviously, Mack and Kyran had bonded to the point they shared one another's power.

It was a painful reminder that she and Orlando weren't as close as the other mated couples and she wondered if she would ever share his empathic ability. She'd never had a special power and didn't know what it would be like to have one.

An enormous dragon rounded the corner and she prayed it was Nate. The enormous beast had slate gray scales and a head as big as her body. If not for the familiar glint in its red eyes, she would have believed it to be demonic. She'd recognize Nate's peepers anywhere and hope sparked they might defeat the enemy.

Nate breathed sheets of fire to her right, reminding her to focus and stop gawking. When she looked back to the fight, she noticed that countless tiny men were running towards her, shouting as they waved small machetes in the air. Their crazy red hair flew about and their pointy shoes were comical, but what stood out most to her were the razor-sharp teeth they sported.

Thinking they had new demons to face, she lifted her sword, but Mack placed a palm on her arm, stopping her. "The gnomes are with us. They were helping Nate," Mack said before she turned and lifted her hands in the air. "Leave some for me, dammit," she shouted.

Ember shook her head. She had not spent enough time at Zeum with her mate to understand anything going on in his world. She'd kept him from all of this. She was shocked that he didn't hate her. She'd never forgive him if he'd denied her the pack and her family.

"Doona worry, Firecracker. You're still beating me," Kyran called out. It took a minute for Ember to realize he was talking to Mack.

The female kept hold of her sword and hacked the head of a Sheti then turned with a pout on her face. "Yeah, but I want to be on the top of the killboard," she complained.

Ember wondered what they were talking about, but what was clear to her was that this was a very competitive group and Mack strived to be the best. She couldn't help but smirk at her filthy pink shirt that read *It Wasn't Nice Knowing You But It Sure Is Nice Getting Rid Of You.*

"This isna the time for foreplay, mate," Kyran growled with glowing gray eyes.

The battle shifted with the help of the gnomes and Nate, leaving few Sheti to kill. Ember looked for Orlando and saw him making his way to her side. He'd shifted back and was bleeding from several cuts.

Shifters weren't shy about nudity and she was glad about that as she watched him saunter in her direction. She would never get enough of admiring his sexiness. He made her mouth water and her body ache. Foreplay indeed, she thought. She'd never thought fighting as particularly arousing, but given that anyone of them could have died in this battle she was oddly turned on to see her mate so victorious.

Orlando reached her side and pulled her into his arms. His kiss was passionate and ignited more need. Now was not the time to get lost in her desire for her mate. They were standing in the middle of a battleground with onlookers surrounding them.

Staying close, she broke the kiss and took stock of the others around her. Everyone was injured in some way, except Nate, she noticed when he finally shifted back. He had a large dragon tattooed on his chest that matched the color of his eyes. And, he was just as muscular and hot as the warriors. This was no fluffy butler, she noted.

Orlando led her into the house as the gnomes began the process of piling the bodies for disposal.

"Thank the Goddess the Rowan sisters are here to replace the protections," Bhric muttered as he followed them inside. "Fuckers kept gnawing at the spell until it crumbled."

"I wondered how they got in again," Orlando

commented. "How is Caell? I saw you pulling him off the field," he asked her. She sensed how worried he was for his friend.

"I don't know. He was alive when Zander grabbed him, but he was in bad shape. His skin and his leg..." Ember trailed off and chided herself as she felt his concern deepen. "But, he said Cailyn was going to heal him."

Orlando's question seemed to mobilize everyone as they all began running for the front doors. Ember followed behind, her own worry escalating. They entered a room to the right that looked big enough to house fifty people. Caell was laid out on the floor and his twin was sitting by his side, reprimanding him for rushing into the sunlight.

Jace knelt next to Cailyn and placed his hands over the male's leg. "I did everything you told me and his skin healed, but his leg, it won't heal," Cailyn blurted as tears brimmed.

"You've done, great, *Shijéí*. You saved his life. If Ember hadn't acted quickly, he wouldn't have made it," Jace assured her.

"So he'll live?" Ember asked as she stood alone wringing her hands. She felt awkward because Orlando had followed Nate to get clothes, but she needed to know if the male was going to make it.

"Yes, thanks to you two. Now, let's see if I can save this leg without surgery," Jace said as he turned to Cailyn. "I need more saline in this area."

The two worked quickly as the group hovered, waiting to see what happened. Elsie broke away from Zander and approached Ember. Suddenly, she wished the ground would open and swallow her. The vampire queen didn't like her and the feeling was mutual, but standing around as they waited to see whether a fellow warrior would live was not the time to get into it with the female.

"Thank you for what you did for Caell. He's new here, but part of our family and it would've been devastating to lose him. Listen, Ember, I know we haven't gotten off on the best foot, but I want you to know you're always welcome in this home," Elsie said, surprising Ember.

"That means a lot. I never realized how close knit a family you are. It's something anyone would be blessed to be a part of," Ember replied. She doubted she and Elsie would ever be best friends, but it was a start.

Thankfully, Orlando returned a second later and wrapped her in his arms. Elsie clapped him on the arm before she returned to Zander's side. Ember felt his emotions before he opened his mouth and wasn't surprised by what he said next.

"Liege. I'm sorry I wasn't here to help sooner. If I had been, Caell could've been spared this," Orlando confessed.

"Doona blame yourself. We have known they were lingering around the property, but didna know they were eating away at the spell. You have a mate and need to be with her. We all understand," Zander told Orlando.

Ember heart dropped at his words. She was the one to blame. She'd been selfish and hadn't given one thought to what her mate needed or wanted. She expected him to leave everything for her, and, he did, without complaint. Even now, he wasn't blaming her or mad at her. She had to believe her position within the pack was more flexible than she claimed.

Despite the attacks, she knew the demons weren't specifically targeting the shifters. She suspected they were trying to divide the power in the realm.

"Come on, Wildcat. Let's go back to my old rooms and

shower. I don't want to get black blood all over my leather seats," Orlando murmured. He leaned down and kissed the top of her head. She shook her head at his comment. Her mate and his obsession with his damn vehicle.

"He's going to be ok?" she asked as they walked away.

"Yes. The demon blood didn't infect the wound so Jace will be able to heal him," Orlando replied as he ushered them up the stairs. What he wasn't talking about was the weight that weighed heavily on his heart. And, like it or not, it was the same one weighing on hers.

CHAPTER 25

"I didn't realize how nice your bathroom was," Ember said as he led her into the large area. He reached into the shower and turned all four showerheads to hot, anxious to get his mate naked.

"We haven't spent much time in here," he observed. "Here, let me help you with that."

A smile stretched across her face. "Such a gentleman," she purred as she ran her hand up his chest.

Reaching for the hem of her soiled top, he lifted it over her head and tossed it aside. "I have learned a thing or two in my time. Just like I know that you aren't in the mood for a gentleman tonight."

Her bra followed her shirt to the floor, allowing her lush globes freedom. They bounced, drawing his attention. Damn, he loved her breasts and couldn't resist palming and squeezing them. She leaned into his touch and fire ignited in her amber depths.

"What gave me away?" she asked as she grabbed his shirt with both hands and ripped it down the middle. His shaft went rock hard and his balls drew up tight at her display while his hands flew to her waist.

He was completely out of control and wanted to ravage her. His sultry mate drove him to the edge of sanity.

"That feral look in your eyes might have been my first clue," he murmured as he allowed a partial shift and shredded the fastening to her jeans. He pushed them down her long legs, along with her silk panties, and watched as she stepped out of her shoes and kicked the fabric aside.

She stood before him and her nipples puckered under his scrutiny. His eyes roamed downward to the landing strip between her thighs.

Sexiest. Sight. Ever.

"How can one female be so perfect?" he asked. Unable to stop himself, he leaned down and took one nipple into his mouth. Her eyes slid closed and her head fell back.

"Not perfect," she panted as she arched her back.

"Open your eyes, Wildcat," he ordered.

"I love when you call me that..." she moaned.

He lifted his head and her taut nipple popped from his mouth. Her mewls of objection had him chuckling.

How could he not love the fiery female who accepted him even when he was shattered in a million pieces? Time and again she'd jumped by his side without hesitation.

"I have so little to offer you and I'm certain I drove you to the point you've questioned if we even have a future. But, I promise to love you with all that I have and I will never stop trying to deserve you," he promised.

Steam filled the room as their heat burned out of control. His leopard clawed at his mind, demanding to be set free. Not until he had his fill first.

"I love you, Orlando, and always will. I am the one who

doesn't deserve you—" he put his fingers over her lips, cutting off her reply.

"My mate is perfect in everyway. I'll not have you defiling her good name," he teased. "I love you."

"I want you inside me," she pleaded as claws extended from her fingertips.

"I've got this. Your sharp tips are way too close for Mr. Happy. One cut and the night would be cut short. I have plans for you, Wildcat," he said with a wink.

Leaning down, he kissed her lips as he shucked his jeans. Her hands went to his chest and around his neck. Her touch calmed and inflamed him like none before her. It took great effort to keep control and not rut on her like the animal inside wanted to do.

He picked her up and groaned when her legs wrapped around his waist and brought her dripping core in line with his cock. He tightened his arm around her waist to stop her frantic movements as he walked them into the shower.

"You're a cruel, cruel male," she muttered before she nipped his lower lip.

Looking deep into her glowing amber gaze, he saw his future and was floored all over again that this incredible female was *his*. She objected when he set her on her feet.

"I'm hungry, love, and you promised me a feast," he murmured.

"Yes, I remember." she replied then slightly widened her stance. Her arousal was a thick cloud in the bathroom and drove him to the brink. His leopard roared again, making it difficult for Orlando to hold back his beast.

He knelt at her feet and gazed up at heaven. Ember braced her back on the white tile and her brown hair stuck to her face as the water poured over her head. Her eyes hooded and she bit her lower lip between her teeth, giving him a hint of her raging desire.

"You are exquisite," Orlando observed as he ran his hand up the back of her leg.

He leaned in and kissed his way from her knee to the spot where his world revolved. Hovering inches above her mound, his breath left him in pants and he noticed her stomach quivering in anticipation.

Closing the distance between their bodies, he ran his tongue through her slick folds. Her flavor awakened his taste buds with a punch. Growling against her flesh with his animal close to the surface, he licked over and around her clit then devoured her sex.

Her hands grabbed the short strands of his hair as her back arched off the wall. Her nipples glistened under the water, beckoning his touch. One of his hands went north to tease her breasts while the other reached between her legs.

"Oh Goddess, yesss," she hissed when he inserted one finger. "I'm so close."

Sucking her clit into his mouth, he added a second finger and pinched her nipple. It didn't take much more and she exploded above him. Screaming his name, he watched the pleasure consume her as she writhed against his mouth. He did that to her. Male pride swelled in his chest that he was the one that had caused her to cry out in ecstasy.

EMBER OPENED her eyes and shivered as the tremors traveled through her body. Orlando was grinning at her like the cat that ate the cream. His satisfaction and fulfillment over her pleasure was as evident through their bond as it was on his face.

"Come up here," she instructed with a crook of her finger.

He stood slowly, allowing his body to rub along the front of hers. His hard chest was heaving and his eyes were twin emerald beacons. His white-blond hair was slicked to his head and he looked feral as his leopard prowled just beneath the surface.

Never in her life had she imagined being so complete. There were no words to describe the connection she shared with Orlando as his Fated Mate.

Their souls had joined and intertwined to the point where there was no differentiation between them. Where they used to be two entities, they were now one. She didn't lose part of her identity when she met Orlando, but gained a side she had never realized was missing.

His large arms wound around her middle at the same time he claimed her lips. His kiss had an edge of need she hadn't experienced since the night of their mating. She understood and felt the same frantic need for him.

They could have died earlier and both needed the reassurance the other was alive and well.

The moment he broke the kiss, she slid to her knees on the tile floor. The hot water dripped off his downturned head, softening his savage edge. "My turn," she announced as she grabbed the base of his long, thick cock.

Her fingers barely fit around the base, reminding her of the delicious stretch when he entered her. Her core spasmed, needing to be filled. This was where they always got sidetracked. He smelled her arousal and allowed it to override everything else. Not this time, she vowed. She was going to taste him for once.

Before he could reach for her, she closed her mouth around the spongy head. A loud groan left his lips as his head fell back. His hand fisted in the back of her hair and held her in place while she sucked him down.

When he reached the back of her throat, she expected her gag reflex to kick in, but surprisingly it didn't. She relaxed and set a rhythm of licking and sucking. She explored his entire length, paying extra attention to the slit on the tip. When she swiped her tongue across, sampling his slightly salty taste, he groaned and she felt him tense. Through their bond, she knew exactly what she was doing to him and felt the pleasure she provided, adding to her own desire. It made her want more.

His hips started moving and she sensed the battle he waged with his wayward body. "Let go," she murmured and knew the vibration of her voice sent him to a higher peak. She grabbed his balls and gave them a not too gentle squeeze.

"Fuck," he groaned as his hips picked up their pace and the head of his cock hit the back of her throat.

She reminded herself to relax and swallow him down. She'd fantasized many times about doing this to him. She hadn't performed oral sex but a few times in her life and had doubted her performance, but she could feel his pleasure and reveled in the way his hips swiveled with her movements, as well as, the growls coming from his throat.

His cock swelled in her hand, signaling he was close. "You have to stop," he croaked. "I'm going to cum."

Rather than release her hold, she tightened her grip and doubled her efforts. She wanted everything he had to give her. Needed to feel his release through their bond. This was something she'd never done with anyone else, but was an intimacy she wanted to share with him.

"Ahh, Em!" he shouted right before the barb extended beneath the head of his cock.

His body stiffened above her and she closed her mouth slightly, keeping pressure on the barb. It was difficult to relax enough to swallow the hot seed that spurt into her mouth, but well worth it as he let himself go. His climax ripped through his body and she felt the same rush wash through her veins.

She understood the smug satisfaction she'd sensed from him as she watched him collapse against the tile wall, panting. She'd been created to give this male pleasure and she loved seeing his satisfaction.

"Let me wash your body while I recover. Then I'm taking you to bed," he said, his husky voice arousing her to a fever pitch. He pulled her to her feet and she wrapped her arms around his waist.

"Deal," she agreed. He grabbed the shampoo bottle and squirted some into his palm. He took his time washing her, paying extra attention to her breasts and between her legs.

By the time they were done washing each other, their need was as frantic as when they'd entered the bathroom. Flipping off the shower, Orlando reached out and snagged two towels from the warming bar and wrapped her in one. Doing a hasty dry on his body, he tossed the towel aside and picked her up before she was even done.

Cradled in his arms, she kissed and nipped his neck while he carried her to the bed. He pulled the towel from her body as he tossed her to the mattress. She was still bouncing as he prowled the mattress to drape his body over hers.

A soft sigh escaped her lips the second his flesh touched hers. She loved the electrical current that came with physical contact and was glad its effect on her had not diminished in the slightest. It still had every nerve-ending begging for more.

"I love you, Wildcat. I know I'm difficult and a pain in the ass most days, but I'm the luckiest male alive to have you." His confession brought tears to her eyes and reminded her how much he had done and sacrificed for her without asking for anything in return.

"I love you, too, and I will spend the rest of my life making sure you never regret mating with me," she admitted.

Before he could respond, she pressed her lips to his. She reached between their bodies and palmed his erection while she licked and teased his mouth. Their tongues tangled wetly and his shaft jerked against her hand.

Guiding him to her core, she rubbed the head through her sensitive folds. She broke her mouth away, unable to hold back her moan of pleasure.

His hips shifted and he took over torturing her as he coated himself in the process. His mouth continued a path down her neck to her collarbone and stopped at her breast. Teasing one turgid peak, he sucked it into his mouth while pinching the other.

A fine sheet of sweat coated their bodies and the rub of his flesh over hers brought her to the edge and had her growling. He twined their fingers together above her head and looked down to capture her gaze as he aligned his cock at her entrance.

Pushing in, Orlando stretched her to that point of plea-sure-pain as he filled her. Sliding through her heat, she saw the threads of control snap and he surged forward, going balls deep inside her.

Orlando grunted and thrust his hips, surging in and out of her. His pace increased, creating a delicious friction. His fingers tightened and his body moved with a frenzy that spoke to the animal within. He'd made love to her countless times since they'd mated and she loved it when he was raw and out of control. He was more a wild animal than anything soft and gentle. He was huge and strong, and all hers.

Ember was lost in the maelstrom, couldn't move or breathe and didn't want to. She felt him swelling inside her and the barb extending. Clenching her eyes tight, she gave herself over to the mounting pleasure and burst apart, stars exploding behind her eyelids.

Orlando slammed into her one last time and held still. As her core spasmed with the aftershocks of her orgasm, she felt his hot seed jetting deep inside her womb. Panting, he collapsed on top of her.

"You've drained every ounce of energy I have," he admitted. "I can't move."

"That's okay, I can't either. Besides, I like your weight on me."

"I'm too heavy," he protested and with a surge of energy she couldn't muster, he switched their positions so she was on top and he was on bottom while his shaft remained locked inside.

She shifted until she found a position that was comfortable for their bodies then relaxed against his warm chest, listening to the rapid beat of his heart.

"Do you think it will always be this great between us?" she asked as she thought about the intense pleasure he'd given her. She didn't want it to ever end.

"Mmmm, I think it will get even better," he responded and she felt his hardness pulse inside her. As always, her body responded and arousal shot through her system. She would never tire of this male.

"We can rest for just a little bit then we can head back to

your, I mean, our place," he murmured without opening his eyes.

He still saw the cabin as hers. In his mind, it wasn't their home, but he was trying because he wanted her happy. The Goddess's words echoed through her head solidifying her decision.

"I can have my mom bring Brantley home to us. We don't have to go anywhere," she offered.

His eyes flew open and he watched her closely. "What? What are you saying?" he asked.

Letting out the breath she'd been holding she decided to go for broke. "I've been a selfish mate. You have spent weeks giving me everything while all I have done is ask for more. I didn't listen to the Goddess and that changes right now," she admitted.

"That's not true. It's my job to ensure your happiness," he replied as he sat up and kissed her lips.

Holding herself up by her elbows on his chest, she smiled at him. "There isn't a better mate alive, but we both need to compromise to make this work. I see how much Zeum and everyone here means to you, as well as, how much they need you. It's my turn to sacrifice and move in with you."

He sat up and scooted them so he was leaning against the headboard. Running his hands up and down her back, he rubbed circles against her flesh. "You don't have to do that. I know what the pack means to you and being close to your family and Faith."

"This is something I must do and it's not up for debate. Besides, I imagine Brantley misses everyone here, too."

Hugging her close, he whispered in her ear, "I really am the luckiest male alive. But, we can have both places. You don't have to give up the pack."

"I won't. I have no intention of giving up my position as a C.L.A.W. and I'll drive there to fulfill my shifts and then drive back."

"Of course, you're going to stay a C.L.A.W., but what I meant was that we can stay at the cabin part of the week and be there for the hunts and other pack gatherings," Orlando said.

"That's perfect. I know Hayden has enjoyed having you around. But, you'll still need to build onto the cabin. Brantley is getting older and having him sleep in our room won't work much longer," she said as she gestured to the crib along the opposite wall.

Orlando chuckled and palmed her ass, giving it a squeeze. "You're right about that, love. We can move his crib to the living room until better accommodations can be made at both homes. Maybe we could even convince Santi and Tori to join us at the Grove," Orlando suggested.

"Hayden would bust a nut if both of you were there for hunts. He is so proud of his Dark Warriors and enjoys showing you off," she agreed.

Orlando's face suddenly sobered and he pulled her closer. "The fact that you would do this means everything. *You* are the key to every hope and dream I've ever had. You own me body, heart, and soul forever."

"And, I vow to spend the rest of my days being your best friend, lover, and mate. All I've ever wanted is you," she professed as emotion overwhelmed her. Snuggling closer, she laid her head in his neck, and for the first time, Ember had hope for their future.

S ix months earlier...

Moving was difficult and breathing was next to impossible. But that wasn't what had her heart racing in her chest and sweat slicking her palms. Blinking rapidly and taking in the odd pointy ceiling, she grappled to not only determine *where* she was, but *who* she was. All that met her considerable efforts to jog her memory was a big, fat blank. Nothing at all came to mind when she attempted to pull up her name.

Tears burned her eyes and threatened to spill down her

cheeks. What had happened to her that she couldn't remember anything?

To make matters worse, she had no idea where she was or how she got there. How she came to be in her current predicament seemed like a pretty important issue given she could still be in danger.

And, she was exhausted. Her body felt as if it had been asleep forever, yet gotten no rest whatsoever. Lethargy pulled at her limbs, making them heavy and cumbersome, but thankfully it was passing. Much more rapidly than she would have expected if she were ill or injured. This was all kinds of screwed up and had her mind whirling even more while her body went rigid.

Chastising herself for wallowing on her predicament, she forced herself to focus on the last thing she could remember. Faceted green eyes flashed in her mind only to be washed away, followed by utter terror.

She may not know who she was or where she was, but she understood that someone had meant her harm. A sudden gratitude at being alive replaced her fear and panic. Her situation could be so much worse. She could be dead.

Unfortunately, feelings of being lost, alone and frustrated returned, making her fists clench as she fought back tears.

Not wanting adversity to immobilize her, she tried to grab hold of memories that were just out of reach. Details hovered at the edge of awareness, but she couldn't touch any of them.

A sudden, intense pain wracked her middle and she clutched her stomach. The pain spread from her abdomen to her limbs and her whole body throbbed.

Water. She needed water.

Her mouth was dry and she was parched as a desert, but

it wasn't just thirst she needed to assuage. What she desperately craved was being submerged in water and she had no idea why that need was so urgent.

Shaking her head at the absurd thoughts racing a million miles per hour, she sat up slowly and glanced around. She was lying on a surprisingly comfortable surface, given the stone and rock that surrounded her. Further inspection told her she was lying on a bed of some kind. Feathers, her mind automatically supplied. How the hell could she know that fact and not her own name?

Frustrated tears bloomed again and her heart sped up. It was difficult to concentrate with the roar of blood rushing through her veins and the waterworks that blurred her vision.

With a swipe of her arm, she cleared her eyes and noticed she was in a dimly lit cavern. *Ok*, she told herself. *Focus on what you can make sense of and leave the rest for later.* It was easier when she pushed aside the fear and annoyance.

The pointy stones she had noticed upon waking were stalactites growing from the cave roof. Again, her mind provided more useless details, but held the most important ones at bay.

What had happened to her, she asked for the hundredth time. Chastising herself for getting stuck on minute details when she could be in danger, she finally managed to calm down. Dripping water was the only sound that could be heard, telling her she was probably alone.

Swinging her legs over the side of the platform, she looked down and saw that the feather bed rested on a natural stone platform, keeping her off the hard, damp floor and the illumination came from floating balls of light.

Magic, her mind whispered.

Ignoring the mounting irritation, she felt a pulse of foreign power surrounding her in the cave. It grated against her skin like sandpaper, highly irritating and uncomfortable.

There was a long, low table with various objects spread out across it, and, wanting to get a closer look, she lowered herself to the ground. Testing her legs, she faltered and nearly fell to the ground. Weakness had her gripping the platform to keep her from a bad tumble.

Taking a minute to steady herself, she laid her head down on the plush feather-bed. The sheets were so soft compared to the rougher material of the blue dress she was wearing. Looking down, her eyes landed on the plaid pattern of the navy skirt of the dress. The sight brought a lump to her throat and had her heart skipping a beat, but she had no idea why. To her knowledge she'd never seen the dress before.

Refusing to get bogged down by the confusion, she lifted her head and noticed the soft pillow she'd been laying on appeared clean, as well as, the sheets. Her mind told her she'd been asleep for a long time and unless there was someone taking care of her, the items should be filthy.

For that matter, she should have been soaked to the bone given the damp atmosphere. The stone was slick and shiny from the water dripping down. The stalactites above her were the same. Dirt covered the floor and there were bugs everywhere...but none near her. Another glance at the magical balls of light told her there was more at play.

As she focused on the ceiling, a drop of water made it's way down a formation towards her. Expecting it to fall into her hair, she was surprised to see it hit an invisible barrier and roll away from her to the edge of the cavern.

There was definitely a force field surrounding her. Question was, who caste it? Whoever did it wasn't out to harm her or she'd be in much worse shape.

She wouldn't go so far as to say this person meant her *no* harm. She was, after all, in a strange cave with no recollection of how she got there or who she was. The only explanation that made sense was someone had her under a spell. But why?

Bracing her weight against the platform, she slowly maneuvered toward the adjacent table. Critters couldn't get through the barrier, either, she acknowledged, as she watched a beetle attempting to cross to her side.

She shuddered and silently thanked whoever had set the enchantment. It would have been all kinds of creepy to wake up soaked, filthy and covered in bugs. Who knew what kind of damage those little critters could have caused her body while she was unaware.

She had to maneuver around stalagmites growing from the floor, although there were fewer growing in her bubble compared to outside it. No doubt the shield had prohibited growth, but how long had she been there?

It should've been impossible for her to survive long enough for the development of stalagmites. Water and nourishment were required for any living being to survive. She hadn't eaten or drank anything, so surely she hadn't been there long. Unfortunately, the evidence around her suggested otherwise.

Before letting go of the bed, she grabbed the sheet off the platform and wrapped it around her shoulders. The short-sleeved dress didn't provide enough coverage and the cold air was seeping into her bones.

Taking slow steps, it took several minutes for her to cross the few feet to the table. When she got closer, she realized it was a wood and not a natural part of the cave. Glancing back over her shoulder she examined the platform she'd been sleeping on. It wasn't a natural part of the cavern, either. It was a dark wood platform with four sturdy legs the size of tree trunks.

Returning her gaze, she noticed various object on the table. A couple bowls held liquid in them. Leaning over, she sniffed and recoiled at the bitter smell. Even though she was thirsty as hell, she wasn't about to drink whatever that was.

Shoving aside a stack of paper with foreign writing, she gasped at the glow coming from a small disc she uncovered. The round metal was engraved with runes. Squinting her eyes, she picked it up and held it to the light. The amulet said something about sleep and protection, if she deciphered it right.

An object nearby caught her attention. It was a seashell and she was drawn to it. Reaching over, her hand hovered over the object as faint tendrils of magic buffered against her palm.

Before she could understand its significance, the air thickened with a cold blast that made her skin prickle. Wrapping the sheet closer, she rushed back as fast as her weak legs would allow and crouched behind the plateau that had been her bed.

When bright light filled the cavern, it forced her to shut her eyes and avert her head to avoid being blinded. Footsteps had her heart pounding and sweat beading her cold skin. She cracked opened her eyes while remaining crouched and alert for danger.

A couple blinks later and large, muscular thighs encased in a dark blue fabric entered the room. Her eyes trailed up and over a wide chest covered in soft tan fabric to intense black eyes. Scrambling away from the male in front of her, her dress snagged on the bed. Terrified for her safety, she pulled and tore the fabric then hurried to the opposite side of the platform.

"Keira," the voice intoned and held out his hand.

Blinking, she looked to him. "Is that my name?" she finally asked when he made no move toward her. The name resonated, making her believe that it was, in fact, her name.

He cocked his head and his long blond hair fell across his face. "You don't remember?"

"No, I remember very little," she admitted. She hated revealing any vulnerability, but she had no choice. She was flying completely blind here. "And, who are you?"

"Shit, an unfortunate side affect. My name is Cyril and I mean you no harm. I'm not like the monster, Angus, who put you here," he spat.

The tone when he said Angus's name had her protectively wrapping her arms around her middle. It also made her hide the soft smile playing at her lips when she heard the name.

"So, you know how I got here? Tell me, please," she begged, hoping details would jar her memory.

"It's no longer safe here. If I sensed the spell breaking, Angus will to. Come with me and I will tell you everything," he promised.

Her gut was in knots and she had no way to judge this male's character. He could be dangerous, but she was left with no other option, unless she wanted to take her chances with this Angus. His name may have made her want to smile, but she had gotten there somehow and Angus could pose an even bigger threat.

From the frying pan into the fire, she saw no way out of her predicament and placed her small palm in his outstretched hand.

AUTHOR'S NOTE

Authors' Note

With new digital download trends, authors rely on readers to spread the word more than ever. Here are some ways to help us.

Leave a review! Every author asks their readers to take five minutes and let others know how much you enjoyed their work. Here's the reason why. Reviews help your favorite authors to become visible. It's simple and easy to do. If you are a Kindle user turn to the last page and leave a review before you close your book. For other retailers, just visit their online site and leave a brief review.

Don't forget to visit our website: www.trimandjulka.com and sign up for our newsletter, which is jam-packed with exciting news and monthly giveaways. Also, be sure to visit and like our Facebook page https://www.facebook.com/TrimAndJulka to see our daily themes, including hot guys, drink recipes and book teasers.

Trust your journey and remember that the future is yours and it's filled with endless possibilities!

DREAM BIG!
XOXO,
Brenda & Tami

OTHER WORKS BY TRIM AND JULKA
The Dark Warrior Alliance

The Rowan Sisters' Trilogy

The Rowan Sisters' Trilogy Boxset (Books 1-3)

NEWSLETTER SIGN UP

Don't miss out!
Click the button below and you can sign up to receive emails from Trim and Julka about new releases, fantastic giveaways, and their latest hand made jewelry. There's no charge and no obligation.

Sign Me Up!